Changeling Press, LLC

ChangelingPress.com

Daddy's Kitten
Razor's Edge Daddy Dom Erotica
Wanda Violet O.

Daddy's Kitten
Razor's Edge Daddy Dom Erotica
Wanda Violet O.

All rights reserved.
Copyright ©2024 Wanda Violet O.

ISBN: 978-1-60521-892-2

Publisher:
Changeling Press LLC
315 N. Centre St.
Martinsburg, WV 25404
ChangelingPress.com

Printed in the U.S.A.

Editor: Margaret Riley
Cover Artist: Angela Knight

The individual stories in this anthology have been previously released in E-Book format.

Table of Contents

Daddy's Kitten
A Razor's Edge Daddy Dom Erotica Short
Wanda Violet O.

Life doesn't always happen as we expect. When I found myself in the hands of a sexy Daddy Dom in the form of a powerful billionaire, I wasn't sure what to expect. What I got was more pleasure and satisfaction than I'd ever known. But my Daddy pushes me. Sometimes further than I ever thought I could go. How I respond is up to me. But the last thing I want is to disappoint the man who's come to mean everything to me.

Daddy Takes A Pet

My name is Isabella. Not so long ago, though it feels like a lifetime, I was a college student floating through life with no real idea what I wanted -- no ambitions or goals. Twenty years old, in my fourth semester, my major still *Undecided*, I knew I was going nowhere fast. An only child born to older parents, I had been pampered and coddled all my life. When they were both killed in a car accident, I was left with but no one to take care of me.

Until Daddy. He offered me protection. He offered me a life of luxury. He offered me everything I'd ever dreamed of, including love and acceptance. A life free of worry. But his offer came with a price.

Daddy told me he wanted me to be the little girl and pet to his Daddy Dom, but not until I was ready. As I was to find out, that wasn't all he wanted of me. Soon, he'd demand so much more. Was I willing to give what he demanded? Could I?

My first week in Daddy's mansion was like a dream. I was grieving hard and had trouble focusing on what he wanted, but he was patient. At night, he held me while I wept. During the day he spoiled me beyond belief, buying me anything I desired. "Anything to make my little princess smile."

He bought me clothes -- a few cocktail dresses and sexy shoes, but mostly he bought me cute frilly panties, adult onesies with my choice of color and design, tight little shorts with sassy sayings across the ass, and tiny T-shirts that showed off my tiny tits. My nipples are rather prominent, especially when I'm aroused, and being near Daddy always made my pussy cream, so I was always walking around with my nipples sticking out. At first, it was uncomfortable, but

Daddy always praised me for wearing what he wanted.

"You're so beautiful, princess. So fucking beautiful. I'm looking forward to sucking those pouty little tits. When I do, I'll make you scream." Daddy has a growly voice when he's turned on. He never tried to hide his cock from me either. When he was hot for me, his dick would stick out proudly from his expensive slacks. He'd yet to show himself to me completely naked, but I'd felt his cock snuggled against my ass more than once as he held me.

Nighttime was the worst. The first night, I cried myself to sleep only to wake up with Daddy wrapped around me, his cock nestled between my cheeks, but doing nothing but drying my tears and petting me into relaxation. After that, he always had me sleep with him. He moved all my clothes into his room, but kept my toys and anything I didn't need at night in my room.

After the first week, I was feeling better. Daddy still hadn't made a move on me, but I knew he wanted to. Apparently he was looking for a signal from me, so I wandered through the enormous walk-in closet to select an appropriate outfit. There were so many to choose from! And all of them were brand new. Chosen specifically for me.

One outfit caught my eye. A black top that said "Daddy's Little Kitten" written in white, with a black-and-pink plaid skirt, black-and-pink-striped socks and pink combat boots. There was a black satin choker with a pink bow and black thong panties that said "Kitten" on the front over my mound. To top it off, there was a pair of barrettes with black furry kitten ears to fasten on. In my blonde hair, they stood out beautifully. Just the thought of Daddy seeing me like this made me long for his cock in all the appropriate -- and inappropriate -- places.

I took a shower, taking care to shave every part of my body, wanting to be smooth and silky for my Daddy. I took care with my hair and makeup, ensuring the colors went well with the outfit. I painted my lips the same shade of pink as my skirt and lined my eyes similarly. My lashes were extended and darkened, my brows expertly groomed and painted. My vivid green eyes stood out starkly with the black mascara. The cute crop top hit just above my belly button and the skirt just below. The narrow expanse of skin seemed to beckon a man's touch. Would it be enough for my new Daddy to give in?

I slowly made my way down the stairs, taking my time to settle my nerves. I wanted to show Daddy I was ready. If I was too nervous, he'd never believe me.

Once I got to his study, I stood outside the door, fluffing my long blonde hair, letting it settle over my shoulders, the purple-tipped strands caressing my slight breasts where my hair draped over my shoulders. Taking a deep breath, I knocked on the door, then stepped back, putting my hands behind my back.

At first there was nothing, then the door opened, and I was greeted by a man I didn't know. His face held no expression. I could hear other men in the background but not my Daddy. I knew this was his study, but was he not here? "I apologize," I whispered, trying not to sound as panicked as I felt. "I must be in the wrong place."

"No," the man said, his face still not betraying his thoughts. "You're not. Mr. Blackstone, I believe you have a visitor."

"Thank you, Victor."

I nearly sagged in relief when I heard my Daddy's voice.

"Everyone, this is Isabella. You will rarely see her, but when you do, remember she's taken, and she's very special to me."

All eyes were on me. Several looked me up and down, like they'd either love to have their way with me or were disgusted by my mere presence. Others just gave me a flat stare. All in all, there were twelve men in the room, not counting Daddy. I've never felt so self-conscious in my life.

"Come to me, Isabella," Daddy said.

I did, without hesitation. "I'm sorry, Da- Sir," I whispered. "I didn't mean to interrupt."

"You didn't, sweetheart. And you know I'm not your Sir," he said with a frown. "Say my name, Isabella."

"I..." I wasn't sure what he meant. Surely he didn't want me to call him Daddy in front of his guests.

When I hesitated, Daddy turned me around gently, held up my short skirt, and placed three well aimed, hard smacks to my ass cheek. I gasped in a sharp breath, shocked before a wave of scalding humiliation washed over me.

"What do you call me, Isabella?" His tone was stern, and he didn't put my skirt down. Instead he gripped my hips, holding me still and facing the group of men sitting at the table quietly watching our interaction.

"D-Daddy," I replied softly.

"Good girl." He gestured to the floor beside him. "On the floor close to me. Get comfortable because once you settle, you're not to move without permission. Do you understand?"

I didn't, but I'd follow his instructions to the letter. My bottom stung from the earlier correction, and I wasn't sure how to feel. I thought I might want to cry. I'd come to Daddy to let him know I was ready to move forward and gotten more than I'd bargained for. When I didn't immediately answer, Daddy gave me three more swats, harder this time. I couldn't help but cry out and stumble forward. My hands landed hard on the desk, but Daddy steadied me before once again gripping my hips with my skirt still above my ass.

"When I ask a question I expect an immediate answer, Isabella. Do you understand your instructions?"

"Yes."

Unexpectedly, he spanked me again. Three more smacks to my ass. These were the hardest yet. Every eye in the room seemed to bore into me, witnesses to my humiliation.

"Yes, what?" he asked. His voice held no inflection. He didn't sound angry or irritated. In fact, I suspected he'd anticipated this exact scenario.

"Yes, Daddy," I gasped.

"Good girl," he said, lowering my skirt. "That's a very good girl."

I sighed in relief, and several of the men around the table chucked, including my Daddy. I wanted to glare at them but didn't dare.

"Get little Isabella a pillow, Victor. I don't want my new pet to be uncomfortable."

I gasped. *Pet?* But I thought I was his little girl. I looked up at him, wanting to ask, but not daring. He raised an eyebrow with a slight grin as if to say, *"Problem?"*

I immediately lowered my gaze, but Daddy caught my chin and lifted my face to his. "It's OK, princess. I just need you to understand what I expect from you. You're fine. Trust me to protect you." He placed a soft kiss on my lips. "This is about my pleasure and what I want, but I'll never abuse you, and I promise I'll always give you pleasure. All you have to do is be what I tell you to be."

I nodded and whispered, "Yes, Daddy."

Daddy smiled, then positioned the pillow under the table and between his spread legs. "If you need my attention you are to place your head in my lap. While you're my pet, your name is Kitten. You will still call me Daddy, do you understand, Kitten?" I was sure he repeated my name to emphasize it for me.

"Yes, Daddy."

"Take your place, Kitten."

I did, curling up on the plush red pillow. It was large and velvet soft. Had I been an actual kitten I would have purred. I accidentally let out a soft moan of pleasure as I laid my head down. I was against Daddy's calf, but he didn't move. I took it as a sign he didn't mind my touch.

With me out of the way, the meeting continued. I didn't pay attention to anything but Daddy's voice. It was gravelly but pleasing. I loved to listen to him, especially when he praised me. His voice sent shivers through me. Now, with my hot bottom and knowing how that voice sounded when he got stern, that voice made my pussy clench. I wondered what it would be like to hear him scold me for being naughty. What it would sound like if he commanded me to come for him. I squeezed my legs together to get friction on my clit at the thought. I rolled my hips slightly, needing to have Daddy's hands on me.

"Excuse me, gentlemen," Daddy said.

Uh oh. His voice sounded irritated. Why?

"You'll have to forgive me. My pet is new and is still not sure how to behave."

"Better to correct naughtiness as it happens," Victor said. "Otherwise pets become confused."

Daddy rolled his chair back and gave me a hard look. "Up, Kitten," he said softly. I hesitated, but one look from him had me scrambling to my feet. He held my arm and turned me around to face the group at the table again, pulling my skirt up and tucking the hem into the waistband. He pressed me forward so I was bent over the table. My breath hitched, then I started to hyperventilate. "What were your instructions when I told you to sit, Kitten?"

I thought for a moment, and it cost me. Daddy smacked my ass. Hard. I yelped, but it definitely jogged my memory.

"I wasn't supposed to move once I settled," I said in a rush. "I was to place my head in your lap if I needed something."

"And what were you doing, Kitten?"

"I moved," I said softly.

"You were *squirming*," Daddy corrected.

I hung my head. "I was squirming, Daddy."

"Now. Before I give you your punishment, I want to know why you were squirming not fifteen minutes after you settled in." He rubbed my back from my neck to the base of my spine just above the curve of my ass.

I knew better than to hesitate. Daddy commanded instant obedience. Also, if I were honest, I was afraid I'd think up a lie if I thought about it too hard. If I did that, Daddy might get really angry. "I was listening to your voice, and I liked it, Daddy."

"I see. Explain why you liked it, Kitten."

I sighed, not wanting to tell him but knowing I

had to. "I wanted to hear you telling me I was a good girl."

"And?"

Could he read my mind? "And I wanted you to tell me to come." This last sentence was nearly a whisper. I could only hope the other men couldn't hear me.

"I see," Daddy said again. He moved his rubbing down to my ass. In praise? "Anything else, Kitten?"

"I wondered what you'd sound like scolding me, but I found that out now," I said, cheekily. More than one man chuckled. I thought Daddy did too, but when I looked over my shoulder at him, he wasn't smiling.

"The sass is more than it should be, but I'll ignore it this time. Since you told me the truth, I'm only giving you ten spanks. You will count them, Kitten."

"Yes, Daddy."

The first smack landed on my right cheek. "One, Daddy."

"Very good. Just like that, Kitten." Then he landed the second spank on the other cheek.

I winced, but didn't cry out. "Two, Daddy."

The third was back on the right cheek. The fourth as well. Left. right. Left. Left. By this time, my ass was beginning to really hurt. Each smack was harder and harder until I wasn't sure I was going to make the last strikes.

"Eight, Daddy! Nine, Daddy! TEN, DADDY!" I cried out the last of the spanks. My eyes were closed, and tears leaked from the corners, but I braced myself on the desk and took my punishment as best I could. I wouldn't embarrass Daddy by making a scene. Well. More of a scene than I already was. I was in a room full of men in a meeting with my Daddy, and they were watching him spank my bare ass. Yeah. No spectacle there.

When he was finished, he took off my skirt and panties, pulling me into his lap. I was sitting there in my T-shirt with no bra, my socks and boots. Oh. And the cat ears. The really weird thing was, though I could feel the eyes of the men on me, none of it mattered. Only my Daddy mattered.

He wrapped me up in his arms, careful of my hot bottom. At first I sat stiffly, uncertain what to do. I looked up at him, the question in my eyes, and he smiled down at me tenderly. "Put your arms around me if you want to, Kitten. Use me for comfort."

"But I was bad," I whispered so softly I wasn't certain he heard me.

"You weren't bad, Kitten. Just naughty. Kittens sometimes have trouble staying still, and I know that. Your behavior has been corrected, and all is forgiven."

"Thank you, Daddy," I said with a small, broken sob. Then I wrapped my arms around his neck and sobbed silently into his chest.

I'm not certain how long that continued. With the spanking, the nerves, and the crying, with Daddy's warm, strong arms wrapped around me, I soon started to drift.

The next thing I knew, there was a deep chuckle beneath my ear, followed by several more in the room. I gasped, jerking a little and sitting up slightly.

"Seems my little Kitten wore herself out," Daddy said. "And she has the cutest little snore." More chuckles all around. I gasped, looking up at him in horror. Had I embarrassed Daddy? He gripped my chin with his fingers and tilted my head up, placing a soft, lingering kiss on my lips. "My adorable little Kitten," he cooed. "Can you curl up on your pillow at my feet and nap?"

I nodded, nervously glancing around the room.

"Words, Kitten."

I swallowed, nodding again. "Yes, Daddy. I can sit at your feet now."

"Down you go then," he said, helping me to my feet. My bottom was hot and uncomfortable, and I rubbed it absently to more chuckles.

"Someone is feeling her punishment," Victor said, amusement in his voice. Automatically, my gaze shifted to him, but the man was just too intimidating. I lowered my gaze and sank to my pillow bed beneath the table and between Daddy's legs.

"Do you need a blanket, Kitten?"

I looked up at Daddy and shivered, my nipples puckering beneath my T-shirt. "Yes, please, Daddy."

"Very good," he praised. "Victor?"

The other man got me a soft, fuzzy blanket. Instead of handing it to me like I expected, however, he leaned down and draped it over me carefully. There was no expression on his face, but he gave me a shiver with his intensity. I glanced up at Daddy, not sure what I should do.

Daddy nodded at me. "You may allow Victor to pet you, Kitten. It was his suggestion your behavior be corrected here. If he wishes to comfort you, I'll permit it."

I shifted my gaze to Victor, who gave me a soft smile. Gently, he petted my hot bottom through the blanket. "I'm sorry, little one. But it was the right decision. You want to be with your Daddy, right? If he can't trust your behavior, he can't allow you to be with him like this."

I nodded my understanding. I hadn't thought about his logic, but it made sense. I certainly wanted to be with Daddy every chance I could.

Then Victor was gone, and Daddy moved his chair back into place. As before, I leaned against his thigh as I rested. But I couldn't doze back off.

I lay as still as I could, listening to the voices of the men around me. My Daddy's was the sexiest. I didn't pay much attention to what he said, but I let the timbre wash over me. It was deep and gruff -- he wasn't a smooth-talking man -- but then I'd learned that over the week I'd been in his company. He'd been unfailingly gentle with me, meeting my every need as soon as it was presented to him. Today was the first time he'd ever been harsh with me.

Voices continued around the room, sometimes rising in intensity. It disturbed me when they did. I found I didn't like the aggression from the other men, even if it wasn't directed at me.

I thought for a moment. My instructions were to lay my head in Daddy's lap if I needed him. I assumed that meant he'd stop and attend to me. Did I need him enough for him to stop his meeting? To disturb him twice in the same sitting? What if he wouldn't bring me back again? No. That was unacceptable. Instead of interrupting him, I scooted closer to his calf and stuck two fingers in my mouth. I should have known Daddy would notice.

He shifted slightly. When he did, I looked up to see him peering down at me with a hard gaze. Then his expression softened a little. The meeting didn't stop, for which I was glad. First, I wasn't sure my poor bottom could take any more. Secondly, I didn't want to be a burden to Daddy. Instead of interrupting the flow of the meeting, he unzipped his fly and patted his thigh for me to come to him.

I obeyed, settling myself between his legs and

wrapping one arm around his waist. Was he offering me his cock? My mouth watered for him. Not so much for sex, though I found I wanted that very much, but for the comfort. When I was distressed, I used to bite my nails. Long ago, I'd broken that habit, but not the oral fixation I needed from it. Which was why I put my fingers in my mouth when I was in distress or upset.

Daddy nodded down at me. I took it as an indication I could take out his cock and eagerly reached for it. He was semi hard but sprang to full life before I got his dick out of his fly. I glanced up at him. There was no change in expression, but his eyes glistened with lust. It was all the encouragement I needed.

The second I took his cock in my mouth, peace surrounded me in a warm blanket. I didn't bob my head and pump his shaft like I'd normally suck a cock. I simply held him there and sucked softly, like I did my fingers. I couldn't help the soft moan of pleasure. Then I sighed and settled myself comfortably, my head on his thigh, and closed my eyes.

A euphoria enveloped me, and I drifted. The voices hadn't stopped, but they were muffled and didn't matter anymore. I didn't have to worry about them getting upset or angry. All I had to worry about was Daddy's cock. Which wasn't a hardship.

When a drop of precum hit my tongue, I shivered. My hand crept up to the base of his thick dick, and I curled my fingers around it. Daddy's fingers tunneled through my hair, petting me but flexing every so often to pull my hair. The slight pain was erotic, and it wasn't long before it made me whimper softly.

Voices continued in what I thought was a heated debate. Though I still had no idea what they said, the noise was too much to ignore now. In an effort to block out everything once again, I put more effort into sucking Daddy's cock. I needed to focus solely on Daddy. To block out the meeting and the angry, hard voices.

I did my best to stay quiet, and if all I was doing was sucking Daddy's cock, I could have managed it. At least, sucking it at my own pace. I could set the tempo to match my instructions. But the voices became heated and harder, almost angry now. I needed to lose myself in pleasing Daddy to block them out, and now wasn't the time or place for that. So I accidentally whimpered. Once.

"Stop," Daddy's said in that gravelly voice of his that sent shivers through my pussy. This time he was so commanding, he had the same effect on the mean voices as he did on me. Everyone stopped instantly. No one protested. "Kitten?" His voice was gentle now. "Tell me what's wrong."

I shook my head slightly, my lips still around his cock. I'd stopped moving my mouth up and down as if trying to milk him of his seed. Instead, I sucked softly once more. I winced, expecting him to get strict with me for disobeying, even as I couldn't help my first instinct to deny answering him. I didn't want him to think I couldn't handle being with him during his work. I wanted to sit or lie at his feet every single day! Instead of giving me that hard look he had before though, he just patiently stared at me until I let his erect cock slip from my mouth to answer him. To give myself time, I tucked him back inside his pants before sitting back on my heels. I'd never felt more ashamed in my life.

"Everyone is loud. Their anger scares me. I'm so sorry, Daddy. I'll try to be braver."

He leaned down to rest his forearms on his knees. "Kitten, you don't have to be brave. It's my job to protect you, and you'll learn how seriously I take that job. So this is on me. I should have expected you'd be sensitive to other Alphas." He didn't move, but his gaze shifted up, likely to the men at the table. "I know what each of you has riding on this deal," he began. "But you will keep the discussion orderly and your voices under control."

"Because of a woman you're playing with?" The question held a snort of derision. "Hell, you'll tire of her soon enough, Blackstone. When you do, one of us will find her and have our turn. She's just a bitch. We all have them. Who fucking cares if they get their delicate sensibilities offended? They're a dime a dozen."

The voice came from the far end of the table. Shame scalded me. I knew I wasn't good enough for Daddy. He'd taken me in and given me so much already, and I'd repaid him with this.

"Hell, I could probably come up with ten whores just like her who're better looking, better fucking, and much better behaved. Maybe you need to give her a harder demonstration of how a fucking pet should act." The voice had a condescending bite to it. Like he was challenging my Daddy in something more than simply how Daddy treated his pet.

Daddy looked down at me, and I ducked my head quickly. Gentle fingers cupped my cheek and urged me to look at him. Tears dripped down my cheeks, and I couldn't hide how I felt from him.

Without a word, Daddy reached for me and pulled me up gently to stand before him. I was so small next to Daddy. So insignificant. And now he'd put me at the center of attention. When he urged me to turn around to face the table, I shivered but obeyed him. I stared down at the table, unable to look at the other men in the room.

"Courage, Kitten." This came from Victor. It shocked me enough I gasped a little and peeked up at him from beneath my lashes. The man looked as impassive as ever but nodded his encouragement.

"I believe I mentioned when I first introduced Isabella that she was very special to me." He reached for my long hair and tugged gently but insistently until I raised my head to counter the pressure on my scalp. "I don't take kindly to tears on her lovely face I didn't cause with a punishment. I also don't like it when another man puts them there without my permission. I especially detest someone who wants something from me, putting tears on her face by trying to shame or humiliate her."

I finally saw the man in question and had to stifle my gasp. The other male was a well-known businessman. A shark who always got what he wanted. Everyone knew the man on sight, and most of his peers were afraid of him. Some said he was the most powerful man in the country, but Daddy was calling him out? Over me? I wanted to peek over my shoulder to look at Daddy, but didn't dare.

"Never thought I'd see you roll over and show your belly for a little fucking whore, Jacob," the man said with a chuckle and a shake of his head. "That's a move you may regret if you're not careful."

The room went utterly silent. There was more going on here than I understood, but I knew I needed to remain absolutely still. The belligerent man still grinned and looked around at the men closest to him. Looking for support? If so, none of them showed it outwardly. In fact, the three closest to the mean man kept their gaze on Daddy or Victor.

"That slight I won't forgive, Ronald. You may take your contingent and leave."

"You can't do that," Ronald snapped. "You need me, Blackstone. More than you'll admit, but you know you need me."

"No. I do not. You're nothing but a drain. Every deal with you ends up costing more than it's worth. The only reason I've done business with you is because of the relationship my father had with yours. My father passed away last month and with him the loyalty of this company to yours also died. Good luck with your future dealings, but we will no longer stake your schemes." Daddy raised his hand, snapping his fingers once. Out of the shadows, two muscled guards appeared to escort the men out of the room.

At first, Ronald protested. Then one of the guards calmly tazed him. He and his team went without a word. Most of his team seemed resigned, but Ronald? Well, he wasn't coherent.

"He'll give you trouble," one of the others advised softly. "We'll all stand with you, but he'll smear your good name and try to ruin your company."

I felt Daddy shrug behind me. "He won't be the first to try. Certainly not the last. He'll meet the same fate as all the others before him." Daddy turned me to face him, gracing me with a soft smile as he stroked my cheek, gathering the stray moisture before bringing his finger to his mouth and taking my tears into him. "I give him a month before he's completely and utterly broke. No bank or business will touch him. When it's all said and done, he'll be lucky if he can get a job at a fast-food joint. His company? His holdings and hotels and everything he holds dear? All gone."

"If you'd do this because of a girl, I'd hate to see

what you'd do for your family."

I had no idea who asked the question. My eyes were on Daddy. But Daddy didn't hesitate in answering. "She *is* my family. No one is more important in my life than her."

My breath came in quick pants, my mind blanked. The only thing that registered was the declaration from Daddy. We hadn't been together long, but he'd made me promises. While I believed him, this was more than I'd ever thought possible. He defended me with swift, sure justice. Even against such a powerful man! My Daddy was ruthless!

"Daddy," I breathed. I was sure my heart was in my eyes. He looked down and smiled at me.

"What did my little Kitten expect? No one insults you or belittles you. For any reason. No one touches you unless I allow it." He wrapped his hands around my waist and lifted me onto the table, wedging his hips between my spread thighs. "You're mine in all respects, Kitten. I protect what's mine."

Before I could respond, he leaned down and kissed me gently. Then with more and more heat. Before I could process the whole scene, he was kissing me greedily. His tongue tangled with mine, driving me higher and higher. I hadn't been aroused before, but now I was spinning out of control.

Maybe it was because I'd been sucking his cock. Maybe it was the possessive claim he'd just staked on me, or the vicious way he dealt with a powerful man who'd slighted me. Whatever it was, I was now going mad with lust. I had to have my Daddy. I clutched at him, fisting my hands in his immaculate shirt.

When he pulled back, he grinned down at me. "My little Kitten is greedy."

"She was very good, Mr. Blackstone," Victor

said. "She held her ground and trusted in you."

Daddy glanced at Victor then back at me. "You think she deserves a treat?"

"Just as it's important to correct bad behavior when it happens, you should reward good behavior in kind, sir."

Daddy just smiled. "I couldn't agree more."

With gentle hands, Daddy pushed me back on the table to lie on my back. My legs were draped over the edge, but he quickly wrapped his arms around my thighs and pulled me to the edge.

"I'm going to eat this sweet little pussy, Kitten," he said. "Because you were so good and put your well-being in my hands so beautifully, you may come anytime you feel like it. Since this is the first time I've touched you, I want you to understand it will not always be so. I own your orgasms. I own your body. You are never to touch yourself or make yourself come without my permission. Do you understand, Kitten?"

"Yes, Daddy," I said, following it with, "I am never to touch myself or to come without your permission."

"Very good girl," he praised. Then he sat in his chair and moved closer between my legs. Inhaling deeply, he sighed. "Such a sweet, sweet pussy. How does it taste?"

"D-Daddy?" I knew my eyes were wide, my breathing brisk.

"Shh, Kitten. Just relax and enjoy."

I sighed happily. "Yes, Daddy."

Then he winked at me before lowering his lips to my weeping cunt. I couldn't contain the sharp gasp, but bit my bottom lip before I could cry out. It earned a sharp slap to my inner thigh from Daddy.

"Don't hide your responses from me, Kitten. No

matter where we are or who's close when I take you, you do not hold anything back from me unless I tell you to."

"Yes, Daddy!" I screamed. There were a few chuckles from the remaining men at the table, and I blushed furiously but focused on Daddy's dark head between my thighs.

He held me open and flicked my clit with his tongue several times before kissing it and sucking it between his lips gently. I gasped, my hand going to his head before I snatched it back, not wanting to muss his hair.

Daddy chuckled. "Go ahead, Kitten. Touch me all you want. This is your reward."

I sighed and reached for him again, loving the look of his dark head between my pale thighs. The rough stubble of his cheeks abraded my inner thighs, leaving red marks in his wake. We were such a contrast. Light and dark. Smooth and rough.

Daddy licked me close to orgasm. Though he said I could come when I wanted, I was acutely aware he was reading me and controlling my orgasms just as surely as if he'd told me not to come. He might have told me I could come when I wanted, but it was all an illusion.

"Daddy!" I gasped after the third time I'd failed to fall over the edge.

There were chuckles around the table, but no one said anything other than Daddy. "What's wrong, my beautiful little Kitten?"

"You said I could come, but you won't let me!"

"Oh? Were you close?"

"Yes, Daddy!"

"Perhaps you should have told Daddy?"

I blinked, lifting my head to look at him. There

was a wicked gleam in his eyes as he licked my pussy. "B-but…"

"Shy about asking for what you want in front of my guests?"

I nodded, my gaze clinging to his.

"Don't be, Kitten. You'll do much more than this in front of them and others just like them. You're my pet. I do whatever I want, whenever I want. I like you sitting with me, so you'll be wherever I am whenever I'm working. Which means, if I need to fuck you, I'm going to do it no matter where we are. And before you wonder how I can do that, I'm one of the richest, most powerful men in the world. I can do anything I fucking want to."

I sighed, and just embraced it. "Please make me come, Daddy."

"That's my girl. Now tell me what you want me to do. And don't stop talking until you come, my sweet pet. I want to know exactly what you need."

He sucked my clit again. I cried out, arching my back. "Daddy! That's so good!"

"You like it right there?"

"Yes, Daddy," I cried. "Will you put your fingers in me?"

"Absolutely, Kitten." He did, pumping and stroking, never taking his tongue off my clit.

"Feels soooo goooood, Daddy!" I writhed on his desk. Then did something I never thought I'd do. I pulled up my shirt, exposing my tits for all to see. I mean, after all, they were witnessing me getting my cunt eaten expertly and listening to my cries of pleasure. "Don't stop, Daddy. Please don't stop…"

"Is my little pet ready to come?"

"Yes, Daddy! Yes! Please lick my little pussy until I come for you!"

"Mmmmm…" He hummed over my clit, which finally set me off. I arched my back and screamed, letting go of everything. Leaving it all to Daddy to take care of.

My orgasm lasted a long, long time. Daddy stayed with me until I came down from the high he'd put me in. Sweat coated my body, and I was completely and utterly spent. With a sigh, I went limp on the table, my legs frogging wide when he let go.

I must have passed out, because the next thing I knew I was in Daddy's arms with the blanket I'd been given wrapped around me securely. Daddy was talking again, but I didn't pay attention to the words. I just basked in his warmth and my post-orgasmic bliss.

"You good, Kitten?" he asked softly as the conversation continued around us. He stroked my back through the blanket while I snuggled into him.

"Yes, Daddy." I sighed softly.

"Good. Stay here as long as you like. When you're ready, you can slide to your bed on the floor. Tomorrow I'll have a proper bed for you to lie on at my feet."

"Do I have to get down?"

"No, Kitten. Not today. I won't always be so indulgent with you, but you've earned whatever pleases you today."

"Thank you, Daddy. I love you, Daddy…"

Then I drifted off to sleep.

Daddy Claims His Pet

Every day when I woke, Daddy was with me. We were inseparable. We woke and showered together then ate breakfast together. Daddy took me to work with him. Sometimes it was to his study in our home, but other times, he took me to the big skyscraper he owned where his office rested at the very top. He always dressed me for our day. If I wore cute, sexy clothing with "Daddy's Kitten" or "Daddy's Girl" on it, we stayed home. If he dressed me in elegant, smart but sexy office wear, he intended to work from his downtown offices.

Always I sat at his feet in my bed under the desk. Sometimes he let me suck his cock when the conversations around us got too heated, but he didn't put me on display like he had that first day.

And he hadn't fucked me yet. He pleasured me. I pleasured him. But there was never any penetration other than his fingers or the occasional slim dildo.

Today, we were headed to the big offices in the city. Daddy dressed me in a soft, pink, form-fitting skirt that hit me at mid-thigh, dark brown, knee-high, stilettoed boots with slightly lighter-colored thigh-high tights that came just above the tops of my boots. That left about an inch of bare thigh visible. My top was black silk and tight with a deep V neckline. No bra, naturally. The outfit was a little racier than he normally dressed me in no matter where we went, but I loved it. The look in Daddy's eyes said he loved it too. I thought I looked a cross between elegant and edgy.

My makeup was tasteful, my eyes lined a smoky gray, my brows neat. My cheeks were contoured to perfection and my lips the matching pink of my skirt. My blonde hair was left loose and flowing down my back in a silky, straight waterfall. Daddy had brought me a pair of pink kitten ears to pin in my hair, but these were different. These were sparkling with little gems that caught the light and twinkled merrily when I moved.

Around my neck was a pink collar studded with clear gems and trimmed in gold. Daddy had placed it carefully around my neck this morning, kissing the skin just above and below the thin collar. "So beautiful, Kitten. You're going to be good for me today, yes?"

"I promise, Daddy," I said softly, looking up into his eyes. Even though I wore boots, Daddy was much taller than me. His body, thick with muscle, made me look and feel positively tiny.

"Good. You know good pets get rewards. Yes?"

"What reward will I get if I'm good, Daddy?" I asked the question eagerly. Though Daddy played with me constantly, he'd yet to actually fuck me. I had no idea why he hadn't, but I was eager to continue to the next level.

"What would my good Kitten want as a reward? Hmm?" Daddy looked down at me with amusement in his dark gaze.

Knowing that I'd have a better chance of getting what I wanted the sooner I asked, I blurted out my wish. "I want you to fuck me, Daddy."

"What?" He feigned surprise. It was obvious by the smile tugging at his lips he'd expected this. "Is my pet eager to become my little whore too?"

"I am, Daddy." Just the thought was making me wet. And I didn't have on any panties.

"You know the rules. You do what I say, when I say it and you'll have your reward."

"Yes, Daddy. Thank you."

He leaned in to kiss me, and I lost myself in his

touch. His tongue swirled against mine as he cupped my jaw. My hands went to his crisp, dark shirt. The feel of the soft cashmere blend was heavenly. The soft material made me want to curl up on Daddy's chest and purr like the Kitten he wanted me to be at the office.

There was pressure at my neck and, when Daddy pulled back, I found he'd fastened a thin gold chain to my collar. I looked up in surprise but said nothing.

"Today I'm entertaining special clients, Isabella. They expect no interruptions. While I could give a good Goddamn what they want, I'm going to use this situation to test you. Do you understand?"

Not really. My expression must have given me away, because Daddy sighed, amused but slightly... disappointed? Immediately, he scooped me up and carried me to the couch where we sat. I was allowed to curl up in his lap and get comfortable before he started speaking.

"You don't have to do anything you don't want to, Isabella. But I need to know now before we leave. I will push you today if you let me. But once I start, I can't stop. If you don't obey me, you will be punished, and you may not enjoy the outcome."

I thought for a moment, then ducked my head a little. "Will you tell me what you'll want me to do, Daddy?"

His expression softened, and he leaned in to kiss me once more. Before I could lose myself in him again, he pulled back. "Just that you do exactly as I tell you immediately." He smoothed back a stray lock of my long, blonde hair. "Once we get to the building, the second we exit the limo, you're my Kitten. I'll hold your leash." He indicated the golden chain he'd fastened to my collar. "You'll be at my side the entire time, but I will lead you in. There will be no mistake what you are to me. Can you handle that?"

Could I? This wasn't a huge leap. I'd already been playing the part once we were in his office. Most of the top floor at least knew about me. Only one person had dared to snicker at me. She'd been dismissed on the spot.

Though I didn't associate with the office staff or any of Daddy's associates, I wasn't deaf. I heard the rumors. The woman who'd been fired had been unable to find a job anywhere in the city. No one would touch her. Some even said she'd been unable to find a job outside of the city.

Not only that, but Ronald, the businessman Daddy had kicked out of the first meeting I'd ever attended, was said to be penniless. My Daddy's reach was long and strong, and he was merciless to his enemies. Everyone knew this. After the incident with the woman in the office and with the businessman, if anyone had thought badly of me, they never voiced it or let it show in their expressions.

"Yes, Daddy," I said softly. "I can handle myself if you wish to test me."

He looked at me for long moments. "Are you sure? I don't want you uncomfortable."

"I'll keep my focus on you, Daddy. If being there as a kitten gets to be too much or I'm afraid, I'll rely on you to keep me safe."

That must have been the exact right thing to say because Daddy's face lit up with pride. "My very good Kitten," he murmured. "You will be magnificent."

The anticipation of what was to come during the ride there was nerve racking, but I sat quietly, only speaking when Daddy asked me a question. I tried to lose myself in the sensations around me. The cool leather on the backs of my thighs. Daddy's subtle cologne. The onlookers gawking at the limo as we sped by. Once we stopped at the front of the huge skyscraper, my pulse was racing. Outwardly, though, I kept my calm facade firmly in place. Discipline. I had to have Discipline.

A man opened the door to the limo and Daddy slid out, elegant as a jungle cat. He reached for my hand, and I followed.

"Deep breath, Kitten. Courage." His voice was deep and rumbly. It settled me as nothing else could.

"Thank you, Daddy," I said looking up at him. "I got this."

He chuckled. "I know you do. Because you're my brave, fearless Kitten." The praise settled over me like a warm blanket on a crisp morning. I could do this. For Daddy, I'd do it with gusto.

He took my chain in hand and let the length sway between us. I followed, though Daddy slowed his pace for me to catch up to him so we walked side by side. I kept my head up, my expression haughty. Kittens might be cute and cuddly, but they were also princesses. In my high heels and sexy clothing, I could be a princess. A kitten princess.

We passed by several people who looked at me curiously, but no one said a word. I did my best to walk through the enormous foyer without a thought other than to keep pace with Daddy. He took his time. Probably allowing for my heels, not wanting me to fall and injure myself. As if Daddy would ever allow me to fall.

I noticed Daddy glancing at me often as we walked to the express elevator that went to the top floor where his offices were. At some point, I became that kitten princess. I held my head high, and anyone who did glance my direction got a look of haughty disdain. Princess to peasants. My hips swayed with every step, and I thrust my shoulders back in pride, which pushed my breasts forward.

We stepped into the elevator alone. The second the doors closed, Daddy was on me. "Fucking little tease," he hissed.

I was shocked. I wasn't trying to tease anyone. Fear coursed through me. Did he think I'd betrayed him? I only ever wanted Daddy! Not some other man or woman. "Daddy?" My heart pounded in fear and panic.

"You walked across that lobby like you owned the fucking place. Do you know how fucking sexy that was? You're just daring me to fuck you in front of everyone so they know who owns you, aren't you, Kitten. You think I won't?" He didn't look angry. Only extremely lustful.

I raised my chin, taking a chance. "I know you will, Daddy. Maybe it's what I want."

"Fuck," he bit out before shoving his hand up my skirt to sink into my wet pussy. I cried out, my head resting on the wall of the elevator. "So fucking wet," he bit out. He jerked the chain on my collar up, forcing my head back. "My fucking little whore."

Daddy pumped my cunt with his fingers for long moments before he swore viciously and sank to his knees. He shoved my tight skirt up above my hips and wedged his shoulders between my thighs. Gripping my ass in one hand my hip in the other, he covered my pussy with his mouth and sucked.

"Daddy!" I cried, my legs trembling as the pleasure engulfed me.

"Mine," he hissed. "This pussy is all mine."

"Yes, Daddy! It's yours!"

"All to do with as I please."

"Yes, Daddy!"

He continued to suck me, flicking my clit with his tongue and taking me straight to the edge of madness. But he didn't let me fall over.

"Daddy! Please let me come!" I begged him, trying not to make it an order. Last thing I wanted was to get in trouble.

"No!" he snapped, not even considering it. For good measure, he smacked my ass hard. "You come, and I'll bend you over the first desk we come to and whip that little ass with my belt." Then he continued sucking and flicking my clit.

I gritted my teeth. Counted backward from ten. I screamed, pushing his head away in desperation as I neared an orgasm I wasn't sure I could contain. "Daddy! Please!" I wasn't sure if I were begging to come or for him to stop. Either way, something had to happen now.

Abruptly, he pulled away, tugging my skirt back to rights and wiping his face with a handkerchief just as the elevator door slid open. I was gasping for breath and turned slightly, hiding behind Daddy. He merely took his time as if nothing were amiss. The door stayed open for a few seconds as I tried to gather myself. Daddy had stepped half in, half out of the elevator to keep the door open.

After a moment, he gave my chain a gentle tug to get my attention. "You ready, Kitten?" His voice was gentle now. Not at all the growling caveman he had been.

I cleared my throat and put my shoulders back. There was probably still a glazed look in my eyes, but if Daddy could do this, so could I. "Yes, Daddy."

He gave me a look so filled with pride I wanted

to purr. "Such a good Kitten," he praised. "Shall we then?"

Again, we made a long walk through the spacious lobby of the penthouse offices. More people up here paused to glance at us than had on the lower floor. It was usually the other way around, but Daddy had never dressed me thusly, nor had he led me with a leash. I was acutely aware of the eyes on me, out of sorts as I was. My body felt like it was completely on fire, burning from Daddy's masterful touch.

I tried to put on my haughty princess routine, but my body didn't feel like my own. Needing to be grounded, I glanced at Daddy. He looked almost angry as he moved through the spacious floor to his office.

My world was off center. My confidence was shaken. Daddy had brought me to the brink of orgasm but refused to let me fall, then shoved me out into the world where all around me greedy, hateful eyes watched back. All because I belonged to Daddy and they didn't. I felt like I'd done something wrong but didn't know what. Because of all that, my temper spiked when I was supposed to be docile, a domesticated kitten.

When I got a sneer from a woman who'd been trying to get close to my Daddy, instead of ignoring her as I usually did, I turned my head and hissed, lunging slightly and pulling my leash. Daddy stopped and stared at me, a faintly startled look on his face.

"Explain yourself, Kitten," Daddy said softly.

I wanted to demur, but knew there was no way I could manage it. Not in my current state of mind with my emotions running high and my need of Daddy so strong it was a physical ache. "*I'm* your Kitten, Daddy. Not her."

It was all I said, but I could see Daddy

understood the deeper meaning. His gaze flickered to the bimbo in question. She was better than the woman my Daddy had fired, and this was a different situation. The woman carefully blanked her face before looking slightly confused, as if she had no clue what I was talking about.

"Sir, I put on coffee for your ten o'clock meeting. Should I order some baklava as well?" Oh, she was good, playing the encounter off as if nothing had happened. I wanted to claw her greedy little eyes out.

She was a beautiful, sophisticated woman. Tall. Elegant. Sexy. She wasn't a peer of Daddy's, but she knew his business. The things important for him to succeed. She would be a much better partner for my Daddy than I was. All I could do was take from him when he gave me so very much.

The look she gave me said she knew she'd won. Naturally, I hissed again. This time, Daddy laid a firm hand on my shoulder. "Not another sound, Kitten," he said softly. "I'll deal with you later."

I should have been grateful he didn't punish me in front of the whole office, but all I could see was the woman in front of me making a play for my Daddy. I might have been in big trouble except for one thing. When Daddy told me he'd deal with me, the bimbo flashed me a triumphant look. Immediately, Daddy's mien hardened, his gaze snapping back to the woman. Then back to me.

"How long, Kitten?"

I wasn't exactly sure what he meant by his question. Daddy was notoriously closed lipped, never using two words when one would suffice. At least, that's the way he was when he was working. With me, he explained things thoroughly so there were no misunderstandings.

I held Daddy's gaze like I'd never done before. I wasn't defiant, but I didn't back down either. "Since my first day. And every day since. You just don't see it because it's about you, not me."

Daddy was silent for long moments, holding my gaze. It was if he were trying to pull the information from my head, to see what I saw and why I'd drawn those conclusions. Then Daddy looked back at the woman and studied her. She held Daddy's gaze, too. But her gaze was hungry. Grasping.

His head jerked slightly. Then he looked back at me. "Go inside my office, Kitten. Wait on your bed for me and be in position."

I wanted to protest. Wanted to see what happened. I had a sick feeling in my tummy. What if Daddy chose her to be his Kitten? Worse, what if he chose her as his *woman*? With another hiss at the woman, I did as Daddy instructed. I'd probably pay for that little show of defiance, but it was worth it.

Once the door to his office was closed, I moved to my bed at the foot of Daddy's chair and flopped down. My outfit wasn't conducive to flopping, but I managed. What was happening outside the office? Was he promising her pleasure? Did he want to make her his woman? What was a Kitten to a man like Daddy anyway? Once those thoughts entered my mind, the tears came in a flood.

I was so busy feeling sorry for myself I nearly forgot to get into position. Daddy had taught me how to present myself soon after the first time I'd submitted to being his Kitten. Now, I hiked up my tight skirt. Sitting back on my heels, I spread my knees wide, placing my hands on my thighs palms up. Then I waited for Daddy with my head bowed so he wouldn't see my tears.

It seemed like forever before Daddy opened the door and walked in. I could feel his gaze on me, but I wouldn't look up. I refused to look into his eyes when he told me he didn't want me anymore.

"Kitten, look at me." I sat so still, not wanting to look up at him. Not wanting to see the look in his eyes when he rejected me. "Kitten. I gave you an order. Will you not obey?"

Instead of answering, I just shook my head.

There were footsteps as Daddy walked toward me. The next thing I knew, he was kneeling in front of me, his hand gently urging my face upward to do as he commanded. "Kitten, why the tears? You know I'd never give you more punishment than you could handle."

I tried to turn away, but Daddy held me firm. "Talk to me, Kitten. We can't make this work if you won't talk to me."

"Are you replacing me with her?" My voice was stronger than I thought it could be given how my throat was burning with tears. A few fell, but I refused to let any more. If he was done with me, I knew my heart would shatter.

"Would it upset you if I did?" Daddy's voice had no inflection.

It was a simple question. I knew I needed to stay quiet and keep calm, but I felt anything but calm inside. "Yes, Daddy! It would upset me a whole lot!"

"Why would it upset you, Kitten? Would you miss my money that much?" The corner of his lips turned up slightly as if it were a joke, but I wasn't amused.

I flinched back away from his grip. I felt like he'd slapped me. Tears did fall then whether or not I wanted them to. "Do you really think I'm that bad of a person?" I didn't even address him as Daddy when he'd been nothing but that to me since the day I moved in. This hurt. "I love you! Not your money. I've never wanted your money. All I've ever wanted or looked forward to is your time. I just love being with you!"

Daddy reached for me, pulling me into his arms. I resisted at first, but he scooped me up and went to the couch, sitting down and positioning me so I straddled him. My skirt was halfway over my ass now, my pussy hovering over Daddy's lap. He still had his slacks on, and even though I was hurt and angry, I still didn't want to ruin those expensive pants. When I struggled to get down, Daddy jerked my skirt up to my waist and smacked my ass three times.

"Sit still, Kitten," he said firmly. He reached between us and unzipped his fly, pulling out his erect cock. Then, without preamble, he tucked the head against my opening and shoved himself inside my cunt.

"Daddy!" I gasped as I realized he was actually inside me. For the first time! Daddy was inside my little pussy, and I didn't know whether to sob in relief or grief. Was this goodbye or the next step in our relationship?

"I told you to sit still, Kitten. Obey me or I'll spank that ass red while I fuck you."

"Are you sending me away, Daddy?" I couldn't keep the small, frightened note from my voice, and the tears came harder no matter how hard I tried to stem them. In the short time we had been together, Daddy had become my world. The one person I never wanted to be without.

"No, Kitten. I'll never send you away. Especially not for a woman like her. She's gone now. Never to come back. Just like the other one." He cupped my face in his big hands, brushing my tears away with his thumbs. "You are my Kitten. My woman. You're mine. No one else, Kitten. I want no one else but you. Do you understand me?"

"Daddy?"

He urged me to move on him. Just a little. I moaned, my body shuddering at the unexpected pleasure in the midst of such sharp pain in my heart. "Answer me, Kitten. Do you understand?"

"You're my Daddy?"

"Yes, Kitten."

"Always?"

"There's no other woman for me. No other man for you. There will be times when I let other men fuck you, but only when I say. There will be times you'll want to share me as well. Again, only when it pleases you. When those interludes are over, they're over. It's always going to be me and you, my sweet Kitten."

I was very still for a long time, just looking into Daddy's eyes. I needed to know he was sincere. That he truly meant what he was saying, because I needed to grab it with both hands and hold it to my heart. When the truth finally sank in, I dissolved into tears, throwing my arms around Daddy's neck and sobbing. Daddy just held me, murmuring to me reassurances I couldn't understand.

"I mean this much to you, Kitten?"

"Y-yes, D-Daddy," I said, brokenly. "L-Love y-you s-so much!"

"I love you too, my precious, precious Kitten."

He held me for a long time, his cock throbbing inside my pussy. I was turned on beyond belief, but so relieved all I could do was sob. Once I was more in control, Daddy started fucking me in earnest, moving me up and down on his thick, hard cock.

He lifted me only to pull me back to him, using me to masturbate his cock like he might using a fuck doll. I bucked my hips at him, trying to give Daddy as much pleasure as I could. I wanted to please him. Wanted to keep him happy so he always wanted to keep me.

"My little pet," he cooed. "Your pussy is so hot and tight around me."

"I love how you feel inside me, Daddy. It's even better than I imagined." I whimpered a little when his thumb found my clit and circled it lazily. "I'm sorry I doubted you, Daddy."

He paused. "Doubted me?"

I nodded vigorously. "Yes, Daddy. I should have known you wouldn't replace me so fast. At least, I should have trusted you wouldn't without telling me what I was doing wrong and how to fix it."

The expression on his face was at once cunning and stern. "That's right, my little Kitten. You should have trusted me. I'll forgive it this time. You've been under a tremendous amount of stress adjusting to this life. I tried to give you time, but you thought you were ready, and I'm proud of you for that. But now that you're all in, I need that trust, Kitten."

"But, how do you know, Daddy? That I'm the one for you when you could have any woman you wanted?"

"Do you honestly think I brought you to me out of the kindness of my heart, Kitten?" He surged up into me several times for emphasis. "I studied you long before your parents were killed. Knowing you'd be out in the world alone moved my plans forward, which was why I wanted to give you all the time in the world to decide if this was for you. To ease you into it. When that accident happened, I knew I couldn't let you go,

Isabella."

Daddy always called me Kitten now. Even when we were at home. I thought he needed the role play as much as I did. When I was Kitten, I didn't need to worry about anything but Daddy. Incidents like this one were why. With him calling me Isabella instead of Kitten, I knew he was as serious as he could be.

"I'm not letting you go. Not ever. Tell me you understand me."

I nodded. "I understand."

"I understand, Daddy," he corrected, holding my gaze intently. I realized then he might be as shaken as I was.

"I understand, Daddy."

Daddy grunted his satisfaction, then wrapped his arms around me and surged into me over and over, harder with every stroke. This wasn't how I envisioned my first time with him, but it felt right. Satisfying. It was exactly like it was supposed to be.

"Yes, Kitten," Daddy praised. "You're accepting me. Accepting us."

"Yes, Daddy," I gasped. "Feels so good…"

"I know, baby. But you're not to come. Do you understand?"

"Daddy!" It was a protest, but I'd obey the order.

Daddy smacked my ass twice. "Don't. Come."

I whimpered, but kept riding him. When it became not enough for Daddy, he picked me up and turned to lay me on my back on the couch. He gripped my waist and fucked me as hard and fast as he could. His lips peeled back from his teeth, and he growled at me.

"Fucking pussy is so fucking hot," he bit out. "Needed it so fucking long."

"I need you too, Daddy," I whimpered. "Fuck

me. Take what you need from my body. I'm yours to do with as you please."

"That's right, Kitten," he growled. "Your body is mine." Daddy continued to fuck me, pistoning in and out of me. "Your orgasms are mine. All of you…" he bit out as he fucked me harder and deeper, "…is fucking mine!" With one last thrust, Daddy came deep inside me. I hadn't been allowed, but it was OK. Daddy came inside my pussy. He'd given me all of himself. And I was greedy for more.

After several moments, Daddy moved off me. Wiped himself with a handkerchief, then tucked his cock back inside his pants. He reached out a hand and pulled me to my feet.

"Come with me, Kitten. We'll get you cleaned up then it will be time for my meeting. Remember what I told you before we left home?"

I nodded. "I'm to do what you say without question."

"That's my good Kitten. You'll do exactly what I tell you to do without hesitation. You are as important a part of this meeting as anything else. Normally, I'd make other arrangements for this, but I need to push you. To get you used to doing as I ask, no matter what. I'll never let it go beyond what I believe you can take, and I need to know you trust me in that. Do you?"

"I do, Daddy. I promise to do whatever you ask."

"No matter what, you do not make a sound unless I say you can. This is most important."

"I understand, Daddy. Not a sound."

"My good little Kitten," he praised. That praise washed over me like a warm bath. Soothing and wonderful.

I redid my makeup just like Daddy instructed that morning. When I was presentable, he led me back to his place at the long meeting table. A plush bed with thick pillows and warm blankets looked inviting and wonderful. I looked up at Daddy, and he nodded to the bed.

My appearance was flawless. I looked exactly like Daddy wanted me to look. Daddy sat in his chair, and I settled between his legs in the pet bed he'd provided. I curled up, resting my head on his thigh, but instead of facing inward to focus on Daddy, he wanted me facing outward so I could see the others when they sat at that table. I noticed several large, thick pillows spaced perfectly around the chairs so that each person sitting would have access to a pillow. They were large and plush. Big enough for someone… or me… to sit on. Or kneel on.

I looked up at Daddy. He grinned down at me, a lustful gleam in his eyes. Then I glanced down at his cock. Despite just emptying himself inside me, he was stirring once again. Whatever was about to happen, Daddy was looking forward to it.

It was ten minutes until the meeting, but both Daddy and I sat in comfortable silence. I leaned against his thigh, my hands on the other thigh, and Daddy petted my hair in a soothing rhythm. It didn't help with my nerves, but it made me feel closer to Daddy. I rubbed my face against his crotch once, needing to feel his hardening cock against my cheek. He groaned, but made no other move.

When the door opened to admit several men. all of them were talking and laughing, either unaware or uncaring of me and Daddy sitting there. To be fair, they might not have noticed me in my bed on the floor, but they definitely should have noticed Daddy.

"Jacob!" One of the men greeted Daddy with a friendly smile as he strolled in. When Daddy didn't immediately stand, the other man glanced down, and his expression softened. "I see you've been holding out on us. Have you finally found your special pet?"

"I have, Giovanni. She's precious to me." Daddy continued to stroke my hair. I closed my eyes into his touch, focusing solely on Daddy. I found it easy to block everything out when Daddy had meetings. After the first encounter, I'd even learned to block them out when things got heated. Also, I had the option of sucking Daddy's cock if I needed help concentrating on nothing but Daddy.

"She's a very beautiful pet. I hope she fulfills you." He raised an eyebrow as if it were a question, his gaze flickering to me then back to Daddy.

"She most certainly does." Daddy cleared his throat. It must have been a signal to bring everyone to order. "Everyone, I'd like to introduce you to my little pet. Her name is Isabella, but she answers to Kitten."

There were murmurs of appreciation and congratulations. Most nodded at me in acknowledgement but didn't address me directly.

"If you'll take your seats, we have a full day ahead."

The meeting started, and I leaned my head against Daddy's thigh and closed my eyes. The ebb and flow of this meeting was nothing like others I'd been to. These men were closer to Daddy than most others. It was almost like they were all fast friends.

There was a whisper of movement, and I opened my eyes. Daddy had taken out his cock. Immediately, I reached for it, taking hold of the base before engulfing the head in my mouth. I wanted to whimper in pleasure, but managed to remember my order to stay silent.

Wrapping my arms around his waist, I took him

deep, not bothering with the soft sucking I usually took such great pleasure in. I was greedy for the taste of him. Daddy grunted and gripped my hair in a firm hold. I was aware of the murmur of voices going quiet but didn't bother to process it properly. Instead, I kept moving on Daddy.

"You'll have to excuse me," Daddy said, his voice husky. "My pet is quite eager."

"Wonderful she's so eager to please you, brother," a man said.

Daddy chuckled. "You don't understand. Sure, she wants to please me, but more than anything, she's simply greedy for my cock." That got several chuckles around the table. "Please," Daddy said. "Don't stop the report on my account. Continue."

They did. I didn't concern myself with any of it. Only with Daddy's cock. And keeping silent.

It didn't take long before Daddy let out a groan, then pulled me to my feet. He hadn't come so I was confused. I looked up at him to find a look of deep lust so intense I gasped softly.

"That's a sound, Kitten," he bit out as he turned me around and shoved up my skirt. The tight garment stayed bunched at my waist. I had on no panties, so my ass was bare. Daddy shoved me against the table and delivered several hard slaps to my bottom before dipping his fingers to my pussy. I managed to hold in my cries, more from the sudden pleasure in the midst of the pain than because of the spanks.

"I love that shocked look on her face," one of the men murmured. I recognized the voice and glanced his direction. Victor. Again, he sat at Daddy's side. "I see she's come a long way since I last saw her."

"She's my greatest treasure, Victor," Daddy admitted, which both shocked and pleased me. "I will never give her up to anyone."

Then Daddy tucked his cock against my entrance and planted himself inside me. As instructed, I didn't make a sound. I had to bite my bottom lip to keep from it, but I was silent. Being inside me seemed to help Daddy. He sighed as if in relief, then addressed the men at the table.

"Please, continue. Sometimes I find I simply need to fuck my pet."

"Quite understandable, Jacob." I didn't know that man, but he was soft spoken.

I'm not sure what I expected, but for them to actually continue their meeting as if nothing were happening as Daddy started to fuck me wasn't it. Perhaps it should have been degrading or humiliating, to be fucked in a room full of men without them seeming to care at all. But I felt empowered. Sexy. My Daddy needed me so much he took me even in the middle of his meeting. The feeling was nearly euphoric.

As Daddy increased his pace, I let my eyes close, and I knew the dreamy smile I felt showed on my face. My lips were parted slightly and each time he surged into me, the breath exploded from my lungs. Still, I held any sound from escaping. Just as Daddy commanded.

Daddy rode me harder and harder, his grunts and growls growing loud when I was forbidden any sound. I was glad I'd been instructed to be quiet, too, because I found Daddy's noises both exhilarating and satisfying.

With a nearly deafening roar, Daddy came. As his cock pulsed inside me, he reached around and found my clit. "Come for me, Kitten," he whispered at my ear. "I want to hear it. Scream it out."

I did. The instant my orgasm crashed over me, I gave a shrill scream that completely shattered the flow of the meeting and should have embarrassed me. Instead, I felt a flash of pride. I'd done exactly as Daddy had instructed. If he'd wanted me silent, he'd never have told me to scream.

"That's it, beautiful Kitten." Daddy ran a hand down my back. I still had on the silk blouse, but it clung to my skin, sweat making it stick. "Stand up for me," he commanded, his cock never leaving my cunt. He reached around in front of me and unbuttoned my blouse, exposing my tits for all to see. My skirt followed so I was naked, Daddy's cock still inside me, his cum dripping down my thighs.

"We seemed to have brought the meeting to a standstill, Kitten," he said, amusement in his voice. The eyes of every single man in that room were on me. There were soft chuckles all around. Daddy didn't acknowledge them but kept his focus on me. "You see these men? They are my most trusted -- my brothers. They will never harm you, and they will never tell you to do something I'm not comfortable with. You're mine, Kitten, but you will obey them as you would me unless I'm with you. They may want to use your mouth, Kitten. That is always allowed. Anything else needs my express permission. Do you understand, Kitten?"

I got the feeling that command was as much for the men as it was for me. Daddy was setting boundaries. I also now knew what the large pillows were for. To my shock, the thought made me shiver with anticipation. Daddy didn't miss a thing. "I understand, Daddy."

"My good, beautiful, greedy Kitten," Daddy chuckled. "You are a rare treasure."

"Thank you, Daddy." I turned my head to look up at him, my heart in my eyes. "I love you, Daddy."

"I love you too, Kitten." He leaned down and took my lips gently. His softening cock slid out of me along with more of Daddy's cum. "Now, Kitten. Clean up then come back to your bed."

"Yes, Daddy."

Once I was clean and settled at Daddy's feet, I thought about everything. We were starting our life as Daddy and Kitten in earnest now. I knew he'd push my boundaries, and that I'd sometimes be uncomfortable. But I also knew Daddy would always take care of me. I found I was looking forward to the challenge.

With that last thought, I drifted off to sleep. Right at my Daddy's feet.

Kitten's Playdate
A Razor's Edge Daddy Dom Erotica Short
Wanda Violet O.

Daddy takes such good care of his Kitten. He even brings me a playmate just to brighten my day. But Max is more than just a partner to play with. He's supposed to be another layer of protection for me in the form of a sensual pet. Trouble is, Max has been badly damaged. But I think I can heal him.

Question is, can Max be what I need, or will Daddy need to make some adjustments?

Kitten's Playdate

A warm breeze tickled my shoulders, waking me gently. The big bed I shared with Daddy was perfect, just like everything else about our time together. Daddy was protective and gentle with me, though I had seen the surface of his ruthless side. All someone had to do was cross him regarding me, or have word get around someone was being mean to me and Daddy shut it down. Sometimes I saw it when he wanted to push my comfort zone, but he always seemed to know just exactly how far I could go. Didn't mean he didn't push me further the next time, but he always stopped before overwhelming me too much.

Smiling, I stretched and rolled over... to find an empty space next to me for the first time since Daddy had made me his kitten. I gasped, sitting up, my gaze darting around the room, looking for Daddy. But he wasn't there. I hated how dejected I felt, but I was used to having Daddy's full attention. We hadn't been apart in weeks. Wherever Daddy was, I was there. He'd kept me close by his side every single day. So, where was he?

That was when I noticed the note on his pillow beside me.

Kitten,

Don't fret because I didn't wake you before I left. I assure you it was a hard decision on my part, but you needed your rest for what I have planned for you today. I've prepared an outfit for you. You'll find it in your sitting room. You are to wear everything I have out and nothing more. Come downstairs when you're ready and we'll begin.

Always remember you are mine, Kitten. You're mine and I'm yours. You're my kitten. But you're also my woman. Make me proud today. Wear what I've put out for you. Be honest with me. Open your mind and trust me to take care of you.

> *Love,*
> *Daddy.*

This sounded serious. Was Daddy upset with me about something? He was careful to reassure me, but I was still nervous. I held his letter for several moments before crawling out of bed and heading to my sitting room. The outfit he had for me made my heart accelerate in both nervousness and excitement.

Daddy had picked out a plain, pale blue sleeveless dress that hit about mid thigh. No panties. Also, there was a tail attached to an anal plug. The tail was the same pale blue as the dress with the fur as soft as mink, and black ears of the same soft fur. There were tiny glittering blue gems in the fur that sparkled under the light with every movement. The plug was small, but still large enough to hold the weight of the tail. It was shaped so that, when inserted into my ass, it would turn up just beneath the hem of the dress Daddy wanted me to wear.

The previous day finally made sense. Daddy had hired a woman to wax me and do my nails. She'd given me a wonderful massage and I'd been so relaxed Daddy had just laughed and carried me to the bed where he'd made gentle love to me. It had been an indoor spa day. A day for his princess. One I'd thoroughly enjoyed. Daddy had done it for me, but he was also preparing me for today.

I showered and dressed. I dried my hair in long spirals, leaving it to hang loose just like Daddy loved it. I had trouble with the plug and tail, but did the best I could, knowing the important thing was doing what Daddy ordered. When we were in sexual situations, Daddy demanded total obedience.

Taking one last look at myself in the mirror, I fluffed my hair once more then headed downstairs. I found Daddy in the great sitting room where we usually entertained guests. He was sitting on a loveseat, watching the stairs. When he saw me descend wearing the outfit he'd planned he smiled warmly and stood.

"My beautiful princess," he greeted. "Did you have trouble with the tail?" His grin wasn't mocking or unkind, just like a man who knew his woman and knew she'd try her best to do as he'd asked.

I rolled my eyes and blew a curl out of my eye. "Yes, Daddy. It's making my dress flip up and show my ass." He chuckled and reached for me.

"Come. Turn around and I'll fix it for you, Kitten." As he manipulated the tail, it moved the plug inside me, making me squirm. "Does my beautiful Kitten like the way the tail plug feels inside her?"

"I do, Daddy."

"Mmm… maybe it's time to plug you more often. Get you ready for my cock. Hmm?"

I shivered, looking at him over my shoulder. "I'd love that, Daddy."

He turned me and placed a gentle kiss on my lips. "You're my lovely little kitten. My perfect woman. Are you ready for today?"

Again, I shivered, goose bumps erupted over my skin and my nipples puckered. My pussy clenched and leaked out moisture. "I don't know what's happening."

"But I can see you're excited."

"I trust you, Daddy. Anything you do, you do for your pleasure, but you've always made sure I enjoy it as much as you do."

Daddy pulled me into his arms, hugging me tightly before kissing me. "Our guests will be here in a few minutes. Shall we go over the rules?"

"Rules, Daddy?"

He chuckled. "You know there are always rules. This is your first playdate so I will be lenient, but there are a few things I want you to concentrate on. Everything I do has a purpose and this is just one step in making you my perfect pet."

"I understand, Daddy."

"Good. Now. Before I begin, I want to make sure you understand you're mine. You're my pet and my woman. Anything we do is strictly for us. I won't enjoy it if you don't, so it's very important for you to tell me if you're uncomfortable. That being said, I want you to give everything we do an honest try. I wouldn't ask you to do something if it wasn't what I wanted. Do you understand?"

"Yes, Daddy," I answered, then repeated what I understood. "I will try anything you expose me to. If I can't find a way to enjoy it or I'm too uncomfortable physically or emotionally, I'll let you know immediately."

"Good, Kitten. Use the red, yellow, green system. Red, we stop. Yellow, we slow down. Green, all is well."

"I understand, Daddy."

As if on cue, the doorbell rang. Daddy smiled down at me. "One more thing." Daddy brought out a metal collar. It was a deep blue with clear gems embedded in it. Instead of a thin band, it was more like a wedding ring -- a thick metal about a half inch wide. He fastened it around my neck and it rested comfortably against my collarbone. "You will wear this as a symbol of my ownership whenever we have guests over, or whenever we are outside this house. You've had one before when we've gone to the office, but this one is your responsibility. Any guests we have, anyone I introduce you to will respect that symbol and my claim on you. Do you understand?"

"Yes, Daddy. Do I have to take it off?"

He smiled softly at me, as if the question pleased him. "You don't, my sweet Isabella. You may wear it as often as you like."

I wrapped my arms around his neck and kissed him. "I love you so much, Daddy."

"I love you too, Kitten. Now, go sit on your cushion by my chair. And remember. Look to me if you're nervous, or if something is set in motion by someone else you're not sure about. This isn't a test. You're not going to disappoint me. I'm not going to be angry with you. The only thing I would ever be upset over is if you had any doubt whatsoever and didn't bring it to me. Do you understand?"

"Yes, Daddy," I answered softly. "I'll look to you for anything I'm unsure about."

Daddy nodded crisply, then went to the foyer to receive our guests.

As I sat on the cushion, my arms resting on the seat of Daddy's chair. I noticed a second cushion next to the plush chair across from Daddy's. Mine had been there since the first day I'd agreed to be Daddy's kitten. This one wasn't needed. What was going on? Was Daddy taking a second pet? Was that why he kept reaffirming that I was his and he was mine? Why he stressed to me that I needed to give what he wanted for us a good try and not dismiss it out of hand?

My nerves were getting the better of me when I heard male voices coming close. There was Daddy, but I thought I recognized the second voice as well. Was that Victor? He was one of Daddy's closest friends and part of his innermost circle. He was also the man who'd suggested Daddy punish me when I'd squirmed under his desk when he'd specifically told me to be still, and the man who'd suggested he reward me for being such a good kitten later in the same meeting.

"I appreciate the invitation, Jacob. I admit I was surprised you asked me to bring Max. he's a bit more... aggressive than I'd have picked for your kitten."

"She's stronger than you give her credit for. I wouldn't have asked for Max if I hadn't been certain he was what she needed."

Daddy and Victor entered the room. Behind them was a man I didn't know. He wasn't as tall as Daddy or Victor, but was every bit as big and muscular as them. He wore black leather pants, a loose white shirt opened half way down his chest, and no shoes. At his throat was a black studded collar attached to a silver leash. Victor had a firm grip on the leash. At his crotch was a steel tiger cock cage. It seemed to be attached to a hole in the front of his pants. While his cock was encased in the thing, his balls were also caged in the same silver steel. He was locked in with a tiny padlock. While not preventing an erection, the device would make it uncomfortable should Max become aroused. The second the big man saw me, he moved in my direction, a lustful gleam in his eyes. I whimpered, my gaze going immediately to Daddy. The leash pulled tight and the man growled as he was stopped abruptly.

"Max!" Victor snapped. "Kneel!" The big man sank to his knees beside Victor, but his gaze had locked on my cowering form. "Are you sure about this? The very last thing I want is to be responsible for that sweet girl's fear or for her getting hurt."

"Which is why you'll discipline your pet and

teach him patience," Daddy said. There was no heat in his voice, just calm instruction. "Max has needed discipline for a long while. We both know it. This is to help you as much as it is to help me."

Victor sighed. "He's just been through so much. I wanted him to have as free a rein as I could."

"As you should have. Max has been through a lot in his young life. But it's time for him to be tamed. He's not a feral cat. He's a proud, fierce tiger. And tigers have patience on the hunt." Daddy looked at Max as if speaking to him instead of Victor. Maybe he was. I tried to keep my own eyes focused on Daddy, but my gaze occasionally darted to Max. A wary prey keeping an eye on the predator.

Daddy turned to me and sat in the chair. I moved so that I sat between his legs, taking my cushion with me. I wrapped my arms around one thigh and lay my head in his lap. Immediately, Daddy's hand was buried in my hair.

"It's all right, Kitten. Remember what I told you."

"You won't let anyone hurt me."

"Good girl. Now, just sit here. You may hang on to me as much as you need to."

I nodded and two of my fingers immediately went to my mouth. Daddy just continued to pet my hair, soothing me. Normally, he'd have offered me his cock to suck, but not this time.

"Stand, Max," Victor said. His voice was hard but not harsh. Max obeyed, his gaze never deviating from me. "What were your instructions before we came?"

"To stay at your side until you give me leave to move away." The man's voice was husky. Rough. I shivered with equal parts fear and arousal. I loved

Daddy's rich, smooth voice. Max was the exact opposite of Daddy, but I was drawn to him in a primitive way. It frightened me because I only wanted Daddy. I never wanted to be without him!

"And what did you do?"

"I went for little Kitten when I saw her."

"And what did I tell you about Kitten?"

Max sighed. "She's precious." He said it wistfully, but with a sneer. His gaze was focused on me. I tried not to whimper, so I turned my head and looked up at Daddy. My fingers were still in my mouth and I sucked softly. This guy really didn't like me at all and I had no idea why.

Victor didn't speak for a long time. "Max," he finally said. "You know you have to be punished. Right?"

It sounded like Max snorted before saying evenly. "Of course, Papa." Max shrugged out of the shirt and turned around, his back to Victor. I gasped, my whole being rebelling at what I was seeing. Max's back was crisscrossed with scars of all kinds. It looked like he'd been tortured repeatedly.

"No," I whispered. "Don't hurt him, sir," I plead softly. I looked from Victor to Daddy, tears in my eyes.

"Shhh, Kitten," Daddy urged. "Let them work it out. Remember your own punishment the first day we spent together as Daddy and Kitten?"

Daddy had spanked my bottom. It had hurt but hadn't harmed me. "I do, Daddy."

"Victor will do no more than that to Max. Only in a different way. One more suited to his body type and strength. It will be harsher than your punishment, but no more than something meant to correct his behavior. Neither Victor nor myself would ever harm him like you see he has been harmed in the past."

Slowly, Max looked over his shoulder at me, his brows drawn in confusion. "You'd take up for me? When I was about to pounce on you?"

I shrank back, but looked up at Daddy. I was sure my eyes were wide with fear and confusion. Daddy just nodded at me, a silent command to answer Max.

"You've been hurt enough," I said. "I don't like seeing that you were hurt when you're so beautiful and proud. You're a lion and should be king of your pride." I spoke softly, still clinging to Daddy. Unexpectedly, tears burned my eyes. "I don't like knowing you were hurt."

"You just met me, Lil'bit. I'm more animal than man." He shifted his gaze. "Animals only respond to pain."

"Animals respond to pleasure, too," I whispered.

"This is a punishment, Kitten," Victor said to me patiently. "Just like your punishment. What happened after your punishment?"

I thought back. "Daddy held me until I stopped crying and told me all was forgiven."

"So what do you think will happen after Max has had his punishment?"

"You'll forgive him, too?"

"Yes, Kitten," Victor said gently. "All will be forgiven and Max will know what is expected of him in the future."

I nodded my head, one tear trailing down my cheek as I held Max's gaze. "I understand."

Victor turned to Max. "Do you understand, Max?"

The big man lifted his chin, never breaking eye contact with me. "I do. I'm sorry, little one," he said to me. "I would have tried to take what you weren't ready to give. Your daddy would have killed me before that happened." Max looked to Daddy. "Perhaps that was what I was hoping for." He bowed his head. "I'm glad you weren't forced to witness that violence. A creature as gentle as you shouldn't have to see something like that."

Daddy and Victor exchanged looks. For a brief moment, Victor looked stricken. Then his expression blanked and he acknowledged Max. "I'm proud of you for explaining your thoughts. I must stress that, before your demons get that bad, you should talk to me or Jacob. We can help you, but only if you let us."

Max straightened, his head once more going up proudly. "I understand, Papa. From now on, I'll come to you when I can't control the demons --"

"No!" Victor snapped. "You come to me when they start whispering to you! You will never endanger yourself in this manner again. The only acceptable reason to ever put yourself in danger is to protect our little Kitten." Victor indicated me with a wave of his hand. "And only if her daddy is unable to protect her. She is precious and to be protected, but she has many looking out for her. You will be her last line of defense."

Once again, Max gave me a measured look. One of a fierce warrior given a reason to *be* a warrior. "She will be protected. I will not be reckless with my life, Papa."

"Good. Now. Are you ready for your punishment?"

Max turned his back to Victor. "I am, Papa."

Victor brought out a crop. "Step out of your pants and place them on the chair across from Jacob."

"Yes, Papa," Max murmured. The man was completely submissive without looking submissive. I got the feeling that, in the right circumstance, unless Daddy or Max's papa was on hand, the man would be the dominant in the room. Especially with me. Daddy obviously had plans for Max. While I wasn't sure if I was going to like Max or not, I trusted Daddy. If he said we needed Max for something, then I'd do whatever he told me to. And I'd welcome Max with open arms.

"Count your lashes," Victor ordered.

Max did. While the strikes with the crop reddened Max's ass, he never flinched or in any way indicated his punishment hurt or that he was angry with his papa for the punishment. In fact, once the last of his twenty lashes was done, the man turned and knelt at his papa's feet. Looking up at Papa Victor, he said, "Thank you. Daddy."

I, on the other hand, winced every single time the crop landed on Max's ass cheeks. More than one errant tear tracked its way down my face.

Victor looked more pleased with Max's response than I expected. It was as if Max had conceded much by calling the other man "Daddy" instead of "Papa."

"You're quite welcome, Max. Come sit beside me while Jacob and I talk."

Max took his time getting situated on the cushion. His ass had to be hurting, but he gave no sign of any discomfort. My own bottom ached in sympathy and I shifted my weight so I sat on my hip. I still clung to Daddy, but I now studied Max. And he studied me.

"Kitten is so empathetic," Victor said. "She seemed to take Max's punishment harder than Max did. I will refrain from further punishments in her presence. I have no wish to cause her distress."

"My Kitten is strong. She may not like it, but I believe she understood the issue and wouldn't have wanted the outcome Max envisioned. Besides, I'm certain Max wouldn't want to cause Kitten distress. I have no doubt he will act the part she set for him. King of his pride." Max looked at Daddy with dignity and a fierce pride. He did seem a little startled but lowered his chin in acknowledgement.

I studied Max as the conversation continued between Daddy and Victor. *Papa* Victor. I knew I needed to remember that, should I need to address the man directly. He wasn't my papa, but he was Max's. Which made him Papa Victor in my world. Anything less now wouldn't be appropriately respectful. And I liked Victor. He was just as compassionate as Daddy and had helped me ease into my role as Daddy's pet when I'd anticipated being his little girl. Now that I thought about it, I was much better suited to being Kitten than Baby Girl.

Max was as intent on me as I was on him. I wondered what had happened to him, but I knew it wasn't my business. He sprawled lazily next to his Papa, both legs bent, one on the cushion he sat on, the other up so he could rest one forearm on his knee. He's gaze never wavered from me as he seemed to be sizing me up. Trying to figure out what my angle was. I could have told him my only angle was making Daddy happy. I owed him so much and loved him more than anything. No matter what he asked of me, I'd do my best.

Papa Victor reached toward a bowl of fruit and snagged an apple. Without a word, he handed it to Max. Max murmured his thanks then bit into juicy fruit. He held the apple in the hand he'd rested on his knee. His chewing and swallowing fascinated me. I couldn't take my gaze away from his throat. For some reason, the act was erotic. Especially when he grinned at me as if he knew how he was affecting me.

I ducked my head in shame. I didn't want this man. Not like that. Did I?

Daddy's hand found its way to my hair again, stroking me, comforting me when I hadn't indicated I was distressed. "It's OK, Kitten." Daddy leaned down and murmured in my ear. "You don't have to suppress your interest. I brought Max here for *you*. Not only is he a strong male, but he's intensely sensual."

"But… Daddy…" I felt tears burn my eyes. "I don't want anyone but you."

"I know, Kitten. Consider Max a gift. Victor is my right-hand man. He is not only a partner, but a protector. He has many pets who serve as guards. Pets can protect in the bedroom where you and I would normally be alone. Victor has convinced me of the benefits of having a pet like Max of my own."

"And you want Max?"

"I do. He's fierce. Strong. He'll protect you with his life."

"But I don't want him to protect me, Daddy. He needs to protect you! Nothing can happen to you!" Tears fell freely now. "If Max is that good, he needs to protect you!"

"I have my own guards, Kitten. Since I found you, I've been searching for the perfect guard for you. While I've had men protecting you, I've wanted someone with you at all times. For him to give his all, Victor believes Max needs to bond with you. You'll always be mine, Kitten. Isabella. Always mine." He smiled gently at me. "But I want you to be safe when I can't be with you, or when you just prefer to sleep in rather than leave the house with me. Max will be a friend as well as a protector. You need to bond with him. It's a lot, I know. But you're easy to love, Kitten."

I glanced at Max again. He grinned at me, then took another bite of that apple. The man oozed sensuality in every move he made.

"Come, Max," Daddy said, beckoning him over. "Feed my little Kitten. Let her get used to your touch."

I clutched Daddy's pants but took a breath, trying to push myself out of my comfort zone and let another man close in an intimate situation. Hadn't Daddy told me there would be times he'd want me to please his friends? I remember being a little intimidated at the time but hadn't really thought much about it. Looked like maybe I should have.

Max grinned again, then took the apple in his mouth and crawled to me in a sensual glide.

"Yeah, that one's a natural," Daddy chuckled.

"I have no doubt he can please her. It's his self-control I'm concerned about." Papa Vincent tossed Daddy a small key. "To his cock cage. May I suggest you keep him locked when they're alone unless you intend him to seduce her."

"Agreed. While I trust Isabella, Max has yet to prove himself. Or fully appreciate the position he will be in." Daddy gave Max an encouraging smile. "But I have no doubt he'd soon earn his full freedom. We'll set boundaries and he'll see that his needs will be addressed and taken care of in the appropriate time and place. I have faith in Max."

Max didn't seem to be paying attention, his entire focus on me as he crawled to my side and crowded my space on the cushion. Nevertheless, he acknowledged Daddy. "I appreciate your confidence in me, Daddy Jacob. I won't let you down." Max didn't take his gaze from mine as he offered me the apple he'd been eating. When I reached for it, he pulled it back, shaking his head, then brought it to my lips. He wanted me to eat from his hand?

I glanced up at Daddy, who nodded at me encouragingly. Looking back at Max, I leaned in and took a nibble from the sweet fruit. I chewed and Max smiled at me as he took his own bite. Again, he offered me the apple. I took another nibble, but he shook his head and held it to my lips again. He thought I needed a bigger bite? When I opened my mouth and took a larger piece, he gave a satisfied purr.

"Very good, Max," Daddy praised. "It's important for her to eat to keep her strength." Daddy looked at Papa Victor. "You've trained him well."

The other man shrugged in acknowledgement. "To meet your needs, he must protect and care for her. I stressed one was just as important as the other, but I believe your kitten won his heart with her defense of him."

Daddy looked at me with pride. "She is a prize beyond measure. Max will be the man I trust with my heart. For that, I'll allow him liberties I would normally reserve for my most trusted friends. Liberties I might not give even those few men."

I met Daddy's gaze as I finished chewing. "Max. You may play with my kitten if you do it gently. I know you'll be uncomfortable in your cage, but I'm not removing it immediately. As Victor said, you'll be wearing it when I can't be with Kitten so you need to be used to it."

"As you wish, Daddy Jacob. I'll earn your trust, and that of little Kitten. Given your unfamiliarity with me and the way I presented myself at the beginning, your caution is wise." Max set the remains of the apple aside and reached for me. "Little Kitten. Will you allow me to play with you?"

As always, I looked to Daddy. "This is your

decision, Kitten. This isn't a test. I wouldn't have offered you to him if I was opposed."

"You're still my daddy and I'm still your kitten?"

"Always, Isabella. You're also my woman. And I'm your man," he repeated.

"Thank you, Daddy," I said. Then I looked back to Max. He reached for my hand and I took it.

Max pulled me into his embrace, kneeling and urging my legs over his thighs and around his waist. I was still dressed in the dress Daddy had picked out, but I had no panties. Max petted my thighs as he looked into my eyes. Judging my comfort level? My breath came in little pants and I gripped his muscular shoulders. As he slid his hands up my thighs, I whimpered and found myself riding my pussy against the bridge of the cage that held his cock in check. Max slid his hands around to grip my ass and squeezed.

"You smell good," Max growled as he kneaded my ass. "Daddy Jacob. May I remove Kitten's dress?"

"You may." Daddy sounded proud that Max had thought to ask. I hadn't thought he'd have needed permission, but it seemed important to Max not to mess this up.

Instead of whipping my dress over my head, he took his time, leaning back to slide his palms underneath the hem, up my ribcage, then urging my arms above my head so he could slip the flimsy material off my body. Rather than tossing it aside, he folded it neatly and laid it on the table beside us.

His hot gaze roaming over my body, Max stroked fine strands of hair from my face before cupping the nape of my neck and bringing my lips to his in a searing kiss. He let me take my time adjusting to him, but Max was insistent in his kisses. He licked the seam of my lips until I opened willingly to him.

With a satisfied grunt, he wrapped his arms tighter around me and deepened his kiss, taking me with him on a ride of sensual carnality. I heard my own whimpers as he refused to allow me to be afraid of what he was doing to me. He just kept kissing me, making my head spin with the intensity of the lust he generated within me.

"That's it, Max," Daddy said. "You're taking such good care of my kitten."

"She tastes good," Max said between kisses. "So fuckin' good."

Daddy and Papa Vincent both chuckled. "That she does," Daddy agreed. "There is more of her to taste, you know. I give you free rein to do anything other than penetrate her tender body, Max. Show me how you can pleasure my kitten, and I might let you fuck her before you leave."

I squealed into Max's mouth. Did I really want Daddy to let him fuck me? I thought I might. As long as Daddy was with me and giving permission, I could do whatever he wanted. And I knew I'd enjoy this time with Max. Daddy certainly knew what I needed. Better than I did.

Max lifted me, moving me to my back on the plush carpet, before settling his body between my legs. His upper body pressed me against the floor as he wrapped his arms around my torso and found one nipple to suck on. I cried out as my fingers threaded through his thick, long mane to hold him to me.

I was losing my grip on anything but the pleasure. Needing to ground myself I turned my head to give Daddy a desperate look.

"You look beautiful, Kitten," Daddy said, smiling at me. "You always do when you're lost in your own passion. Let Max tend to you. You may come as many times as you need, but you mustn't hold back. You have to voice your pleasure. Scream if you need to."

"You're a very lucky man, Jacob," Papa Victor said. "She's so passionate."

"That she is. And very responsive. Look at her little nipples. So hard and puckered. Max," Daddy said. "Pull back and show us her pussy. Is she wet?"

"She is, Daddy Jacob." Max did as instructed, raising himself off me and pressing my knees wide. With his thumb and forefinger, he opened me up so Daddy and Papa Victor could see my soaking wet pussy.

"Taste her, Max," Daddy whispered. "Taste how sweet she is."

To my surprise, Max hesitated. He glanced at Papa Victor then back to Daddy. "Respectfully, Daddy Jacob. I'd request my papa get the first taste of her. I'll gladly feed him from my fingers if you prefer, but my papa deserves to taste Kitten before I do."

Daddy raised an eyebrow, glancing at Papa Victor. "Indeed."

Papa Victor raised his hands as he chuckled. "Don't look at me, brother. That was his own suggestion. I know I could taste your sweet Kitten if I asked. We all wanted you to cement your bond with her before taking anything you might offer."

"Fully aware of that, brother," Daddy said, grinning at Papa Victor. "You want a taste of her? I highly recommend taking it straight from her pussy, but I'll leave the manner in which you get your taste up to you."

Papa Victor held his hand out to me. "Come here, girl." Max helped me to rise and urged me to stand in front of Papa Victor. I looked over my shoulder at Daddy. He was sitting in his chair with a contemplative look on his face. A little smile graced his generous mouth. "Don't be afraid, Kitten. Let him have his taste."

I stood between Papa Victor's spread legs. His cock tented his pants, but he made no move to free himself or to relieve the pressure. "Only one taste, little Kitten," he said. "Though, I have no doubt I'll crave more. You're Jacob's Kitten. His woman. I only take when he allows."

"Yes, Papa Victor," I murmured.

"Spread your legs, Kitten," he instructed. When I did, Papa Victor leaned in, his tongue snaking out to lick between my folds. I jumped and cried out when he rasped over my clit. Max had to hold me upright with one strong arm around my body. "Fuck me," Papa Victor whispered. "That has got to be the sweetest pussy I've ever tasted."

"Now you see why I'm so smitten," Daddy said with a chuckle. "I've shared pets in the past. Pets who were never meant to be with me long. I tried to find them good homes, but Isabella will be forever mine. Sharing her will not be an easy thing, Victor."

"Nor should it. Doesn't mean I won't ask to taste her again," he said with a wry grin.

Daddy laughed then. A full-bodied laugh born of pure amusement. "We've been friends for more years than I care to think about, Victor. Even though I love my Isabella very much, you know I'll always share with those closest to me."

"As we all will, provided your Isabella is comfortable with it should the time come."

"Let's hope that time comes for you all soon, my friend. The feeling I get from her is indescribable. She is everything I could want in a pet or a woman."

Papa Victor paused, then grinned. "One more

taste before Max continues?"

Daddy chuckled again. "Of course. In fact, make her come. Max? Your job is to support her. She puts everything she has into her pleasure. If she has to stand on her own, she'll fall."

"You can count on me, Papa Victor. I'll protect little Kitten from anything." He gave me a cocky grin when I looked over my shoulder at him. "Even rogue orgasms."

That got a laugh from everyone. Even me. Until Papa Victor leaned in to lap at my pussy again. This time, he gripped my hips and pulled me closer. Max moved with me, keeping me upright and comfortably on my feet…

Until Papa Victor groaned and urged one of my legs over his shoulder. Once he did that, my mind got scrambled. Daddy Victor licked all around my pussy. Between my folds, around my lips, my clit, my opening. There wasn't a millimeter of skin he didn't savage. He wasn't as gentle as I'd have thought. The first lick might have been gentle and coaxing, but this was an assault. One I wasn't sure I liked. Wasn't sure I *didn't* like it, either.

Papa Victor drove me higher and higher. It happened so quickly I couldn't process everything happening. The sensations were overwhelming and massive, and all I could do was scream as I came in a wet rush. My body went limp but Max held me fast while Papa Victor drove me higher and higher. One orgasm turned into two. Then three. All in the space of a few minutes. When Papa Victor finally let me go, I was sobbing. I had no idea if I was frightened or just needed fucked into oblivion.

When Papa Victor finally let me go, sweat covered my skin. My legs were too weak to hold me and tears stained my cheeks. Max wrapped his arms around me, trying to steady me. I clung to him, but all I really wanted was my daddy.

I tried to turn in his direction, but Max held me tight. He was moving with me, murmuring to me. *Growling*. At me?

"Give her to me." That was my daddy. Max set me down gently, then Daddy's arms were solidly around me and he held me tightly. "You're OK, Kitten. Shh, shh. It's OK. I've got you."

"Daddy," I whimpered. "Daddy!"

"What the fuck?" That was Max. Pets were never that disrespectful. Littles either. Obviously, Max had had a tough time adjusting to his role, but something was off. "You hurt her!"

"Max! Kneel!" That was Papa Victor. Just the sound of his voice made me bury my face in Daddy's neck. There was an enraged roar, then the sound of a scuffle. "Max!" Papa Victor sounded angry. Was he beating Max?

"No," I whimpered. "Don't hurt Max! Please!"

"You better go to him, Kitten," Daddy whispered in my ear. "Max needs you."

I looked up at Daddy. He looked worried but smoothed the damp hair from my face, stroking my cheek soothingly. He didn't urge me to get up or to move in any way. I'm sure had I wrapped my arms around his neck and hid in his wide chest, he'd have let me. But I could tell by the sound of his voice and the way his brow furrowed slightly that something was very wrong.

I turned my head in Max's direction and saw him standing over his Papa where the other man still sat in his chair. Max's fists were clenched, one raised over his head. Max looked like he'd just thrown a punch at the other man. Victor got to his feet. He didn't retaliate against Max, but his expression was thunderous.

"I will never kneel for you again," Max spat. "I trusted you!"

"And you still should," Victor said, his voice mild, but he looked wary of Max. Like he knew the other man was just waiting to pounce on him.

"No one hurts Kitten! No one!" Max yelled. His rough voice was even harsher when he raised his voice.

"Max, any lesson you get from this will be harsh. I understand your feelings, but you only get one chance."

"You weren't gentle! You're the one who told me I always had to be gentle with Kitten!" Max was going to fight Victor. It was in every line of his body. The clenched fists. The muscles bulging in his arms and shoulders. I was sure Victor could defend himself, but if he did, and Max lost the fight, then Max would be punished. Might still be punished.

"No!" I shoved free of Daddy, stumbling to Max. I put myself between him and Victor. "Please, Max," I whimpered. "Please don't!"

I wrapped my arms around Max's waist, trying to walk him away from Victor, but Max just pulled my arms free and gently urged me behind him. "Go back to Daddy, Kitten. He'll protect you."

"You're supposed to let Daddy defend me," I said, my voice wavering even as I tried to calm myself. "You're supposed to let Daddy go first. Remember? You're to put yourself between me and Daddy when there's danger! Daddy will take care of it!"

Max looked down at me, then back to Victor and bared his teeth. He clamped one arm around me, twisting so that he pinned me to his back as he moved away from Victor toward Daddy.

I peeked around Victor and saw the anguish on his face as he shook his head and dabbed at his lip where Max had hit him. Blood continued to trickle from the cut. Max continued to back me away from Victor until he was behind Daddy.

"I don't know the layout of this place, baby," Max said. "But you need to go to your room and lock the door."

"I'm staying with you and Daddy," I said. My voice was still shaky but I was at least holding myself up. Mostly.

OK, almost mostly.

"It's all right," Daddy said, finally standing. It struck me as odd that Daddy hadn't already taken a stand. Did he not think Victor had done anything wrong? "Stop, Max," he said. "Bring Kitten back to me."

Max growled, shaking his head slightly, but finally giving in and moving toward Daddy. He still kept me behind him, his arm holding me securely to his back.

"I'm so sorry, little Isabella," Victor said, looking as if he truly meant what he was saying. "I didn't want to frighten you. I needed to test Max. I needed to know that he would protect you from any threat. Even me."

"What?" I peeked around Max, not believing what I was hearing. I wiggled away and stepped close to Daddy, but finding Max's hand and keeping a hold of it. "You... did that on purpose?"

"I did," he said, wincing as he spoke. "Max has the most important task of his life. He can say he'll protect you, but I needed to know he was willing to do anything to keep you safe."

"He passed with flying colors," Daddy said.

"The second he realized you'd gone from enjoying yourself to overwhelmed and scared, he pulled you back and got you to safety."

"Daddy?" I looked up at him, stricken. "You let him hurt me... on purpose?"

"No, Kitten," Daddy said, his jaw clenching and unclenching. I realized now that Daddy had been holding on to his temper when he was comforting me. He'd been angry at Victor and trying not to show it.

"No," Victor said softly. "That was all me, Isabella. I'm so sorry for frightening you. But it was more important to me to make sure Max could be what you needed."

"I already told you Max was the one," Daddy snapped. I never thought he'd talk to Victor this harshly.

"I know. But I'm the one giving you Max. I wasn't about to take the chance that he'd balk when it was important. If he'll defend her from me, he'll defend her from anyone. Even you."

I gasped, looking from Victor to Daddy. The men stared each other down.

"You know she'll never have to be protected from me, you son of a bitch."

"I know. But you're going to put her through a lot. Max needs to focus on her and not worry about who is giving her orders. Only about her comfort and safety."

Daddy sighed. "Fuck." He scrubbed his hand over his face. Then he turned to Max. "Have her show you to our room. We'll continue there." He paused before continuing. "You did well, Max. I owe you."

Max never took his gaze from Victor. "Do I belong to Kitten's Daddy Jacob now?"

"You do," Victor said. "He's your new master.

You will address him however he sees fit."

"We can discuss that later," Daddy said. "For now, see to Isabella. Take her to our room and I'll be with you shortly."

Max nodded, his gaze never wavering from Victor. There had been trust lost tonight. More than Victor frightening me with the way he played my pussy into staggering orgasms. He'd dealt a horrible blow to Max's trust, as well. "I'm so sorry, Max," I whispered.

"Not your fault, Kitten," he murmured as he continued to back us out of the room. Once in the hallway, he scooped me up and headed for the stairs. "Which floor?"

"Third," I said, clinging to Max and burying my face in his neck. "At the end of the hall."

Max went swiftly up the stairs. It didn't seem to faze him at all carrying me. He had to be nearly as strong as Daddy. Once inside our suite, Max took me to the corner behind the big bed I shared with Daddy. We were away from prying eyes and he could still see the shadow of the door when it opened. He held me in his lap, his arms securely around me. "Are you OK?"

His voice soothed me just like Daddy's. Instead of the smooth, deep timbre of Daddy's, though, Max's voice was rough and so full of emotion I had to focus on him and shake off my fright. "I'm fine, Max. But you're not."

He shook his head slightly, not speaking for a long time. I was afraid he wasn't going to answer me, but he finally did. "No. But I will be. I'll obey your Daddy, but I make my own decisions regarding you, Kitten. If I even think he's hurting you in any way, I'll intervene. Even if it means a beating."

"Max! Why would you do that? I'm nothing to

you! When you first met me, I got the impression you didn't even like me!"

"I didn't," he admitted with a sigh and a shake of his head. His gaze never wavered from the door. "Or maybe it was more that I didn't like the idea of you." He spoke almost absently. Like he was musing to himself. "I saw you as a spoiled pet who got everything she wanted while I had to work for everything I have. Had to endure beatings when your daddy seemed to protect you from everything, even harsh language. And yet I was supposed to protect you. All I wanted to do was make you want to stay away from me."

I was almost afraid to ask, but I needed to know. "What changed your mind?"

"You. You defended me. No one had ever stood up for me like that before." Max tightened his arms around me. "I knew then I'd always defend you. Victor was right. I was born to protect you."

In my heart, I knew this meant I had to trust Daddy completely. I already did, but I needed to really think about my reactions. Daddy wasn't going to like this at all, but it was Max's reality. If he truly wanted Max as my protector, he needed to know this.

The door opened and Max sat me gently on the floor and stepped in front of me.

"Max." Daddy sounded tired. "I apologize. Victor takes my happiness and Isabella's safety more seriously than I realized. He risked sacrificing our friendship to make you prove yourself."

"I'll always protect Kitten," Max said. I could tell he meant it.

"I know you will. Now. I assume you've got her hidden away? Even from me?" I stood without Max's permission. Max gave me a look but, to his credit, didn't say anything. Daddy held out his hand for me. "Come here, Kitten." I did without hesitation. He pulled me into his arms and just held me for long, long moments. "You know Victor would never hurt you. Right?"

I thought about my answer. What Victor had done, while it hadn't hurt me, had shaken my faith. No, I didn't know he wouldn't hurt me because he had. OK, so he hadn't *hurt* me so much as frighten me nearly to death. The pleasure had just been too much for me to handle. But if Max knew I was uneasy around Victor, he'd never let the man near me, no matter what Daddy said. I knew that in my heart.

"I know," I finally admitted. "If there was even a chance he'd really hurt me, you wouldn't have let him pleasure me, and you certainly wouldn't have taken Max from him."

Daddy let out a sigh of relief and sat on the bed. As a rule, Daddy never showed weakness. Not even to me. But now, he looked like he'd given up something. Or, more accurately, like something had been taken from him. He pulled me onto his lap and just held me. He looked up at Max. "You always use your best judgment with her, Max. Pay attention to her. In the heat of the moment, I might miss something, no matter how hard I try. You can't."

Max's chin went up. "You can count on me, sir."

"He said he would obey you, Daddy, but that he'd make his own decisions if he had to. I know he'll always protect me. Just like I know you'll always protect me."

"Of all my closest friends, I never would have thought Victor would harm you." Daddy shook his head sadly. "I understand why he did what he did, but if he'd warned me, I might have found a better way to test Max."

"It's done, Daddy. Don't worry about it. Maybe he was right. Now you know you can trust Max no matter what."

"Yes, but at what cost to Max?" I knew the cost had been very high. "How do you feel, Kitten?"

"I'm good. Victor scared me with the intensity and speed he made me come, but he didn't hurt me."

"Do you think you could thank Max for saving you?"

"Of course," I said, wiggling off Daddy's lap. I reached for Max. "What should I do to thank him, Daddy?"

Daddy handed me the key to Max's cage. "I think you should let him free, then let him play with you. Do you think you can do that?"

I smiled up at Daddy, then turned to Max. "Yes, Daddy. I think I'd love to do that."

When I knelt before Max to unlock his cock cage, he rested his hand on the top of my head, his fingers tunneling through my hair.

"What are my limits, Daddy Jacob?"

"No limits. But you must wear a condom if you fuck her. That is a hard rule from this point forward. Only I'm allowed to cum in her."

Max nodded. "Understood, Sir."

My hands trembled slightly as I fumbled with the key until the lock finally opened. It took some doing to figure out how to release Max once I'd unlocked the cage, but I finally managed to remove it from his cock and balls. His cock was already semi hard. Once freed, he sprang to life quickly.

Max groaned, obviously glad to be free. I wrapped my hand around his cock. He wasn't as thick as Daddy, but he was longer. "Stroke me," he murmured. "Grip me hard and beat my dick for me."

I did as Max instructed, my gaze focused on his beautiful cock. One hand pumped him while I slid the other up his thigh to grip his ass.

"Surely you want more than a hand job," Daddy said with a light chuckle.

"I do," Max said. Sweat had broken out on his brow and he swallowed as he watched me stroking his cock. "It's been weeks since I've been allowed to come," he admitted. "All in preparation for little Kitten. Victor said that if I did well, you'd let me come, Sir." I hadn't missed the fact that Max didn't like referring to Daddy as Daddy Jacob.

"You're free to come whenever you choose, Max. If you need a condom, tell me." Daddy sat in a chair in the corner of the room, watching us with a smile on his face. "I think Kitten likes you, Max."

"Victor was right in one thing," Max said through clenched teeth as I continued to stroke him. "She is precious."

"That she is."

Out of the corner of my eye, I saw Daddy take out his cock and give it a lazy stroke. At some point, he'd taken off his shirt and now sprawled out lazily in his big chair.

"Suck me, Kitten. I want to feel your mouth on me."

I did as Max instructed, taking him as deeply as I could. I dug my nails into his thigh before I slid a hand around to grip his ass. I moaned around his cock, saliva dripping down my chin as I took him as deep as I could over and over. The more I sucked, the more I swallowed so my throat massaged the head of his dick.

Max let his head fall back, his hand gripping my hair as he let out a loud groan. "Fuuuck! That feels fuckin' good!"

I hummed around him, never letting him slip from my mouth. I focused on Max's cock and all the pleasure I wanted to give him. I was beginning to think Victor wasn't as benevolent as Daddy. Had he really denied Max any kind of sexual pleasure for weeks? I couldn't imagine Daddy not pleasuring me for a single day let alone *weeks*!

With that realization, I resolved myself to give Max as much pleasure as he could stand, no matter what I had to do or how. Max would never regret being given to Daddy. And he'd never regret being responsible for me.

Digging my fingers into his ass once again, I bobbed my head faster, always taking Max as deep as I could. I looked up at him, needing to how much he enjoyed what I was doing. The look of utter bliss on his face was everything I wanted to see. Max looked like he was in heaven.

"Fuck... fuck... *fuck*!" Max chanted the mantra over and over, the muscles over his body flexing as he fucked my face. His hips surged forward even as he held my head still by my hair. He'd taken control of the situation even as I knew he would. When he looked down at me, his eyes seemed out of focus. Like he looked at me but couldn't see me clearly. He closed his eyes tightly, then shook his head before taking a deep breath and pulling back. "Goddamn, baby," he gasped. "Your mouth is so fuckin' good. Fuck!"

"You know... " My gaze snapped to Daddy. I noticed at some point he'd zipped up his pants again. Was he angry with me? He'd said I should pleasure Max to show him gratitude. But did he really want me doing this?

One look at Daddy and I could see how turned

on he was. Something inside me settled. I loved Daddy. Wanted nothing more than to be his kitten and his Isabella. If there were never anyone else in my life, I'd always want there to be Daddy. But I found that I wanted Max, too. Not in the same way I wanted Daddy, but I needed him with me.

"You still haven't tasted her, Max."

Max looked down at me, a feral gleam in his eyes. "No," he said, his voice even more rough than usual. "I ain't." He pulled me up by my hair, then abruptly let go, taking a couple of steps away from me. He looked equal parts horrified and angry. "Fuck," he said, scrubbing a hand over his face.

Instantly, Daddy was on the edge of his seat, readying himself to come to me. "What is it?" The question was sharp. All arousal gone and Daddy was all protective.

"I --" Max swallowed. "I pulled her up by her hair. Kitten," he said gently kneeling down but not moving closer to me. "Did I -- did I hurt you?"

"I… what?" I looked from him to Daddy, confusion and lust warring with each other.

"Max seems to believe he got carried away and was too rough with you, Kitten," Daddy supplied as he sat back in the chair. "Was he?"

"What? No!" I shook my head emphatically. I lunged for Max, grabbing his leg before swallowing his cock again.

"God*damn*! Fuck!" Max's legs trembled and he held my head while he pulled out of my mouth. "Get on the fuckin' bed!" he snapped. "I'm gonna fuckin' come before I'm ready!"

I scrambled up onto the bed like he told me. I yelped as there was an uncomfortable pressure in my ass. Then it dawned on me. The tail I'd worn was still in my ass. I glanced at Daddy, who grinned in amusement. He nodded and I pulled it from my body and tossed it in the general direction of the bathroom. Then I lay back. Spreading my legs, I reached down to also spread my pussy lips. "Take what you need, Max." I spoke softly, watching him. The wild look in his eyes made me want to glance at Daddy for reassurance, but I refrained. Barely. If Max thought he was scaring me, he'd never continue this.

Max stood there looking at me hungrily. He shook his head as if trying to clear it, then looked at Daddy. "Sir, I…" He stopped and shook his head again. "I need your help."

"Tell me what you require, Max. You only need to tell me and it's yours." Daddy hadn't hesitated and I could tell he meant it. Whatever Max required, Daddy would provide.

"Sit with her. Hold her." His voice was even gruffer than normal. He seemed to be riding the edge of his control. "I can't risk doing something to scare her."

"Thank you for taking extra care with my kitten," Daddy said as he moved to sit behind me. He pulled me up so that I relaxed against his chest while his legs were on either side of me. I was mashed up against his cock and it twitched like mad at my back. "It's just one more way you're proving you have Kitten's wellbeing foremost on your mind."

"She's precious," Max repeated absently as he visibly tried to get himself under control.

"She is. Now, take what you need. I'll protect Isabella so you can thoroughly enjoy yourself this first time."

"Thank you, Sir."

I looked up at Daddy. He smiled at me before

gently lifting my legs under the knee and pulling them up to spread me wide. "Feast on her, Max," Daddy whispered. "Taste her sweet pussy and drink her up."

Max crawled on the bed, licking his lips as he neared me. He held my gaze as he lowered his mouth to my pussy and started a delicious assault. Unlike when Victor had me, Max was careful of me, doing his best to pay attention to how fast he drove me up. It softened my heart even more toward the big man, even as it made me sad.

"Don't hold back, Max," I said. "Daddy will take care of me. He won't let you go further than I can stand. I want you to enjoy this. You deserve it more than anyone."

Max glanced up at Daddy, then nodded several times before focusing once again on my pussy. "Thank you, Kitten," Then he dove in.

I cried out softly when his tongue flicked over my lips and clit in a long swipe. Then again when he latched on and sucked. I arched my back, the sensations washing over me like a tidal wave but falling just shy of being too much. Max growled and grunted as he licked and nipped and sucked at my pussy, spearing his tongue deep occasionally as if to lick out every available ounce of juice I produced for him.

"Look at her, Max," Daddy whispered. "See how beautiful she is when you eat her juicy little pussy."

Max obeyed, his eyes wide and glassy with lust. "Fuckin' beautiful," he bit out between licks. It surprised me when he speared me with two fingers, curling them to reach that spot inside me that drove me mad. I screamed as I came unexpectedly, my body breaking out in a fine sweat. Daddy kissed the side of my neck, so at odds with the frenzied eating of my pussy Max was doing.

"That's it, Kitten," he soothed. "Is Max making you feel good?"

"Soooo good, Daddy," I gasped. "So fucking good!"

Daddy chuckled, the sound warming me on the inside even as it grounded me in the middle of such pleasure. "Are you ready for him to fuck you, my beautiful, passionate Kitten?"

"Yes! Please!"

Max looked up, his eyes focused on my face. There was a sinister smile on his lips, but I wasn't afraid. I welcomed Max and anything he wanted to do to me. Because I trusted him. And I trusted Daddy.

Daddy reached to the dresser beside the bed and snagged a condom, tossing it to Max. The other man opened the foil packet and rolled the latex over his cock. He squeezed the base for several seconds even as his cock pulsed in his grasp.

"I won't last long," he said, shaking his head as if he regretted it. "But I'll do my best to make you come, Kitten."

"Please," I begged. "I need you inside me, Max!"

Fisting his cock in a hard grip, Max knelt on the bed in front of me and aimed his cock, tucking the head against my opening. With one more glance at Daddy, Max shoved himself inside me.

The pleasure was instantaneous. I cried out, my hands flying to Max's shoulders. His hips surged against me over and over, fucking me with ever increasing intensity. Max grunted, his voice getting louder and louder as he continued.

"Fuck!" he bit out. Max's lips found mine and he kissed me with all the passion and lust he was showing me now. His tongue darted into my mouth, licking all around inside my mouth. I met his tongue with my own, getting caught up in the erotic play. Max raised himself off me slightly, looking down at where our bodies joined the back up at me. Then to Daddy. "You get to fuck her every day," Max said, his voice husky and rough. "This stunning little body is all yours."

"It is. And I do. I relish getting to fuck her. Not only is she physically perfect, she accepts my needs and gives me everything. Playing my kitten. Being my little girl if I need it. Soothing me when I'm restless."

"You chose well, Sir," Max said. Then he looked back down at me. "It's my privilege to protect her, my very good fortune if you ever decide to give me a taste of her again."

"Do the job you've been given and I will reward you, Max. If Kitten's body is what you wish as payment, I'm more than happy to share." I felt Daddy shrug. "On occasion. You'll be given strict rules, but unless you prove you're untrustworthy or that you can't control yourself, I will forgo your cock cage."

"Much appreciated. I'll control myself. You're the only one who can give me permission to touch her."

"That's right," Daddy affirmed. "Now. Make her come and follow her."

Max gave a sharp cry, his cock pulsing inside me. Then he lowered himself over me once more, wrapped his arms around me and *fucked*.

My orgasm washed over me, the feel of Max wrapping himself around me made me feel cherished. It was its own aphrodisiac, one I was helpless to resist. I screamed, my body seizing as a powerful wave of pleasure crashed over me. I clung to Max even as Daddy stroked my head, brushing damp tendrils away from my face.

Max buried his face in my shoulder and shouted, nipping sharply on my skin. I cried out in surprise, but Max laved his tongue over the small hurt over and over, his big body shuddering over me. His cock pulsed in my cunt. Had he not been gloved, he'd have pumped his cum inside me in a hot, wet splash of seed. Daddy had protected me, though. The only cum I'd ever have in my pussy was Daddy's. I knew this emphatically. Much as I liked Max, that was the way I wanted it.

I looked up into Daddy's eyes. His cock twitched by my head in his pants. I'd slipped down his body as Max had taken me. While Max recovered, kissing my shoulder and neck, I unzipped Daddy's pants and pulled out his cock. It sprang free immediately, precum glistening from the tip. Without looking away, I slid my mouth over the head and pumped his shaft.

"Such a good little pet," he murmured in his deep, smooth voice. "You know exactly what Daddy needs, don't you?"

"Daddy…" I breathed his name before taking the head back in my mouth and sucking as I pumped his beautiful cock. It wasn't long before his breathing was ragged and he grunted. Hot cum erupted from the tip and I swallowed him down greedily, whimpering as I did.

"Such a good girl," Daddy grunted. "Such a greedy pet."

We all relaxed in Daddy's big bed. All sated. I was sleepy and I was pretty sure Max had passed out, his head resting on my chest, his mouth sucking gently at one nipple. Daddy chuckled above me.

"My pets seem to have worn themselves out." He stroked my hair soothingly as he grinned down at me. "Let me get something to clean you both and I'll be back."

I murmured my consent as Daddy slipped out from behind me. Max didn't move, his breath even, and he still sucked my nipple. Daddy managed to get the condom off Max with surprisingly little effort. The other man grunted and snuggled deeper against my body. Daddy cleaned me, then Max. Then he covered us all with a large duvet and crawled in beside me.

I pillowed my head on his arm and he pulled both me and Max close. "I'll protect you both," Daddy said against my temple. "You're both mine now."

"Did you intend to claim Max as another pet?" I was sleepy, my words slightly slurred and my voice higher than normal.

"No. Only as a protector for you. But he's broken in some ways. A proud male about to reach his prime. He's young and I'm thankful Victor found him before he completely lost the good man inside him. He's worth saving, but he needs guidance. I'll be that for him. You'll be his reward from time to time. Can you handle that?"

"I can," I said. "But only if it's what you wish, Daddy. I really like Max. Might even grow to love him someday. But only you are my daddy."

"That's right, Kitten. You're mine and I'm yours."

"Yes," I said, snuggling against Daddy for good measure.

"When you wake, I'll probably be gone. You can find me in my study. There may be meetings, but you know you're always welcome. I'll put a chair for Max in the corner if he wishes to accompany you. If he does, his attire is in the guest bedroom. He may choose. You, however, will present naked with only a tail."

I looked up at him in surprise. "Like the tail I

wore earlier?"

"Yes. There are several in your closet now. Choose one you like. Wear the tail and your collar." He fingered the thing band around my throat. "Nothing else."

"Yes, Daddy."

With that, I sighed happily and closed my eyes. I was eager to see what the days ahead held for me. I had my daddy. Daddy had given me Max. Together we were unstoppable.

Naughty Kitten
A Razor's Edge Daddy Dom Erotica Short
Wanda Violet O.

Daddy always takes such good care of his Kitten. But something's wrong. Daddy's in a snit and I don't know why. I'm the only one he doesn't growl at. Whatever's wrong, the only way to find out is to be a very naughty Kitten. And maybe -- just maybe -- that's exactly what Daddy needs.

Naughty Kitten

My life was… *bliss*!

Daddy was the center of my life and he was simply amazing. He made me feel cherished. Loved beyond measure. He took his pleasure in return for everything he gave me, but he always made sure I was pleased just as much as he was. Max was a rare treasure as well. While I loved my Daddy beyond anything in the world, Max was a huge part of our life. One I knew I never wanted to do without. The only thing marring my complete and utter happiness was… Daddy.

Something was wrong. I hadn't yet gotten up the courage to ask him, but I was going to have to. While he was unfailingly gentle and kind to me, Daddy snapped at everyone who came to his home for business. It was worse at the office, even when it was his most trusted inner circle. The men he called his brothers, Victor, especially, suffered. Which I found odd since Daddy didn't hesitate to have the man in the same room with me.

I knew Daddy wasn't still angry about Victor scaring me when he'd been allowed a taste of my pussy. There were even times when he snapped at Max, who took it as a personal failing, when Max had done nothing wrong. This had to stop. Which meant I had to figure out what was wrong with Daddy and fix it.

Today, Daddy was working in his study. There were several men here for meetings throughout the day. I watched them from my perch on the window in the gym while Max worked out. Daddy had growled at Max this morning for not being in our bedroom when I woke up, which wasn't really Max's fault because I woke up an hour earlier than normal.

Max had taken his rebuke stoically, promising Daddy he'd do better. I felt bad, but Daddy insisted none of it was my fault. Now, I sat in the bed Daddy and Max had made for me in the window seat, wrapped in a fluffy pink blanket. I alternatively watched men coming and going from the estate, and Max as his muscles flexed, sweat glistening off his magnificent body. Yeah. He was pushing himself hard today. Likely trying to work off anger and aggression from Daddy's scolding.

This had to stop. Now.

I waited until Max was on the treadmill, his side to me, running in a lulling rhythm that always put me to sleep when I closed my eyes and listened. Max knew it put me to sleep so after a few minutes, as long as I was still, he'd likely focus on his inner turmoil and not so much on me. Sure enough, after about ten minutes, he stopped even glancing in my direction and started pushing himself harder, upping the speed and running faster.

Carefully, I got off the window seat and fluffed my blankets so that, at first glance, he'd think I was napping. Then I crept out of the gym and downstairs to Daddy's study.

I watched, making certain how many men had come into the mansion versus how many had left. If I'd counted correctly, there was only one person left, that man being Victor. Max would be angry with me if I went anywhere near Victor without him, but I'd had time to reflect on that situation. It had truly pained Victor to have frightened me the way he had. Victor had risked Daddy's wrath, the wrath of a man he called his best friend, to test Max to make sure he'd protect me from anyone, including himself and Daddy.

No. Victor wasn't a threat to me. Daddy knew it, too. Max needed to realize it as well.

One problem at a time.

I wasn't dressed for Daddy's study. While he'd never object to me coming to him even naked, I usually at least wore my little shorts and cute tops when I knew other men were going to be present. Today, I wore a dress of the palest blue with spaghetti straps at the shoulders and the hem stopping slightly above mid thigh. I had pale blue kitten ears in my hair to match my dress and a tail plug of the same blue. Both the ears and the tail sparkled with dark blue sapphires. And yes, Daddy assured me they were real stones. I was barefoot except for a sapphire toe ring on my left foot.

I stood listening at the door to Daddy's study. I could hear Daddy, his voice raised as he yelled at someone. The only other voice I heard sounded like Victor's, which I was expecting. Still, I waited a little while longer just to make certain there was no one else. Victor knew at least some of the problems going on, but I didn't want this conversation in front of anyone else.

Finally, satisfied it was only Daddy and Victor, I took a deep breath and knocked softly three times. Then I waited. I heard Daddy yell.

"Who the fuck is that?"

Followed by Victor's soft, "I'm not sure, Jacob. I'll tell them to leave."

"This is fucking ridiculous. I'm firing Raymond. I explicitly told him I was seeing no one else today!"

"Calm down, Jacob."

"Don't fucking tell me to calm down!"

The door opened just as Daddy roared the last bit and slammed his fist on the table. It took everything I had in me not to jump or to look in any way as if I were frightened. I felt the color drain from my face, but I kept my head up and my shoulders back. My hands clasped behind my back were clenched, but no one could see that.

"Jacob," Victor said quietly as he stepped back and opened the door a little wider so Daddy could see me.

Daddy just stared at me a moment before he stood. He looked nearly as pale as I knew I was. "Kitten," he said softly. "Is everything OK?"

"Yes, Daddy," I said. My voice only wavered a little, but I kept my chin up and tried to put a serene expression on my face. "May I come in, please?"

"Of course, Kitten. Come to me."

I did, without hesitation. Victor closed the door softly behind me as I hurried to Daddy. He held out his hands to me and I wrapped my arms around his waist as he closed around me in a solid wall of love. He held me for several minutes, his body shuddering around mine in a rare show of emotion. Daddy always made me feel like he loved me every bit as much as he said he did, but he never acted like he needed me as much as I needed him. I was beginning to think there was much more he needed than he was taking from me.

"I love you, Daddy," I said, knowing he needed to hear it.

"I love you too, Kitten. So damned much." Finally, he let me go only to scoop me up and sit in his chair with me. I curled myself around him, just hugging him, petting him like he might pet me in an effort to comfort him.

"Where's Max? Does he know you're here?"

"No, Daddy," I said softly. "He's in the gym. I needed to talk to you. I know you're busy, but it's important."

Daddy straightened, looking down at me as if he were ready to give me anything in the world I asked. "What can I help you with, Kitten?"

I took a deep breath before taking the plunge. "Something's wrong, Daddy. I can feel it. You're not happy, and I don't know how to make it better."

If I'd slapped him, I'm not sure Daddy could have looked more surprised. "I -- what? Kitten, I'm extremely happy. I've never been more content in my life. You fulfill parts of me I didn't know were empty." He leaned down to place a gentle kiss on my mouth. I turned my face up to meet his happily, but I didn't encourage him to deepen the kiss. "Tell me what's wrong, baby. I promise, I'll fix it."

"It's you, Daddy. I can tell something's wrong. You're so sweet and kind to me, but you're snapping at everyone else. Even Max, and he doesn't know how to react. He's trying his best. What happened this morning wasn't his fault. I got up early. He's never not been there when I woke up before. And you never told him he had to be there. He doesn't sleep in our room so we have privacy, but now he's making plans to sleep outside our door."

Daddy closed his eyes and winced. "I'm so sorry, Kitten."

I cupped his face in my hands, needing him to look at me. "You have nothing to apologize to me for, Daddy. You've tried to keep your temper from me and you've never taken it out on me. But you need to tell me why you're feeling like this." I shook my head slightly. "Is it me? Am I not being the good Kitten you need?"

"No, Isabella," Daddy said immediately. "You're the perfect little Kitten. Perfect in every way. I never have to worry about your behavior. You've never been afraid to do what I ask of you sexually. I can't imagine my life without you in it."

"Then what is it, Daddy? Tell me what you need." I smiled at him. "That's why I'm here. To make you happy."

Daddy sighed. "You do, sweetheart. You absolutely do."

I did my best to do what Daddy always does to me when I'm either afraid to say something, or just struggle vocalizing exactly what I need. I waited patiently, holding his gaze with mine. Finally, Daddy lowered his head, pressing his forehead against mine. "You're the perfect Kitten, Isabella. The perfect woman. But maybe you're a little too perfect."

I stilled. "Are you tired of me, Daddy?" I tried to ask the question in a matter of fact way so he felt free to tell me if that were the case. Much as it hurt to say those words, I had to know the answer.

"Not at all, Isabella. Not at all. It's just… How to word this," he muttered to himself. After a few moments where he seemed to struggle with himself, he finally spoke again. "Sometimes, kittens are naughty. When they are, their Daddies have to correct their behavior."

"Have I been naughty, Daddy? If so, tell me and I'll fix it. Punish me if you feel it's necessary. You know I'll accept your punishment." He'd only ever spanked me once. That first day I submitted to be his Kitten.

"I know you will, baby. I know. But you've not been naughty. You are, quite literally, the perfect Kitten."

Perfect… Too perfect? I thought for a moment. "Are you saying you need to punish me?"

"Sometimes," Victor said, shocking me. I'd nearly forgotten he was there. "A Daddy needs to spank his Kitten. Usually, Kittens are naughty. They act out. Sometimes it's to get their Daddy's attention, or merely because they feel like it. Sometimes Kittens need the spanking as much as their Daddy needs to give it. It's a way to release emotion for both of them. Also…" He grinned. "Sometimes, it's immensely satisfying to see a naughty Kitten's red bottom when Daddy fucks her."

I looked up at Daddy. He glared at Victor, but I could see the truth of Victor's words. "Daddy," I said, putting a hand on his face gently. "Do you need to spank your Kitten?"

He closed his eyes, looking equally unsettled and aroused. That was all the answer I needed. I stood and stripped off my dress. Turning, I intended to bend over the table, but remembered the damned kitten tail stuck in my ass. I reached for it, unsure what to do with it. Then I felt Daddy's hand on one cheek of my ass and smiled at him over my shoulder. Trusting Daddy to take care of my kitten tail, I leaned over the desk and lay with my arms stretched out above my head, my ass ready for Daddy's punishment. I spread my legs apart so he had as much access to me as he needed.

"Look at my beautiful, brave Kitten," Daddy purred. In that moment, I knew I was absolutely doing the right thing. For whatever reason, Daddy needed this. He needed to see the marks of his dominance on my skin. I trusted Daddy never to hurt me, so I'd take this punishment and embrace it.

"What did I ever do to deserve you?"

"Not as much as you should have, but you're making up for it with your indulgence." I deliberately tried to be a brat to lighten the mood. It worked because Daddy barked out a laugh, rubbing one of my ass cheeks in a large circle as he did.

"OK, my sweet Kitten. You know I'd never hurt you or give you more than you could handle. Right?"

"Yes, Daddy. I'm ready for my punishment now. Will you please spank me?" Much as I wanted to do this for Daddy, I really wanted it over with so we could get to the cuddling part. I was willing to do this for Daddy, but… yeah. My poor ass.

"I'll only be using my hand, Kitten. I don't want you to count them."

"How many spanks are you giving me, Daddy?"

"As many as it takes."

That didn't sound ominous at all.

"This isn't a punishment, Kitten, so, if you accept this like a good little Kitten, I'll make sure you receive pleasure after as a reward."

I looked over my shoulder at him, nodding. "Thank you, Daddy."

Again, he murmured, "Such a brave, good little Kitten."

Then Daddy started spanking me. At first, it wasn't so bad. I gritted my teeth and tried to just absorb the punishment. But then my bottom got hot, and his hand grew heavier and heavier until I was certain my ass glowed like Rudolph's nose. Still, Daddy didn't let up. Not until I let out one broken sob. Tears were already leaking freely down my face, but Daddy must have needed that verbal confirmation I was feeling his punishment. He stopped at once and rubbed my poor bottom gently. The second he did, the pain morphed into… something else. The transition was so swift, I gasped and arched into his touch before I could stop myself.

"Need a break, Kitten?"

A break? Was he kidding? "My ass hurts!"

He chuckled. "I know, Kitten. And it's beautiful,

all red and flushed from my spanking. Absolutely lovely."

I looked back at him, pouting. "I don't like being spanked, Daddy."

"Oh? So, if I dipped my fingers into your pussy, I wouldn't find you wet?"

Of *course* he knew. My Daddy knew me so well. "I didn't say that," I said, trying for haughty, but I wasn't sure I pulled it off.

"Shall I test you?" Without waiting for me to answer, Daddy dragged his fingers through my pussy. They came up gleaming with my moisture. The look of supreme satisfaction on Daddy's face was worth any discomfort to my poor bottom. He looked like he'd just scored the best prize in all the world. And that prize was me. "Such a naughty little pussy," he said, clicking his tongue as he shook his head. "I think it wants more. What do you think, Victor?"

"Hum…" Victor grinned and winked at me when I glanced his way. I'd forgotten he was there. "Perhaps she deserves a small reward first? For being so brave and accepting of your needs as her Daddy."

"Good idea." Daddy gripped my hips and lifted me up to the table. My ass was up in the air but he seemed to want me to keep my upper body low. When I tried to rise to my hands, he shook his head. "Uh uh, Kitten. Face and arms on the table. I want nothing in the air but this beautiful ass." Spreading my legs far apart, Daddy kissed each cheek of my butt gently. "Beautiful, Kitten. Absolutely beautiful."

I struggled to stay still, wiggling my ass a little before I could stop.

"Reach back and spread your cheeks for me," Daddy commanded softly. "Let me see your beautiful pussy and ass." I did, without hesitation, spreading myself wide to his inspection.

Since Daddy had invited Max over to play with me that first time, I'd found I loved the waxing treatments. I was ever so glad I'd asked Daddy to keep it up. I thought he might like it too.

I expected Daddy to comment on my pussy and ass. Instead, he leaned in and took a long slow swipe from my clit, through my pussy, all the way up to end licking over my ass. I let out a startled, excited squeal and shivered, torn on whether to push back into him or pull away. The sensations were at once erotic in the extreme, but bordered on sensory overload.

Daddy didn't let me pull back, though. He gripped my hips before burying his face between my cheeks for several seconds. It felt like he was all over the place. I felt him everywhere. But that couldn't be right. Daddy pulled back for a second before groaning and diving back in. This time, he gripped my hips to hold me steady and contained my struggles as I cried out and wiggled.

I screamed, needing to come with every breath I took. Daddy, ever the expert on holding me right on the edge, kept away from my clit except for the occasional swipe to keep me balanced on that cliff without ever actually falling over.

"Daddy!"

"Fuck, Kitten," he said between licks and slurps. "You're fucking delicious."

I thought I was going to die from the pleasure. And I'd die happy. Daddy's lips and teeth and tongue tormented me in the most wonderful way. The slippery slide over my bare pussy and ass was heaven and hell wrapped into one. Every time I thought I'd come, Daddy would move to a different part of my flesh, always keeping me off balance on the verge of falling.

"Please, Daddy! I need to come! Please may I come on your mouth?"

"Not yet, Kitten," he growled. Not till I tell you."

I let out a strangled sob, tears leaking from my eyes. Sweat coated my skin and I shivered continually.

When he finally took his mouth away from my pussy, I sobbed, afraid he'd leave me like this. I should have known better. Daddy promised he'd give me pleasure if I did what he needed and he would.

He pulled me down from the table, putting my feet on the floor and me in the position I was in before. Bent at the waist, laying on the table with my ass up and my legs spread. Then he unzipped his pants, pulled out his cock, and slammed home.

The fucking he gave me was just shy of brutal. It was something he didn't do with me often and never like this. Max usually calmed him down when he got even close to this level of hard. But Max wasn't here. That tempered my lust just a little bit. Daddy let out a brutal yell, the sound of flesh slapping against flesh loud in his study, even over my cries and Daddy's bellow, though I hadn't come yet. His cum filled me in jet after jet of white-hot heat. Filled me to overflowing and I loved it so much. I love Daddy so much.

Just as Daddy bent to press a kiss to my spine, the door to the study burst open. Max was sweating and had a wild look in his eyes. His hair stood on end, like he'd been pulling at it with his hands over and over.

"She's gone, Daddy Jacob!" He burst out. He looked panicked and devastated at the same time. "I thought she was asleep on the window seat and got lost in my mind on the treadmill run and when I looked back she was --" Max's gaze landed on my and he finally realized I was safe and sound with Daddy. He also realized Victor was with us, though the other man still sat on the couch nowhere near me and Daddy.

"I'm fine, Max," I squeaked. I didn't struggle to get up or to do anything other than lay passively still beneath Daddy.

Then Max's eyes narrowed and his gaze zeroed in on my hot ass. Daddy stood and pulled out of me, using a handkerchief to wipe himself off before tucking his dick back into his pants.

"Did you punish Kitten?" He looked at Daddy expectantly. There was no anger or anything. Well, maybe a little anxiety, but that was Max. He always worried about me. It was just a simple question, though his gaze kept darting to Victor as if he expected the other man to pounce on me.

"I did."

"What'd she do?"

"That's between Kitten and me," Daddy said calmly.

I knew that wouldn't satisfy Max, but he wouldn't keep at Daddy with it. He was always respectful of Daddy, no matter what. Which was one of the things that had led me down here in the first place. Daddy yelling at Max and Max not being able to fight back. Even now, I could see the frustration in him as he clenched his jaw and his fists. The tendons and veins stood out in his neck and arms, but he lowered his head respectfully. "I understand, Daddy Jacob. I would never try to interfere with you and Kitten unless I felt she was in danger or unable to tell you she uncomfortable."

"I was naughty," I blurted out. "Daddy was punishing me because I was naughty." I had to do this.

Had to give this to Max because otherwise he'd beat himself up more than he already was.

Max looked startled. "You're never naughty." He even gave Daddy a look that was suspiciously close to being insubordinate, like he didn't believe any of this bullshit.

"But I was, Max."

Daddy put his hand on my back, preventing me from standing up, which made me suspicious of what was to come, but what the hell. I'd do anything to keep Daddy and Max happy. Right now, they were at odds with each other and Max had no way of fixing it. It was up to me. "I left you without telling you where I was going. You know that was naughty because that's why you're so upset now."

Max jerked like I'd struck him before glancing back and Daddy, then, oddly, Victor. "Yeah. I guess you were."

"Since you're the one she wronged, Max, perhaps you should give her your own punishment."

Max nodded, like he was in a daze, rubbing his hand over his mouth. The sudden lust in Max's eyes both thrilled and terrified me. I had a feeling my poor ass wasn't done taking a beating yet. Sitting down was going to be difficult for a few days. But if it cleared the air between the two men, it would be worth it.

"Yeah," Max finally said. "Maybe I should." Then his gaze snapped to mine. He wouldn't ask. I knew it in my heart. Fortunately, he didn't have to.

"Kitten, if you choose to accept Max's punishment, it's possible -- probable, even -- that he won't let you come, no matter what he does. I know I made you promises that I haven't fulfilled yet, but, if you agree to this, Max's punishment will have to be completed first. Do you understand?"

"I do, Daddy," I said, my gaze never leaving Max's. "I was naughty and scared Max. He deserves to be allowed to punish me."

He petted my back. "Such a brave Kitten," he murmured. "Always looking out for me and Max."

"Because both of you look out for me," I said, bowing my head. "I love you, Daddy."

"I love you, too, Kitten."

I looked at Max. I could see the love in his eyes. It was different from Daddy's love for me, but it was there, just the same. "I love you, Max. I know I've never said it before, but you're very important to me."

He nodded, that lust in his gaze punching through me so hard I nearly gasped. "I love you too, little Kitten. I couldn't bear it if something happened to you." Surprisingly, he glanced at Victor once before shaking his head and bringing his focus back to me. "I choose to spank you, Kitten," Max said without further preamble. "Twenty spanks with my hand."

My poor ass! "I understand."

"You don't have to count," Max said, "but I want honest reactions. If it hurts, I want your screams. If it brings tears, I want your sobs."

"I understand," I said again.

"One more thing before we began," Daddy said. "From now on, Max will have a hand in your punishment. Max, you will come to me if you feel Kitten needs correction, but you will not punish her arbitrarily. You always have to discuss it with me first, but if the punishment is your idea, you will be the one to administer it while I observe."

"Understood, Daddy Jacob," Max acknowledged. "Kitten?"

"Yes, Daddy," I said, insanely pleased Daddy had made this step. He'd included Max in my care.

"Begin," Daddy said.

Max moved behind me, rubbing my bottom with one hand as he pushed me against the table with the other. I thought he'd start right away, but he didn't. Instead, he looked back at Daddy. "You've already spanked her. Will you watch and make sure I don't hurt her?"

"Of course I'll watch her, Max. Thank you for being so thoughtful," Daddy answered.

"It's a spanking," I snapped, my nerves getting the better of me. "It's gonna hurt!"

Daddy and Vincent chuckled. Max gave my ass a smart swat. "No sassing."

Daddy moved to sit beside Vincent. I knew Daddy did it to make Max more comfortable. If Daddy was close to Vincent, Max could watch the other man and still take his cues from Daddy. It made my heart swell with pride to know Daddy was taking care of Max the same as he was taking care of me.

"The count is twenty, Kitten," Max said in a stern voice.

"Please, will you give me my punishment, Max?" I said, pouting. And yes. I'd make them fuss over me appropriately and cuddle me the rest of the day.

"Very well, Kitten." Then he started. My ass was already hurting, but Max had no give in him. He didn't go easy on me. With every spank, he fumed. *Smack!* "Do you have any idea --" *Smack!* "How much you frightened me?" *Smack, smack!* "I had no idea where you were." *Smack!* "You deliberately set up your blankets to make me think you were curled under them." *Smack!* "You deceived me." *Smack!* "You may not have said anything, but you might as well have lied to me!" *Smack, smack, smack!* He finished out the remainder of my twenty spanks quick and hard.

I cried out, trying not to tense because I knew it would only hurt worse. The more he laid out my infractions, the harder he spanked me. When he stopped, I thought he'd finished, but when I tried to raise up, his hand pushed at my back until I lay on the table once more.

"We're not done, Kitten. We're only half way." From the sound of his voice, he was eager to get to the next ten spanks.

"Please, Max," I wailed. "My bottom hurts! I'm not gonna be able to sit for a week!" I wailed even as I cried. Tears ran down my face unchecked. I looked to Daddy, but he just looked supremely satisfied. Not like he was ready to stop this anytime soon.

"Naughty Kittens are meant to sit on a hot bottom to remind them to behave. Ten more. Perhaps you'll think twice before running away without telling me what's going on." Max sounded angry. And yeah. I got it. But my ass hurt!

Without warning, Max dipped his fingers to my pussy. I gasped and pushed back into his hand. "I think Kitten is enjoying her punishment," he murmured. "Daddy Jacob put his cum in you so it's hard to tell how wet you are, but your little clit is swollen and throbs under my fingers. Perhaps this wasn't as much of a punishment as I thought it would be."

"Please, Max," I whimpered. "I need to come so bad!"

"I know you do, Kitten. You're such a needy little thing. Only ten more spanks, then we'll see if you deserve to come."

All I could do was sob as I lay passively on the table awaiting the rest of my punishment. Then Max started up again. I cried out with every smack on my ass until I was *wailing* on the last three. Once he'd delivered the last spanks, Max bent to press his lips to my abused flesh. I yelped, but allowed the contact.

Then Daddy was beside me, petting my hair and murmuring how I was such a good kitten and how proud he was of me for taking my punishment so well. Personally, I didn't think I'd taken it all that well. I'd intended on holding everything in, but then Max had to go and order me to let it out. Telling me he wanted my screams.

Daddy handed Max a condom and I sobbed again, this time in relief. I wiggled my ass, telling Max without words what I wanted.

"Oh, you think you're going to get to come?" Max sounded more in control now. I was sure he'd look less wild if I could see him, but I faced away. Every time I tried to turn around, he pushed me back down on the table. "I've still not decided how long to make you hold off your orgasm. I'm sure you should."

"But I've already been punished!" I wailed. "I'm a good Kitten!"

"Of course you are," Max said as he petted my back from neck to the base of my spine. "But you're also naughty. And naughty Kittens don't get to come. At least not right away."

I let out a little sob of frustration then, wiping at my tears with my forearm. "Wanna come," I pouted.

"None of that," Max said as I heard him rip open a condom packet and sheathe himself. Then he gripped my hips and shoved his cock deep inside of me. "So tight," he bit out. "So fucking good!"

"Her sweet pussy grips you like a vise, doesn't it, Max?" Daddy was by my side, his mouth by my ear as he petted my hair away from my face. He leaned in to kiss my lips and I parted them eagerly, wanting

Daddy's kiss desperately. "Such a sweet little Kitten," he praised. "So very good to her Daddy and to Max."

"Please, Daddy," I gasped out as Max rode me hard. "Please let me come?"

"Not yet. This is Max's time and he says your punishment isn't yet over."

Max wasn't gentle. I had to brace myself on the table and just hold on as he gave me a teeth-chattering ride. His grunts filled the room as he fucked me hard, pistoning his dick in and out of my pussy. Though my ass hurt every time he slammed into me, the pain stirred something inside me that threatened to burst. Just the tiniest bit of friction on my clit would send me over, but he wouldn't allow it. Daddy was no help either. True to his word, he let Max control this. I knew Daddy would take care of me later, though.

All too soon, I felt Max's cock swelling inside me. With a brutal shout, Max threw back his head and came. His dick pulsed inside me, threatening to send me over the edge into my own orgasm. But no. I wasn't allowed. Which I'd known going in. But knowing and experiencing are two entirely different things. Still, it was worth it if it put Daddy and Max back on the same page and helped Daddy with his need to dominate and punish me from time to time.

Before I thought too much about it, I got off the table and turned around, sinking to my knees and snagging a box of tissue from the table as I went. Before Max or Daddy could say anything, I took the condom from Max's dick and wrapped it in tissues, then sucked Max gently, cleaning him of his seed. If he tasted a little like latex, it wasn't bad. And it was the least I could do after everything Max had done for me.

"Ah," Daddy said. "Good Kitten. You made Max come then cleaned him up."

"Unlike some of us," I grumbled. Daddy laughed loudly, obviously amused by my sass.

Max delved his hand into my hair and petted me, even as he complained. "Brat. Don't ever leave me again without telling me where you're going."

"You wouldn't have wanted me to leave," I said. "Because you knew Victor was still in the house." I stood and wrapped my arms around Max's neck, nuzzling his neck affectionately.

"Exactly," Max said, glancing at Victor.

"But it's stupid!" I continued, needing to drive this point home. "Victor won't hurt me, Max. If he would, Daddy would never let him near me. You know that! And I had to talk to Daddy. It was important."

There was silence for a long while. Finally, Max lowered his head and kissed me gently. "I know. Victor isn't bad, and he had your well being at heart."

"So you'll forgive him?"

Max sighed. "Yeah, Kitten. I'll forgive him."

I smiled. "Thank you, Max."

With another kiss, Max nodded to Daddy. "I'm through with my punishment. May I go take a shower?"

"Yes, Max. And thank you for always looking out for Kitten. I'm sorry if I've been grumpy and taking it out on you. I couldn't ask for a better protector for my sweet Kitten."

Color swept through Max's cheeks, but he nodded his acknowledgement. He looked at Victor. "I understand what you did. While I still don't like it, I know you'd never hurt Kitten. You were wrong in your methods, but you had her best interest at heart."

"Will you forgive me?" Victor looked and sounded like it really meant something to him. Maybe it did.

"Yes. But I'm not sure I can call you Papa again. Not for a while."

I knew that single word cost Max. When he glanced in my direction, I knew he'd only done it for me and my heart warmed.

Once he'd shut the door, Daddy pulled me into his arms. "You've brought so much into my life, Kitten. I absolutely made the right choice to bring you to me when I did. You are… *perfect*!"

"Perhaps I need to be less perfect," I said with a grin. "Seems my Daddy needs a naughty Kitten sometimes."

He chuckled. "Perhaps I do. But only if you're good with being punished."

"Maybe you need to know I'm not afraid to be naughty more than you need to punish me?"

Daddy cocked his head to the side and thought about that for a minute. "Maybe." Then he grinned wickedly. "But I do so love looking at your red bottom. It fills me with satisfaction. Both that I allowed those lovely cheeks to be reddened by a punishment, and that you agreed to let me put there. So perhaps a little of both."

I smiled, feeling more at peace than I had in the weeks since the incident with Papa Victor. "Whatever you need, Daddy, I'll gladly provide." Then I rolled my eyes. "No matter the cost to my poor bottom."

Pulling me into his arms, Daddy chuckled. "Just know that I'll never hurt you, Kitten. I'll never mistreat or humiliate you in any way. But I won't hesitate to spank your naughty bottom wherever we are if I believe you need it."

I could live with that. I looked at Papa Victor. "I want you to know I'm not afraid of you," I said.

"Daddy was upset with you before, but I know he's happy that he believes without a doubt he can trust Max."

"Thank you, little one."

"Would you be willing to let Papa Victor help me bathe you, Kitten? You went to him willingly before. Perhaps he could gentle you to his touch once again?"

I thought about it, looking at Papa Victor. He smiled gently at me. Yeah, his cock was hard and standing out from his expensive slacks, but he hadn't made any kind of move on me during this whole time. Hadn't tried to get Daddy to let him touch me or even approach me. Besides, Daddy would be with me. He'd told me that sometimes he'd let certain men he trusted have the use of my body. There had been very specific rules laid out for that.

"I think I'd like that, Daddy." I gave Papa Victor a shy smile even as I shivered in anticipation. This would be the first time since Papa Victor had eaten my pussy that Daddy had let anyone other than Max touch me.

Daddy held out his hand to me and I took it. "We'll bathe in here, Kitten," he said. There was a bathroom inside Daddy's study with a large, frameless shower with multiple handheld shower heads, including one in the middle that allowed a gentle flow of water over a wide area. There were benches lining the stall with all manner of shower products and a container filled with condoms. Handy!

Daddy turned on the water, adjusting it to a steamy tropical paradise, just like he knew I loved it. Then he grabbed a couple of shower bombs from a one of the containers on the benches and tossed them into the center where the steady waterfall quickly started to disintegrate them. The scent of jasmine and lavender quickly filled the room, creating a sense of soothing peace.

I sighed happily up at Daddy. "Thank you."

"For what, baby?"

"For telling me what was wrong and how to fix it. I knew you were upset about something. I just didn't know what."

"I was never upset at *you*. You know that. Right?"

"Daddy," I giggled. "I was the only one you weren't growling at. I knew you weren't upset with me." I tilted my head, thinking about that statement. "But, really, it was kind of my fault. You thought I didn't fully trust you enough to act out and be naughty sometimes. When, in reality, I just wanted to be the perfect Kitten. For you. So you always know how thankful and grateful I am for the wonderful life you've given me."

"You've given me much as well, Kitten. But, just so you know, a naughty Kitten isn't a bad Kitten. Be as naughty as you want to be as long as you're willing to accept any punishment I give you."

"I will, Daddy." When he chuckled and pulled me into his arms for a tight hug, I knew I hadn't kept the mischievous grin from my lips.

Daddy stripped, as did Victor. Victor stepped into the shower first, ducking under the hot water with an appreciative groan. Daddy followed, scooping me up into his arms as he went.

"Now, little Kitten," Daddy said. "Let's get you clean so we can dirty you up again."

I raised my arms to circle Daddy's neck and kissed him. "Yes, Daddy."

"No kiss for me?" I looked over my shoulder to find Papa Victor standing there with a cute pout on his face.

I glanced at Daddy, who nodded. "I'm with you, Kitten. Victor knows what's allowed and what needs my express permission. He will abide by those rules. All you have to worry about is doing what he tells you. I'll stop anything I don't approve of before you have a chance to be concerned. You can't do anything wrong with me here, Kitten. Just enjoy yourself and concentrate on pleasing Victor."

"Now," Papa Victor said. "I'd like that hug and kiss, little Kitten."

Shyly, I slid my arms around Papa Victor. I went up on my toes and pressed my lips to his. Victor's arms slid around me, the water wetting our bodies, letting our skin slide together in a sensual glide.

Victor let me kiss him at my leisure for several moments before thrusting his tongue gently into my mouth, more an encouragement than a demand. Sighing, I opened to him, meeting his tongue with my own. His kisses were arousing and I found myself rubbing my thighs together, my earlier denied orgasm starting to take its toll.

"Mmmm…" Victor groaned appreciatively. "Your kisses are as sweet as everything else about you, Kitten."

"Best we wash her," Daddy said, stepping closer so he pressed against mine from behind. His cock pulsed where it was mashed between us. "So we can dirty her up again." Both men chuckled and a flush of desire swept through me. I hadn't realized how much I really wanted to do this for Daddy. Then something occurred to me.

"May I ask a question, Daddy?"

"Of course, Kitten. Anything."

"Were you upset that, because of what happened

with Victor before, because he frightened me and tested Max without telling you first, you couldn't let Victor play with me?"

I looked back at Daddy, needing to see his reaction. When he glanced up at Victor, I knew I'd been right. Quickly, I turned my head to look at Papa Victor. The man held Daddy's gaze easily.

"You need to tell her, Jacob," Victor said softly. "It's not likely there will be a need, but she needs to know in case there is."

"What is it, Daddy?"

He sighed, he turned me around to face him. Gripping my shoulders firmly, he bent down to better look into my eyes. "Nothing is ever going to separate us, Kitten. I'm yours, you're mine. Remember?"

"Yes, Daddy." Where was he going with this?

"In the event something happens to me, as my possession, you will be given to the person I trust most. That's Victor. He would take over the care for both you and Max. For that reason, I need you to feel comfortable with his touch. When things happened the way they did, it put this aspect of our life together on hold. It had nothing to do with my recent foul mood, but your comfort and safety are always a concern for me. With things mended between us all, I can now begin to get you used to Victor."

I frowned. "But what if Papa Victor finds his own Kitten or Puppy? She or he might not want him to have another Kitten in their lives."

"In that event," Victor said, "your daddy and I would choose from his most trusted brothers. He would never risk you not having a good home should he be taken from us. Neither would I, Kitten. You're important to me because of the peace and joy you've brought to my closest friend."

"Enough of this talk," Daddy said. "It's time for your reward for taking my punishment so bravely."

"Good," I said. "About time." I tried to sound bratty and sassy. Truth was, that whole conversation was disturbing. Not because I didn't trust Daddy with any decisions in that regard, I just didn't like to contemplate something happening to Daddy. No matter how much I might grow to like Papa Victor, there was no one in the world who could replace Daddy in my life.

Both men chuckled. Victor reached for the shower gel -- a scent complimenting the shower bombs -- and soaped my skin gently. Daddy took my lips in a gentle kiss that soon turned hot and greedy. I knew my own kisses mirrored his. I needed to be fucked. To be used as Daddy pleased. If he said it was necessary for me to get used to Victor's touch, then I was willing. As long as I got to come.

Victor ran his hands, slippery with the shower gel, all over me, paying close attention to my breasts and, especially, my pussy and ass. Over and over he stroked my bare mound. Petting me. Arousing me. I thrust my ass back to him and he used his other hand to play with my ass, sliding his fingers from top to bottom but never penetrating me. Just like Daddy had instructed all of his men my first day in the office with Daddy's most trusted circle.

"May I dip one finger into her ass, Jacob? She seems to like my touch."

"Yes. She takes tail plugs. A finger or two won't hurt her."

Jacob paused. "You haven't taken her ass yet?"

"No. I was savoring all she had to offer. Stretching her gently and slowly."

Nodding, Jacob murmured, "A wise choice.

Perhaps I could help you stretch her. No more than two fingers."

"I would be grateful." Daddy looked down to my upturned face just as Papa Victor slowly penetrated my ass. Using one finger, he pumped and twisted, circling his finger inside me before adding a second finger.

I gasped, then moaned into Daddy's mouth. My back arched, offering Victor my virgin ass to play with.

"Such a greedy little thing." Victor chuckled. "She loves her pleasures."

"Oh, she definitely does. Use your other hand to stroke her pussy."

He did. "So soft and wet. I feel her quivering around me. She's so needy and responsive to sexual stimulus. Keeping a greedy little Kitten like her satisfied must be a great reward."

"Never have I met her match in passion and giving of herself. She's completely selfless in that regard even as she's a demanding lover."

"I can't imagine this little one being demanding. She's so demure."

"Oh, but she is. You've seen her when she's on the verge of coming and I won't let her. I'm surprised she obeyed Max."

"I'm right here, you know," I snipped. Immediately, I wish I hadn't said it. Not because Daddy or Victor said anything, but because a good Kitten never sasses. Though, to be fair, I'd been sassy most of the afternoon. At least, since realizing Daddy needed a naughty Kitten sometimes. Both men froze.

"I think we've created a monster," Daddy said, eyes wide in surprise before he grinned down at me. "I could grow to crave that bratty tone." I nearly sagged in relief.

"Seems Kitten is impatient." Papa Victor chuckled. Then he stood tall and proud, head high. "I humbly ask your permission to pleasure your Kitten, Jacob. Specifically, I'd like to suck her nipples, tongue her pussy and ass, then fuck her sweet cunt until she comes." The surge of lust was nearly too strong to contain. A gasp left me before I could stop it. I clung to Daddy for support, not because I was afraid. I thought I might want this.

"I owe you much, Victor. You may pleasure Kitten in the way you described." Daddy looked down at me. "I won't leave your side, Kitten. In fact, I may make my own demands of you." His smile was wicked. There was no way to suppress my whimper of need.

"Thank you, Daddy," I said, trying to be a polite Kitten after my naughty outburst.

Victor wrapped his arms around me from behind, palming my tiny tits in his big hands. "Those hard nipples are stabbing my palms," he whispered in my ear. "Maybe I should suck you now. Would you like that, Kitten? Would you let me suck your nipples while your Daddy watches me? Do you think it will make him hard?"

"Yes, Sir," I said with a grin. "I think Daddy likes watching me get fucked sometimes."

"Who wouldn't?" Victor chuckled in my ear, sending shivers through my body. "You're such a beautiful, passionate thing. Turn around."

I did as Papa Victor instructed. Daddy moved to sit on one of the benches lining the shower. Needing reassurance, I looked at Daddy. He was lazily stroking his cock, his gaze fixed on me. With a nod and a grin, he gave me his blessing and I lost myself in Victor's attention.

His mouth fastened on first one nipple, then the other. Over and over he alternated, sucking, nipping, tugging with his teeth until I was crying out in both pleasure and just the smallest amount of pain. It all mixed together to make me writhe in Victor's arms, needing to get closer to him. I wanted to rub my body over his, letting the light dusting of chest hair abrade my poor abused nipples.

With a growl, Victor lifted me in his arms and I wrapped my legs around his waist as he carried me to the bench next to Daddy. He bent me over so that my hands rested on the marble seat so I stood beside Daddy. All I had to do was turn my head and Daddy's cock was right there! Without asking, I stepped to the side so my hands were resting on Daddy's thighs instead of the bench. This way, I could suck Daddy's cock while Victor played with me.

A warm chuckle came from behind me. "She loves her Daddy's cock."

"That she does," Daddy agreed. "And I give it to her whenever she wants it."

I looked up at Daddy. "It's my favorite treat." They both chuckled.

Victor gripped my ass in both of his big hands. I winced.

"Ahhh," Victor commiserated. "Does Kitten have a sore bottom?"

"Yes," I said in a pouty voice. Then I looked up at Daddy and grinned. "But it was worth it. Both times."

Daddy leaned in for a kiss. He thrust his tongue deep, encouraging me to tangle with him as Victor massaged my butt. Then I sucked in a breath as I felt Victor nuzzle between my legs, his lips kissing the inside of my thighs, the slight stubble on his face abrading my tender flesh in an erotic way.

"Going to taste you now. Need another hit of that sweet nectar." Next thing I felt was Victor's tongue at my clit. I cried out into Daddy's mouth, my legs threatening to buckle. Victor kept his grip firm, keeping me from falling to the shower floor. Then his tongue moved to my pussy. Over and over he licked and sucked. His hums of appreciation and grunts every time he got another drop of my honey were loud in the shower.

"Suck my cock, Kitten," Daddy demanded. Without giving me a chance to comply, he tunneled a hand through my hair and fisted it there, forcing me down to his twitching dick. I took him eagerly, keeping my hands on his thighs. Daddy liked for me to use my mouth to take as much of his cock as I could. The more turned on I got, the harder and faster I sucked him. The deeper I took him. When I gagged on his cock, my pussy clenched and Victor groaned as he slurped up my juices.

"Fuck!" Victor bit out between swipes of his tongue. "She's so fucking wet!"

"She's a lusty one," Daddy said through clenched teeth as I swallowed him down.

I was growing comfortable with the rhythm, the feel of Victor's tongue on my pussy when he backed off. When he dove back in, he licked a long, slow lick starting at my clit, to my pussy… then straight up to my ass. He swirled his tongue around several times and I screamed in reaction.

Victor chuckled before inserting one finger in my asshole. "You definitely need to fuck this little ass, Jacob. She'll lose her Goddamned mind when you do."

"Intend to. Right now, though, I'm thoroughly enjoying her hot mouth."

For a long time, they had me like this. Me sucking Daddy's cock, Papa Victor driving me crazy as he tongued my clit, pussy, and ass. In between, he finger fucked my ass and pussy until I thought I'd explode. Daddy hadn't given me permission to come yet, and I was currently gagging myself on his cock.

Sucks to me be me.

When the sensations got to be too much, when I knew there was no way I could possibly hold off any longer, I pulled away from Daddy's cock and screamed. "I need to come, Daddy! Right... fucking... *now*!"

Victor swatted my ass and I yelped. The pain from my earlier spanking didn't help my current predicament. If fact, when it meshed with all the pleasure I was getting, it was the final sensation that pushed me over the edge. I came with a wet rush. Victor's fingers were still in my pussy and ass, so I know he felt it. In fact, I felt myself gushing on his hand with each spasm of my pussy as I came.

"Did you give her permission to come?" Papa Victor glanced up at Daddy who was frowning at me. He ruined the effect when his lips twitched and he had to clear his throat. "Absolutely not."

"Oh, God," I groaned. Daddy pulled me into his lap and gave up the fight to keep from laughing at me. I glared up at him. "I don't see anything so funny."

"You just had to go and be naughty not an hour after your punishment."

"I couldn't help it! Papa Victor had his fingers in my pussy and my ass, and you had your dick down my throat. It was a deadly combination, Daddy."

That got them both laughing. Victor sat on the bench beside us and patted the space in between. "You're priceless, Kitten. Come here. Lay on your back with your head on Jacob's lap. I want to fuck you now."

"And you may come whenever you like," Daddy promised, still chuckling.

I sighed gratefully. "Thank you, Daddy." Again they chuckled.

Victor grinned at me as he retrieved a condom from the container and tore it open. He rolled on the thin piece of latex and gave himself several shallow pumps. "Looking forward to this," he murmured.

Victor urged me to drape my legs over his thighs so my ass was slightly off the marble bench. Then he slid his cock inside me in one slow, sure stroke. "Fuck!" He bit out. "As much as you fuck her and she's still this tight?"

"She is," Daddy said with pride. "Tight. Wet. Greedy for cock."

"That she is," Victor said as he adjusted his position on the bench. Then he started a hard, driving rhythm. Over and over he plunged into me. Fucking me without mercy.

Arching my back, I screamed, gripping Daddy's hand in one tight fist while my other one found Victor's thick wrist where he gripped my waist. He pulled me to him with every stroke he made, fucking me harder and harder with every stroke. "Fucking little kitten whore," he bit out. "Taking my cock so good!"

"I am a little whore," I whispered, my words broken by the jarring of my body.

"You're my little kitten whore," Daddy said before urging my head back to suck at the head of his cock.

My body shook with my fucking. My pussy wept with desire. My clit throbbed whenever Victor brushed it with his thumb. My mind… scrambled. An orgasm rushed through me. Once. Then again. I screamed over and over, my body convulsing and milking Victor's dick, wanting his seed.

"That's it, Kitten," Victor growled. "Take my cum. Take it deep in that little pussy!"

With three more rapid strokes, Victor bellowed to the ceiling. The tendons stood out in his neck, the veins in his muscular shoulders and arms stood out starkly. He held me tightly against him as his cock twitched and pumped his cum into the condom he'd put on before sliding inside me.

When he finally relaxed, he collapsed onto the bench, laying on his back with a loud groan. "Fuuuuuck."

Daddy chuckled, but was already pulling me across his thighs, kissing me deeply before turning me to straddle his lap. Daddy took me bare, as always, and I sighed in contentment. I tried my best to move on him, but Daddy just gripped my waist and did most of the work for me. "Gonna put my cum in you, Kitten. You ready?"

"Yes, Daddy," I cried. "I need your cum! Please! Put it in my pussy!"

With a brutal roar, he did. I felt him pulsing inside me, filling me so full. His orgasm triggered my own and I screamed once more. My throat hurt. My bottom hurt. But when my body finally relaxed, I fell forward onto Daddy's chest with a contented sigh.

I'm not sure what happened next. Papa Victor must have left because the next thing I knew it was just me and Daddy. He still held me in the steamy shower, kissing my temple and stroking my hair away from my face. Telling me how much he loved me and how proud of me he was. "Nothing will ever separate us,

Kitten," he said. "I'm yours. You're mine."

"Yes, Daddy. You're mine. I'm yours. I never want to be apart from you."

Daddy turned off the shower and dried me with a warm, fluffy towel. Then he wrapped me in another dry one and took me upstairs. Max was waiting in our bedroom. Vaguely, I noted the nest he'd made in the corner of the room but was too drained to say anything.

"Not tonight, Max," Daddy said. "You're in bed with us. In you go."

When Daddy took my towel and put me in bed, Max reached for me and I went willingly. Then Daddy was on the other side of me, pulling me close. With the two men who meant the most to me in the whole world wrapped around me, I fell asleep almost instantly.

Later, I'd contemplate all the naughty things I could do to meet Daddy's darker need to punish me. I'd also decide I'd wait a little while to try it. After all, my poor bottom could take only so much.

But that was later. Right now, the only thing I needed to do was sleep.

Kitten's Reward
A Razor's Edge Daddy Dom Erotica Short
Wanda Violet O.

I was very naughty indeed. Now Daddy and Max won't let me come, but they're bent on driving me out of my mind. Not to mention the spanking I earned.

As Max turns my bottom red and Daddy prepares me for what is to come, I can't help but wonder if I'll survive the pleasure.

Kitten's Punishment

"Kitten!" Daddy sounded put out. Probably because I was playing and not paying him any attention.

"Kitten!" Max too. "Where the fuck is she?"

"Relax, Max. She's exploring her naughty side. She knows I need it as much as she does."

"Yeah, well, I *don't* need it," Max grumbled. "But if she doesn't get her ass to me right now, I'm gonna paddle it!"

I tried to stifle a giggle, but Max heard me. I heard his heavy footfalls headed my way and I scooted deeper into the closet. Sure enough, the door was thrown open and Max shoved aside the heavy coats until he found me huddled in a corner in the secret bed I'd made. I gave him a little wave and a bright smile. "Hi, Max."

"You're in so much trouble, Kitten."

"I think I created a monster," Daddy muttered, shaking his head as he smothered a grin. "Get on out here, Kitten. You've earned a punishment."

"Who's idea was it for her to act out?" Max scrubbed his hand through his shaggy hair.

"That would be me," Daddy admitted, his arms crossed over his scrumptious chest. He looked stern, but also amused.

"Well, it was a stupid ass idea," Max muttered, sliding Daddy a glance.

"You're getting awfully snippy yourself, Max."

"Maybe Max needs to be punished, too," I said cheerily, grinning at Max. He gave me a withering look.

"Maybe he does," Daddy agreed. "But not for this. You know Max worries when you're out of his sight."

I sighed, immediately contrite. "Yes, Daddy. I'm sorry, Max."

"Come on, Kitten. Out you go." Daddy didn't sound angry with me. Resigned and slightly amused? Totally. But not angry.

Max, on the other hand…

Yeah, I might have pushed him a little too far. His hair was a wild mess, like he'd run his fingers through it over and over in agitation. I went to him and wrapped my arms around his neck, holding him close. "I'm sorry, Max. I didn't mean to worry you. I was just playing Hide and Seek."

"Who were you playing with? There's nobody here other than the servants, and they were all looking for you too."

I smiled brightly. "See? I had tons of people I was playing with."

"I'm afraid it doesn't work that way, Kitten," Daddy said. "You have to tell people you're playing Hide and Seek so we all know we're supposed to be hunting for you."

I gave him a confused look. "But… you were already doing it. Why would I tell you to do something when it was already happening?" There. That should work.

"Yeah. She definitely needs to be punished," Max said, scooping me up over his shoulder and swatting my ass.

"Hey!"

"I told you, Kitten. Max is allowed to punish you when he sees fit."

"But he has to tell you! You don't have to agree to it!"

Max continued through the house with me, up to

our playroom. Daddy chuckled as he followed behind us. Obviously, Max and I were very amusing to Daddy. It made me happy because Daddy didn't smile or laugh often enough. He was a very busy, very powerful man. If I had to get my ass roasted from time to time to let him play a little, it was a small price to pay. While I was certain Max was genuinely put out, I also happened to know he loved punishing me. So? Win win. Except for my poor ass.

The room was filled with all kinds of toys, including a couple of Saint Andrew's crosses, a Catherine wheel, a stockade, sex swings, and, of course, spanking benches. There were numerous paddles, whips, and restraints, but Daddy hadn't introduced me to much in here yet.

Once inside, Max took me to a spanking bench. That particular piece of equipment I was getting used to. It was Max's favorite place to spank me because it was the perfect height for him to fuck me at his leisure. Before, during, or after. He quickly stripped me, leaving only the metal collar Daddy had given me as a symbol of his ownership. I was allowed to take it off whenever I was in the house, but I loved it so I never did. Max respected that.

"Up you go," Max said, helping me onto the bench. There were two padded shelves for me to place my hands and knees on, with a taller ridge between my legs where I could rest my body if I needed to. Max secured my wrists, strapping me in with leather restraints. He did the same with my ankles. I was able to look back over my shoulder at Max, but not much more. He could have prevented even that if he'd wanted, but neither Max nor Daddy would prevent me from making eye contact with them. At least, not without telling me exactly what was going to happen.

"Now," he said. "What to deliver your punishment with, hmm?"

"What?" Always before he'd used his hand. He delighted in rubbing my ass as he spanked me. I suspected he loved the heat radiating from my skin as the punishment grew more and more intense.

"You didn't think I was using my hand this time, did you?"

"Yes!" I screeched. "Yes, I did!"

Daddy burst out laughing, leaning down to kiss the top of my head. "You pushed Max just a little too far, Kitten. You know how he worries, yet you actually hid from him and stayed hidden even after he called out to you this time."

"I did not!"

"Kitten." Daddy stroked my cheek, catching my chin in his fingers so he could make me meet his gaze. "You admitted you were playing Hide and Seek. Hide is in the name of the game."

He had me there. I pouted.

"Yeah," Max said, running his fingers lazily down my back until he reached the base of my spine. "Pout all you want, it ain't workin'." He gave my ass a hard swat, making me yelp.

"Hey! No fair! You didn't warn me!"

"No one said either of us had to warn you, pet," Daddy reminded me and chuckled. "Remember? Punishment should happen when the infraction happens so as not to confuse a pet."

"That was Papa Victor's stupid idea," I grumbled. "But he's not here so it shouldn't count!"

"Keep it up, Kitten," Max said with an evil chuckle. "The more you protest, the more spanks you get."

I gasped, ready to protest, but quickly snapped

my mouth shut even as I looked over my shoulder. Yeah. One look at Max and anyone could see he wasn't kidding. *And* he was looking forward to the extra punishment. "Why do you have a fascination with spanking my ass?"

"Because your ass blushes beautifully when I spank you. It's my favorite shade of pink." He gave my ass a slap before rubbing the spot he'd just abused. Of course, that got a sharp yelp from me. "Also," he leaned close to my ear as he spoke, "I know what's in store for you tomorrow. It makes me hard just thinking about it, and when I get hard I always want to involve you."

"Well, involve me in the fucking. Not the spanking!"

Max gave me a sinister grin. "But you know how we take such great satisfaction in seeing your red bottom when we fuck you."

"Max can bring that exact shade of pink that drives me wild, Kitten. Bringing him in to help with your discipline was a good decision on my part. Also, I just love watching him move when he spanks you." Daddy winked at me. "It's a work of art."

"Not for my poor bottom, Daddy!" But it was a token protest at best. I'd do anything for these two men. Anything. Because I trusted them, and I wanted them to find enjoyment in my body any way they could.

Max selected a paddle and twirled it in his hand. He'd definitely used it before. I knew I should question what was happening tomorrow, but I was having trouble thinking past the coming punishment. "Daddy!"

Daddy raised an eyebrow. "Let's get on with it so Max can fuck you. Clearly, he's been needing a fix."

I groaned and laid my forehead on the bench. Looked like I was in for a long afternoon. "Please, Max," I said. "Will you please spank my bottom until it's red?" I added the last knowing they'd hear the exasperation in my voice.

"Ready yourself, Kitten." Max leaned down and kissed my bare bottom, first one cheek then the next. I whimpered, but arched into his touch. Yes, punishments hurt, but Max was as adept at knowing my limits as he was at pleasuring me. Only Daddy was better, though Daddy let Max help with my punishment more and more. I suspected it was because Daddy enjoyed watching Max punish me. Max got off on spanking me, and Daddy enjoyed watching the two of us together.

Then the paddle came down on my ass. *Smack*!

I gasped. It had hurt, but it had sounded worse than it really was.

Smack! Smack!

Max stroked his hand up my thigh, rubbing gently. "Very good, Kitten. You're doing so well."

"You only hit me three times!" I wailed my response, knowing there was more to come.

"True," Max said with a soft chuckle. "I imagine it'll get worse before it gets better."

"You're an ape!"

"Now, now, Kitten. No name calling." Daddy moved up to stroke my face. He knelt down slightly, bringing his lips to mine and kissing me passionately. "Now, before Max continues, why are you being punished?"

"Because Max likes spanking me?" That earned me a smack from Max's hand and I yelped. "OK! OK! I'm getting punished because I hid from you and Max."

"That's right, Kitten. And you know how it worries Max when he can't find you."

"Yeah, but what fun would it be if he didn't care?"

"So, you'd rather worry him?"

"No," I grumbled. "I'm just saying."

"That's what I thought. So you'll take your punishment like the good little Kitten I know you are."

I huffed out a breath. "Fine." I looked back at Max. "May I have the rest of my punishment now, Max?"

"Well," he said with a grin, "when you ask so sweetly."

My groan turned into another yelp when he let his paddle fly once more. Over and over he swung his paddle. I tried to hold back my cries, but it was soon more than I could do to keep silent. When Max stopped his paddling, I thought that was it and I sagged in relief. Sweat coated my body and my ass felt like it was on fire. Then he started in with his hand.

"Hey! I thought you were done!"

"I was. With the paddle. Gonna need a few smacks with my hand to get that beautiful shade of pink I'm looking for."

"Fuuuuck!" I groaned, laying my forehead on the bench just behind my bound wrists. I got the feeling Max was just giving me a little extra as a reminder not to play Hide and Seek with him again.

Then Daddy was there, brushing my damp hair away from my face. Kissing me softly. Praising me. "Almost done, baby," he said. "You know Max has to fuck you to finish punishing you."

"D-do I g-get to c-come?" The stammer was partly from crying and partly because I was so fucking turned on I could barely form words.

"Nope," Max said immediately. "Naughty Kittens don't get to come. You know that."

"But this was the worst punishment ever," I cried. "Please let me come!"

"Not this time, Kitten. This is an important lesson. You're *never* to hide from me. What if there had been an emergency? What if the house were on fire and you didn't know it? If I can't find you, I can't keep you safe."

He had me there. "I understand." I sniffed.

I heard Max rip open the condom packet, then he stroked my pussy. Of course, it was dripping wet. I'd learned that I was always fucked after being punished and my body responded like one of Pavlov's dogs. The only question was whether or not I got to come. Either way, I craved it. Craved the sex after Max or Daddy had spanked me. It was always so intense. Even if I didn't get to come it was an experience like no other. I wasn't sure if they'd figured it out or not. If they had, my ass was in trouble. Max, especially, would look for reasons to punish me just so he could fuck me and let me come.

"You ready for my cock, Kitten?" Before I could answer, Max slid inside me in a smooth, wet glide. I was still strapped down to the bench, unable to do anything other than take what he gave me. And give it to me he did. He hardly gave me time to adjust before he began to pound inside me.

Max gripped my hips as he rode me hard. My ass stung when his flesh met mine in a hard rhythm, tempering the pleasure with just that little bit of pain. He was relentless, fucking me harder than he ever had. His fingers dug into my hips as his cock filled my pussy over and over. He growled above me and occasionally slapped my ass with his hand, continuing my punishment even as he took his pleasure.

"Naughty little Kitten," he bit out. "Dirty Kitten. Sweet, dirty little Kitten." The pounding I was taking was teeth clattering. My breast bounced with every surge. His cock fucked in and out of me, swelling as his pleasure built. I could do nothing to urge him on. Nothing but talk to him.

"Fuck, Max! Your cock's fucking me so fucking good!"

"You like my fuckin' cock? Like it in your fuckin' pussy?"

I looked over my shoulder at him and bared my teeth. "Yeah, you bastard," I bit out. "I fuckin' love you fuckin' me like this. Your cock swelling inside me. You using me like a fuck doll!"

"Fuck! Fuck! *Fuck*!" Max smacked my ass again. I thought he might come, but he kept pounding inside me, not relenting or giving into the pleasure. "Fuckin' little bitch! You like me using you? Using you to get my rocks off?"

"I hate it!" I shouted. "Hate every fucking second of it!"

He started, apparently shocked at my response, then narrowed his eyes at me. "Lying to me, Kitten?"

"What are you gonna do about it if I am?"

"Oh, Kitten," he shook his head, his tone going dark. "Now you're gonna get it."

"Do it, Max," I hissed. "Fuck the shit outa me like you want to do."

He did. While I continued to watch him over my shoulder, Max's fingers bit into my hips. His hand kept coming down on my ass as he fucked me. His gaze never left mine. The muscles and tendons stood out in his arms, shoulders, and neck. He was… *magnificent*.

Looking straight into my eyes, Max shouted, his

nostrils flaring as he prepared to shoot his cum inside me. His cock swelled inside me with every thrust. I cried out, my scream broken by his fast, staccato rhythm. Sweat flew from Max's body as it worked mine at a frantic pace. Sweat soaked my own body from the furious way Max drove me higher and higher but refused to give me permission to fly over the edge into my own orgasm.

Then, finally, he roared his release, shoving himself deep inside me. His cock throbbed, beat, stretching me with each pulse as his cum exploded into the condom separating us.

I felt like I was going to explode, I was wound so tight. I've never needed to come so badly in my life.

Max groaned and slipped out of my pussy, the condom still on his semi-hard cock full of his spunk. He gave a satisfied growl before slapping my ass once more for good measure. Then he gave an upward swat to my upturned pussy with the flat of his hand. I cried out, expecting the stimulation to send me over the edge into an orgasm. No such luck.

I groaned loudly, laying my head down between my arms, forehead on the bench. My ass was still up in the air. I knew I was dripping with juice. One strong breeze across my clit would have shoved me over the edge. Just as I was lowering my ass, planning to rest my bare mound on the padded bench I straddled, Daddy stepped forward and swatted my ass.

"None of that, Kitten," he said. He tried to frown, but I saw his lips twitch. He was enjoying himself. "The second your pussy touches that bench you'll come all over it and I can't have that."

"But Daddy!"

"The only *butt* is this one." He smacked my ass again. Then he dipped his hand to my pussy and swiped his fingers through my wet folds before shoving three of them inside me. I cried out, but still didn't come. Daddy dragged his finger upward until he found my asshole with them, rubbing my back opening with his wet fingers. Then he spread my cheeks and dipped his face between them, tonguing my hole before pulling back to spit right on the spot he'd just licked. "I'm gonna fuck this hole now, sweet Kitten," Daddy said. His gentle tone belied his crude, dirty actions. "Unfortunately, you're not going to get to come tonight. That's part of your punishment for being naughty."

I shook my head and whimpered, but Daddy shook his head sternly. "Max is right. You need to learn to not hide from us. If we all know we're playing, it's different, but you knew we were seriously upset and let it play out. Well, this is the end result. You're get a sore bottom and a frustrated night needing to come when you can't."

"If you're good and take your punishment without protest," Max added, "maybe we'll let you come tomorrow." Max had mentioned tomorrow once before. He said he knew what was in store for me tomorrow. I should really try to concentrate on that. Get some information from them. Right?

Then Daddy speared my ass with a finger and my mind blanked. I groaned, rocking back to meet him thrust for thrust. Then he added a second finger. I heard a snap behind me and whipped my head around to look back over my shoulder just as something cool dribbled from the top of my crack over my pussy lips. It was incredibly intimate and embarrassing but I was so far gone I couldn't muster up any outrage. Instead, I arched into his touch.

"Such a pretty little asshole. Tight and

puckered." Daddy chuckled when I moaned, rocking back on his fingers. Especially when I let go a long, keening cry as he slipped a third finger inside me. "That's my girl." Sweat beaded over my skin, letting Daddy's hand glide over me as he stroked a long, slow swipe with his other hand from my neck down my spine to rest at the small of my back. "So responsive." He leaned forward and kissed my burning butt cheeks, one kiss to each globe. "Max, I want you in front of her. If she wants your cock, give it to her. But you are not to come until I give permission. I want your concentration to be on her. If she's uncomfortable, I expect you to tell me. I will not hurt my Kitten with this."

"Understood, Daddy Jacob." Max moved in front of me and knelt to take my mouth in a searing kiss, plunging his tongue inside and licking me with effortless strokes. "Is Kitten on fire?" His voice was a whisper, an enticing layer to the already erotic scene.

"I am," I whimpered. "I need to come, Max. Please. I need it!"

"I know, little Kitten. But you need to learn this lesson more. Now, kiss me again while Daddy finishes preparing you." I did. The more I lost myself in Max's kiss, the more Daddy played with my ass, the tighter I was wound. I felt like a rubber band ready to snap under the tension.

"Now, Max," Daddy said softly. "I'm going to fuck her ass."

I shivered and cried out as Max ended our kiss and stood. I opened my mouth, hoping Max would take the hint and feed me his cock. I was greedy for it. For his taste. For Daddy's cock in my ass, the only place he hadn't yet claimed. I knew this was coming. Had anticipated it. Now, the time had come and I was *starving* for it! Instead of feeding me his dick, however, Max just petted my hair in a gesture I was sure was meant to soothe me. It didn't. It was just one more reminder I'd been denied what I wanted.

I felt Daddy's cock poke my ass. He rubbed it around and around, pressing gently but insistently until I felt my muscles begin to give under the pressure. My breathing quickened. I heard myself whimpering but couldn't seem to stop.

"You ready, baby?" Daddy asked even as he pressed harder until the flared head of his dick penetrated, stretching me with exquisite pain. I let loose a scream -- not in pain, but in frustration. The fullness Daddy created only intensified my need to come. With my legs spread, Daddy holding me off the bench, and my hands lashed, I couldn't get any relief on my clit to push me over the edge.

Fuck. Who was I kidding? Even if I stroked myself into oblivion, I still wouldn't come. Why? Because Daddy hadn't given me permission. I might be naughty, but Daddy had forbidden me from coming for a reason. And I'd never go against Daddy for real.

"That's it, my beautiful little Kitten. You're takin' my cock so good." He pulled out only to push back in. Slowly. Carefully. Then he did it again. And again.

And again. Just the head. Until he slid a little further.

Before I realized it, Daddy's abdomen was against my cheeks. He was fully inside my ass. Seated as far as he could go.

"My brave, beautiful Kitten," he praised, stroking my back again from my neck to the base of my spine. "Now, I'm going to fuck this last hole. Going to cum in you. Then you're mine. Always. Mine to pleasure. Mine to punish. Mine to share. Mine to do with as I please. You belong to me. You're my property. My woman. One day soon, you'll carry my seed and give me a baby in that sexy little belly of yours. You're my everything. And I intend on keeping you." He brought his hand down on my ass once. Twice. I cried out both times but I pushed back into him, needing his hard fucking even as I knew he needed to be careful. I was beyond careful.

"Fuck me, Daddy! Please, oh, God! Please!"

"You want my cock, do you?"

"Yes! I need your cock. I need to come!"

"You'll have my cock. But you will not come. I insist on this, Kitten. You will not come. You will take your fucking. You'll give me all the pleasure I want and take none for yourself."

I sobbed then, rocking my hips as best I could. Circling. Rocking. I was never going to survive this.

Then Daddy began to fuck me. Slowly at first. A steady in and out, letting me adjust. He squirted more lubricant, letting the cool gel coat us both as he continued to move in and out. In. Out.

In. Out. Squirt. Repeat.

He snapped the cap back on the lid before gripping the cheeks of my ass and picked up his pace. His fingers dug into me, much as Max's had when he'd fucked my pussy. I cried out, but kept pushing back to meet him thrust for thrust. My ass burned, my cheeks, too. The scent of sweat, sex, and desperation filled the air around me. I was almost frantic in my need of Daddy's cock. Of Max's.

As if he read my mind, Max gripped my hair in a tight fist. "Daddy Jacob's fuckin' that virgin asshole, isn't he?"

"Uh huh," I answered, looking up into his eyes.

"How does it feel?"

I could tell he was looking for something but I had no idea what. Did he want me to talk dirty to him? I knew it turned him on, but he wasn't fucking me and he wasn't letting me suck him off like Daddy told him to. I'd be pointing that out later. Maybe Max would get tied up and his ass spanked.

"It's filling me," I whimpered. "Making me need to come. Please, Max. Make him let me come."

"No can do, baby. Not this time. Not tonight. Does it hurt?"

"Yes! I need to come so badly I ache with it!"

Max chuckled. "Not your lust, baby. Daddy Jacob's dick. Are you hurting?"

"No. Not from that. I just... there's a pressure inside me. Daddy's fucking my ass so good. Stretching me. Filling me up. I'll die if I can't come!"

"You won't die, baby," Max said, kissing me gently. The gentle way he touched my lips with his was at odds with both his grip on my hair and Daddy's increasingly hard fucking. The longer we went, the harder he fucked. His grip was bruising. His grunts stimulating. Just a whisper of movement over my clit would get me off. Or maybe if he fingered that spot deep inside me.

"Put your fingers in me, Daddy," I begged. "Just for a minute."

Daddy's chuckle sounded strained. He did not finger me. "Trying to trick me, Kitten?" He swatted my ass and I groaned, laying my head back down on the bench. Max pushed my hair out of my face where it was turned to the side. Then he guided his cock between my lips, holding my head steady so I couldn't move. All I could do was let him fuck my mouth as he pleased.

"That's it, Max," Daddy bit out. "Fuck her face

while I put my cum in this greedy little ass. You can come in her mouth if you want."

I squealed around Max's cock, sucking for all I was worth. I wanted their cum. Both of them.

"Fuck me!" Max yelled. "She's so greedy!"

"I know," Daddy agreed. "Fuckin' know! Fuck! *FUCK*!" Daddy pulled me to him, his dick pulsing in my ass as he pumped it full. I felt it run down my pussy as some escaped. Daddy spanked my ass again, even as he continued to fuck me, his cock still hard. "Now, Max," he commanded. "Make her swallow you down!"

Max obeyed. Jet after jet of his hot, sticky cum erupted down my throat. I swallowed greedily. My body was primed and ready. I needed to come like I needed to breathe. But I knew Daddy wouldn't let me and I sobbed even as I continued to swallow everything Max gave me.

The next thing I knew, Daddy and Max were unbuckling the straps, freeing me of the restraints. Daddy scooped me up, praising me and crooning to me as he took me back down the hall to our bathroom. He stepped into the shower with me, Max right behind us. The water turned on automatically, already hot.

"There's a good girl," Daddy praised as he held me while Max cleaned me gently. "We'll both stay with you while you sleep tonight."

"I need to come," I said weakly.

"I know, baby. Just relax."

"You're not gonna let me, are you?" I know I sounded sulky, but I couldn't help it. If I were honest, I was probably too drained to come anyway. At least, not like I needed to.

"No, baby. Not tonight. When you think about not coming when we call for you again, you'll remember this and think better of it. It's all to keep you safe."

I buried my face in Daddy's chest, trying not to cry in frustration. I knew he was right, but I couldn't bring myself to agree at the moment.

"Let's get her dried and in bed, Max."

They did, in short order. I found myself between Daddy and Max. Both men had their arms around me. Max kissed my shoulder, still praising me. Daddy urged my head back so he could kiss my lips softly.

Both men continued to touch and kiss and praise me for a long while. In fact, I drifted off to those sounds and sensations... and slept like the dead.

Kitten's Claws

The next morning, I woke up cranky. My body was sore and I was still horny as a motherfucker. I was not a happy Kitten. The soreness would normally have been a pleasant reminder of all we'd shared together, Daddy, Max, and me, but it also reminded me of unfulfilled lust.

Usually, Daddy was with me when I woke, cuddling me and coaxing me awake like the princess Kitten I was. Not today though. Instead, it was Max who woke me. Fitting, since it was his fault I was cranky in the first place.

"Morning, Kitten," Max purred at my ear before sliding his cock inside my pussy. One of Daddy's favorite ways to wake me in the morning was to gently fuck me until I came in his arms. I could feel the condom separating Max from me. The feel was decidedly different compared to Daddy's bare cock, but it was the feeling I associated with Max. Max usually liked to wake me with his mouth between my legs, but this was good, too.

"What are you doing here." I made it more a disgruntled statement than a real question, still pouting and put out over not being able to come. My pussy welcomed Max, though. It always did.

"Daddy thought since it was my idea to withhold your orgasms last night, I should be the one to deal with your claws this morning." His voice sounded suspiciously amused, even as he started moving inside me in a slow, wet glide. Max had one arm pillowing my head while the other was clamped around my waist, holding me to him. He leaned in and kissed my neck, then licked the spot where he'd kissed.

"Mmmm," I purred. "Feels good…"

"Does it, Kitten?" Again, he sounded amused. "Do you like what I'm doing to you?"

"I love it." I stretched and arched into him, rocking my hips to meet him.

"Good. Unfortunately, we don't have long."

"Don't need long," I said, quickening my movements. I dipped my fingers to my bare pussy, reaching for my clit.

"Uh uh, Kitten," Max said, pulling my hand up to his mouth and sucking on my fingers. So I used my other hand. Max hooked my knee under his arm, then he swatted my inner thigh. "No means no."

"But I'm not being punished now!" I wailed my protest.

Max just chuckled, licking and sucking at the side of my neck under my collar. "Nope. But Daddy Jacob left explicit instructions for me to pleasure you but to not let you come. He wants you ready for today, and to be at peak you need to be so horny you're panting for our cocks."

"I already am! Max! Please!"

"Nothin' doin', Kitten. Take comfort, though. Daddy said if you didn't get to come, we didn't get to come." Then he snorted. "Of course, he's preparing the office in town. I'm here preparing *you*. Thinking I might have gotten the hard end of that deal." He surged forward, working my body with effortless ease. "Then again, it's *soooo* worth it."

Max bit the side of my neck again as he fucked me slowly. I cried out, moving with him as best I could. He still held my knee up, his hand palming my tit. His other hand pulled and tugged at the other nipple. Again, as it did the night before, pleasure threatened to overwhelm me, but wouldn't push me over the edge. My orgasm hovered just out of reach, waiting on permission only Max or Daddy could give me.

"Please, Max," I whimpered. "Please, please, please."

"Can't baby," he said, slowing down his movements so I floated back down. "Daddy Jacob's orders."

I sobbed out my frustration and utter despair. "I can't keep going, Max," I whispered quietly on a broken sob. "I can't survive much more of this."

"You can," Daddy said as he entered the room. "You will. I swear to you, it will be worth the wait, Kitten." He glanced at Max. "I take it she's ready?"

"She is. Though I fear we may have pushed her too far. Perhaps we should have let her come once yesterday."

"Too late for that this time. I want her needy and on the verge of madness. She'll need it for entering the building as well as what's to come later." He looked down into my upturned face. Whatever he saw there made his expression soften. "Oh, Kitten. We have pushed you too hard, haven't we?"

The regret on his face made my bottom lip quiver. "I don't know what to do, Daddy," I admitted quietly. "I need you so much."

"I know, baby. I'm sorry. This is the first time we're doing this and I wanted you so mindless with lust you didn't hesitate when I gave you an order. Perhaps I underestimated your innate passion." He looked at Max. "You know Kitten as well as I do. Probably better in some respects. What do you think? Should we call a halt to this?"

"Your peers will be disappointed. Did you not tell me she was their incentive to get them through the next few weeks?" Max continued to pump inside me lazily, casually pinning my arms out of the way so I couldn't sneak and touch myself.

"True. But I will not overwhelm Kitten. If she can't take this, we'll figure something else out."

"Wait," I said, pushing up slightly. Max let me move, but kept a hand on my hip, never breaking his rhythm. "You need me for something," I said. Not making it a question.

Daddy gave me a long look. Sizing me up? "Ultimately, I'd hoped it would be to your satisfaction. I'd thought that, by using Max's punishment for you and building your lusts and frustration, you'd be so needy and receptive to anything physical, you wouldn't think about anything I was asking you to do. You'd just trust me to take care of you and do what you were told."

I held Daddy's gaze. "This is something you need, Daddy?"

He shrugged. "I can manage without you, Kitten."

"But this is one of the things you told me you'd need to use me for. When I first agreed to be your Kitten."

"First and foremost, you're my woman, Isabella." Daddy only used my real name when he needed to talk seriously about something. "I won't hurt you for their pleasure." He shook his head and winced. "Never. Not for any reason."

Max didn't stop his fucking, but he didn't speed up. Just kept that steady pace. I knew my breasts bounced with every stroke. My pussy was probably pink and weeping. Hell, I knew it was. I hadn't had any relief since before Max had punished me. And I'd loved the rough, harsh way he'd used my body. Loved it with all my might. Daddy had been fantastic when he'd fucked me, too. He'd taken my ass, the very last part of my body he hadn't yet claimed was now wholly Daddy's. I was his. He was mine.

"I can do this, Daddy," I said. "I can do whatever you need."

"Then I have to deny you an orgasm until we get to the office. Once you've done all I require, then I'll let you come to your heart's content. Until then, you'll need to suffer a little more, Isabella. Are you sure you can take it?" Daddy looked like it pained him. "Because I'm not sure I can deny you much more."

I hooked my arm under my knee where Max held me open, taking over so he could grip my hip or where ever he needed as he continued to fuck me. "I'll do what you need me to do, Daddy," I said softly. I know my voice sounded strained and it truly pained me to submit to this for Daddy, but I'd give him anything he needed. Even if it meant my own discomfort. Because Daddy would always see to my happiness. He might withhold my orgasm for now, but he'd make it up to me later.

"Max," I whispered, turning my face to his. He leaned in and kissed me deeply. His cock was a punishing pleasure inside me. The need to come was maddening, but I resolved myself to embrace that need. It would make my climax that much more pleasurable when I was allowed it. "Fuck me until you come."

"Not allowed, Kitten," Max bit out. "Your pain is my pain."

"Not this time," I said. "This is part of why I belong to Daddy. If Daddy needs me stupid with lust, I'll do what he requires. You need to be in control. Anytime Daddy takes us out, you need your control. So take what you need from me." I smiled at him and kissed him again. "Take what you need from my body, Max. Use me for your pleasure."

Max gave a sharp yell, his cock pulsing inside me. Then he started fucking me in earnest. His cock was a piston, plunging in and out of me with brute force. Max had his arms wrapped around me while I held myself completely open to him.

"Love your pussy, Kitten," Max bit out. "So fuckin' juicy. So fuckin' tight!"

"She has the most fuckable pussy in the world," Daddy said, his gaze fixed on the place where Max and I were joined. "The two of you look so hot together," Daddy murmured. "She loves the way you fuck her, Max. And I love watching."

"Daddy," I gasped. "He fills me so good."

"I know, Kitten. Max has a beautiful body and he knows exactly how to work yours."

A wicked thought entered my mind and I gasped, images I shouldn't have flitting through my head. I cried out, needing to come more than ever.

"I think my good little Kitten just had a naughty thought," Daddy said, his eyes narrowed. "Tell me, Kitten. Tell me your dirtiest fantasy."

"I want you to fuck Max, Daddy," I whispered, not hesitating in answering him. It just... fell from my lips. It was a secret I hadn't even known I harbored. I'd never keep anything from Daddy, but it looked like I might have even kept this from myself. "I want you to fuck him while he fucks me."

"Goddamn motherfuck!" Max bellowed to the ceiling as his cock swelled and pulsed angrily. He slammed deep, holding my hips tightly as he came and came and came.

"Fuck, Max," Daddy said, his eyes big. "You came a flood! It's leaking from the lip of the condom across the cheek of her ass." Daddy looked completely shocked, a grin splitting his face as he spoke. "I think you liked Kitten's little fantasy."

"Fuuuuck," Max said, collapsing to his back. I was still on my side when his cock slid wetly out of my pussy. Daddy was right. I could feel his cum trickle down the cheek of my ass to the bed. "That was fuckin' amazing!"

"You want me to fuck you, Max?" Daddy pulled his cock from his pants and stroked it lazily, almost absently. "You want my cum deep in your asshole while you fuck my little Kitten?"

I looked back at Max, rolling to my other side and finding his chest with my hand. His breaths came in great heaves as if he'd just run a mile as fast as he could. Max met my gaze with a heated one of his own. "If Kitten wants it, I'll gladly do it, Daddy Jacob."

"But do *you* want it?" Daddy asked, his gaze intent. "Do you want my cock?"

Slowly, his gaze still on me, Max nodded. "Yes, Daddy Jacob. I've thought about you fucking me while I fuck Kitten. I've thought about fucking you while you fuck Kitten. I've even fantasized about sucking you off while you and Kitten are kissing or you're eating her out. If it has to do with you or Kitten, there's not much I'm opposed to."

Daddy nodded slowly. "We'll revisit this, Max. When we're not in the heat of the moment." Then his gaze landed on me. "But first, I want to paint my sweet little Kitten in my cum."

Daddy stroked his cock faster and faster. I cupped my tits and spread my legs, exposing my pussy to Daddy. "Come on me wherever you like, Daddy. I'll take your cum any way I can get it."

"Then talk to me, Kitten. Tell me what you

want."

"I want you and Max to both fuck me. I want to be covered in both your cum. I want to watch as you fuck Max as he strokes his cock while you do it. I'll suck him and drink his cum down while you shoot off in his ass." I said it all in a rush, realizing it was something I really wanted now that I'd said it.

Daddy nodded. "This is what you want, baby?"

I swallowed. What if I'd done wrong? What if fucking Max wasn't something Daddy could give me? Then I looked down at his crotch where his hand was firmly around his cock. The tip was angry and purple, pre-cum leaking from the tip. That's when I realized he was trying to hold himself off. Squeeze his cock so he didn't come before he was ready.

I nodded. "Yes, Daddy." I got to my knees on the bed and crawled to the edge where he stood. I reached for his cock and circled it with my hand. I couldn't quite get my fist around his girth, but that was no surprise. I loved how big my Daddy and Max were. Two impressive cocks to pleasure me wasn't a hardship. I stroked gently, over and over.

"Harder, Kitten," Daddy growled. "Stroke me harder."

I did, tugging at him as I tightened my grip. His cock pulsed in my hand. When more pearly liquid slipped from the tip, I couldn't resist leaning in and licking that little drop. Daddy groaned and the next thing I knew, he erupted on my tongue and face, jet after jet of creamy cum. Daddy took his cock from me and rubbed the tip over my lips and cheeks where his cum had landed, spreading it around until my face was covered in it.

Max chuckled. "I'm in so much trouble."

Daddy barked out a laugh. "Yeah. You are. I

suggest you stretch your asshole. Don't want to hurt you when this happens. And it will happen. What Kitten wants, Kitten gets."

I sat back on my heels, catching a drop of cum as it dribbled down my chin and licking it off my finger. "Except to come," I said, dryly.

Both men chuckled. "I promise you'll be happy you didn't, Kitten," Daddy said. "I want you ready and horny and needy. You look so beautiful when you're blushing with arousal. You'll make me proud to have you at my side."

I nodded. "Then I'm glad I held off. What is it you need me to do, Daddy?"

"Take a shower, honey," he said. "Let Max help you. I want you shaved everywhere." He turned to Max. "Keep her pleasured so she's on the edge. But do *not* let her come."

"Understood, Daddy Jacob." Max took my hand, urging me from the bed.

"I'll put an outfit out for you, Kitten. You, too, Max. Meet me in the foyer in thirty minutes. We'll leave together."

"Yes, Sir," Max said, scooping me up in his arms. I was covered in Daddy's cum. Rivulets ran down my breasts and I didn't want to get Max sticky. It didn't seem to matter to Max, though. He leaned in and licked a path from my chest to my neck. No way he could have avoided Daddy's cum.

"Mmmm… I might get used to that taste if it was blended with you. Someday soon, I'm going to eat Daddy Jacob's cum out of your sweet pussy. See how much I like that."

That thought made me shiver, the lust inside me that had started to lessen surging back with wicked force. "Max." I knew I was whimpering, but there was no way to prevent it. "That's hot as fuck."

"It certainly will be," Max said.

We didn't talk much after that. Max lathered my skin with a sweet smelling rose and honeysuckle shower gel. Every inch of me. He shaved my legs and under my arms, then, meticulously, my pussy. As he rinsed me, he rubbed his fingers all around my cunt, touching everywhere but my clit. Leaning in, he licked around my outer and inner lips, swiping his tongue up my slit just below my clit.

"Max!" My head fell back and I thrust my hips at him. "Feels so good!"

"I know, Kitten. Your body feels like it's on fire, doesn't it?"

"It does. When will I get to come?"

"Later, baby. I promise. You'll come and come and come and it will feel so fuckin' good you'll want to hold off coming again just to feel so wanton and out of control. You'll enjoy everything that's about to happen and beg for more."

I wasn't coming now. I knew that, but I didn't want Max to stop. Not yet. Not until he had to. As far as I was concerned, he could glide his tongue along my pussy as long as he wanted to. Even if I wasn't getting off.

All too soon, Max turned off the water and helped me out. He took a warm towel and dried me off. I was shivering, but not from cold. I was wound as tight as a banjo string. Ready to snap. When I did, I feared I'd be so wanton, even Daddy wouldn't be able to contain me. But he said he needed this, so I would. If it came back to haunt him, it wasn't my fault. Daddy would never hold me accountable for my actions with something like this. Would he?

Kitten's Reward

The outfit Daddy laid out for me was positively scandalous. Around the house, I'd never hesitate. But Daddy wanted me to wear this to his downtown office. The big skyscraper in the city. Still, I trusted Daddy. If he said it would be OK, then I'd trust him to make sure it would be.

There was a flirty little dark green skirt and a short, fluffy cashmere sweater of the same color. The skirt rode low on my hips while the sweater rode high. There were a couple inches of skin exposed, but that wasn't what had my attention. Daddy had laid out another tail for me in the same shade of green as my sweater and skirt. Diamonds sparkled throughout the soft fur of the long tail and the matching ears I was to wear in my hair. High heeled sandals that wound around my ankles in thin straps completed my outfit. It was even more scandalous than what I usually wore to the downtown offices, but I'd do whatever Daddy required.

After I'd dressed, I leaned over the bed while Max helped me with the tail. It fit perfectly underneath the slinky material. The back of the skirt seemed designed to drape over the tail so it lay perfectly to cover my ass. A long, thin chain of diamonds attached to my collar and I realized that, once again, Daddy would lead me into the building like his pet. Which was what I was. He'd told me on more than one occasion he owned me and had the occasional need to show me off. I didn't mind, but this was a whole other level.

"Courage, Kitten. You know Daddy won't allow anyone to hurt you." Max had dressed in his own outfit for the day. A dark charcoal gray three-piece suit with a darker tie and diamond cufflinks. He looked every bit as powerful as Daddy. Just with an edge showing that Daddy kept skillfully hidden.

I smiled up at Max. "Yes. I know." I took a breath. "I'm just nervous." I gave a short laugh. "And horny. I feel like everyone who looks at me can see how badly I need to be fucked until I come. And he didn't lay out any panties for me, so I feel a little exposed."

"Oh, I'm sure they can tell exactly how horny you are. Believe me, it's an exceptional look on you. Besides, do you really care as long as it's Daddy Jacob who holds your leash?"

"No. Not at all. You have my back, too. Yes?"

"Always, Kitten." Max kissed me. Unexpectedly, he knelt in front of me, sliding his hands reverently up my thighs around to cup my ass cheeks. "You are truly a beauty, Kitten. I'm proud to be your protector." Leaning in, Max lapped at the moisture dripping down my thighs. He ran his tongue lazily over my outer lips, then sucked each inner lip before stabbing his tongue deep to swipe through my pussy. He carefully avoided my clit so he didn't set me off. I gasped and gripped his shoulder to steady myself. Max gave a deep chuckle before standing. Snapping the leash to my collar he led me downstairs.

Daddy was waiting for us just as he promised. His gaze took us both in, satisfaction stamped on his face. "No man could ask for more perfect pets. Or more perfect partners." Daddy's words filled me with happiness. I looked at Max and he'd puffed out his chest just a little.

Grinning, I said, "Shall we go, then?"

Daddy took my leash from Max. "I think it's time." He led us to the stretch limo he used when we went to the city. It was opulent and comfortable. I hoped I could play on the thirty-minute ride.

Inside, Daddy poured three glasses of Champaign. "Today will mark the beginning of a long, arduous siege for my company and the companies owned by my inner circle. We are all working toward a common goal that will give us control of a great section of trade around the world, but most especially in Europe and Asia. It's something that, if successful, will give us all unfathomable wealth and more power than some of my brothers might be able to handle. My hope is, I can keep everyone's eye on the prize and off personal gain by distracting them. You, Kitten, are that distraction. You'll be their reward for keeping this a group effort. That's the only way this venture works."

"So, you're giving me to them?" Even as I asked the question, a thrill shot through me, making my pussy weep, but also a stab of pain to my heart.

"Not exactly, Kitten. I'll be *sharing* you with them. Just like I talked about when we first began our adventure together. You'll always be mine, but I will share your delights with my men. As I told you before, they know the rules. They are not to penetrate you without permission and, even though they all get tested regularly, never without a condom, whether they fuck your sweet pussy, or your delicate ass. That pleasure is mine alone. They may use your mouth and you may swallow their cum if you feel you want to, but that will be the only place their cum is allowed to enter your body. They will not hurt you, or otherwise strike you. Even during sex when Max or I might spank you, they are not allowed that pleasure. Ever. No one spanks you but me or Max."

"I understand," I said softly.

Daddy looked at me a long time before nodding

to the floor of the vehicle. "Kneel between my legs, Kitten."

I did without hesitation, spreading my thighs wide and placing my hands on my legs.

"Such a beautiful, good Kitten," he murmured, stroking a flowing curl from my cheek and tucking it behind my ear. "I can see from your face you have reservations."

"Not reservations, Daddy. Maybe questions."

"Talk to me then. You know how much I need communication about things like this."

"What will I be expected to do today?"

"You won't be fucked by them today, Kitten. I expect Max and I will both end up fucking you for their enjoyment, but they will not do anything more than touch you. I will allow them to taste your pussy and your tits, or lick your asshole as some prefer to give that pleasure, but that's it. No one will do anything else other than touch you."

"Will you and Max always be there?"

"Yes, Kitten. Max will always have eyes squarely on you during this type of event, and I will always be in the room. If Max isn't comfortable with what's going on, he'll stop it until I can assess the situation."

"Will there be times when you let them fuck me?"

"Yes, Kitten. Just not today."

"OK then." I said, looking up at him. "I'd like to play before we get to the office," I said, grinning up at him. "May I have your cock, please, Daddy?"

He chuckled as he unzipped his fly and pulled out his hardening cock. "Yes, Kitten. Suck me down if you want."

"I want," I said, grinning cheekily.

Bracing my hands on Daddy's thighs, I wrapped

my lips around his cock and sucked greedily. I slid his cock deeply into my mouth, as far as I could go before backing off and doing it again. I was careful not to get his slacks wet with my efforts, but it took concentration. When I sucked Daddy's cock, it was hard to focus on anything else. Soon I was humming around him in bliss.

I loved the way he tasted. That salty blend of flesh and precum was addictive. I lived for that hit of his precum. Now, I sucked hard at the tip, trying to coax another drop.

"Fuck, Kitten," he bit out. "So fuckin' good. Can't wait to fuck you later."

"Mmmm…" I moaned in pleasure. I might not be coming right now, but this was its own pleasure. Daddy's responses. The taste of him. The feel of him. I loved how he appreciated my efforts as much as the reward of his cum when I worked him enough.

"She's a hot-blooded thing," Max murmured. "As responsive as she is sweet."

"That she is. You enjoy her as much as I do, don't you Max?"

"I do." Max moved to sit beside Daddy on the luxurious seat. He took out his cock and stroked as he watched me sucking Daddy. I glanced up at his face and saw his gaze was focused intently on me. Grinning, I shifted until I knelt between them both, taking Max's cock in my hand and pumping him with a firm grip. His head fell back and he groaned loudly. "Fuuuuck."

"Suck him, Kitten," Daddy commanded.

I obeyed. I took Max deep, humming in appreciation around him as I worked his cock with my mouth and hand before moving back to Daddy's cock. I did this several times. Moving between the two of them. I loved hearing their obvious enjoyment as they groaned and praised me, telling me what they wanted me to do.

"Gettin' close, Kitten," Max said between clenched teeth. "So fuckin' close…"

"You're gonna take his cum," Daddy said, his breaths coming in shallow pants. "Then you're gonna take mine. You ready, Kitten?"

"M'hmm," I said. Then I swallowed Max deep. That was all he could take. With a loud bellow, Max shot his cum inside my mouth. Down my throat. I swallowed greedily, taking every drop he had to give.

Max had just stopped shuddering when Daddy grabbed a handful of my hair and pulled me to him, forcing me to swallow his dick. The second I had my mouth around him, Daddy filled my mouth with cum. He thrust his hips, fucking my throat as he continued to come. It was all I could do not to lose some of it, but I swallowed as fast as I could.

It was several long moments before Daddy let me off him. His cock was still hard as it ever was, the orgasm he'd just had in no way taking much of an edge off. I looked up at him to find a look of frustrated lust.

"This is gonna be hell," he muttered. "I need to fuck that sweet pussy in the worst way."

I kissed the head of his cock before crawling up onto his lap, straddling his hips. Daddy's hands clenched my ass, but he didn't let me do more than kiss the tip of his cock with my pussy. "Not now, Kitten. Soon, but not now. And you have no idea how hard it is stopping you from slipping your sweet pussy around my dick."

"But… why? Why would you stop me?"

"Because my brothers in that building will likely

be eating out your sweet pussy and they may not enjoy the taste of my cum as much as they do yours." He gave me a wry grin. "But don't worry, Kitten. I will give you as much as you can take once they've all tasted their fill. Now. Kiss me before we go inside."

I did, letting Daddy taste himself on my tongue. He kissed me back just as deeply before passing me to Max.

"Kiss our little Kitten, Max. Then we have to go inside."

"Courage, Kitten," Max said after kissing me just as passionately and affectionately as Daddy had. "You'll enjoy this as much as they will."

"I know." I gave them both a contented smile.

To me, walking inside the building was always the hardest part. No matter the situation, I knew everyone in that place knew what I was there for. I also knew more than one woman -- and man -- envied me my position in Daddy's life. No one would ever admit it, though. I never failed to put my shoulders back and prance through the lobby with my head held high and a secret little smile on my face. Today, however… Yeah. I was a little apprehensive.

"Don't look so upset, Kitten," Daddy said, kissing me gently once more. "I'm not taking you through the main lobby."

"You're not?" Relief poured over me, but I tried to hold it in. I wasn't ashamed of the way Daddy and I chose to live and Daddy always protected me from anyone who tried to be mean to me. But I really didn't want to parade through the place in this getup.

"No, baby. We'll go in through the back and up the private elevator. I will, however, take you through the upstairs lobby. I'm just bastard enough to want to show you off." He gave me a slightly sheepish grin. I was glad I didn't have to parade around in front of people in the whole building, but I had to admit, doing it on the top floor was kind of titillating. I knew most of the people there and it didn't seem as scary.

I gave a relieved sigh. "Thank you, Daddy."

Daddy did exactly as he promised. When we got to the lobby on the upper floor where Daddy's huge office was located, he took his time before getting off the elevator. I looked around and realized he was letting the majority of the people in the area get back to their own offices or cubicles before taking me across the room to his office.

I looked up at him with a smile. "I'm ready, Daddy. You don't have to wait until it's only upper level people milling around. I'm good."

"You continually surprise me, Kitten." He leaned in and brushed a soft kiss over my lips before moving into the lobby, Max solidly behind us.

I got more than my fair share of stares, but then, so did Max. More than one of the more aggressive women in the office approached as Daddy led me on my diamond leash to his office.

"I get off at five," one woman said as we passed. I glanced over my shoulder to see she was talking to Max, trying to stop him as he followed me and Daddy. "Take me out for drinks. I know a great club opening tonight."

"Not interested," Max snapped as he continued on, never breaking stride.

"I can meet you somewhere. Surely Mr. Blackstone doesn't monopolize all your time."

"Never said he did. Now excuse me."

I turned my head and frowned at the other woman. She sneered at me. I narrowed my eyes. No fucking way.

"Daddy," I said as Daddy held his watch up to the lock panel to his office door.

"Yes, Kitten." At first it had made me uncomfortable to address him as Daddy and him address me as Kitten. Now, I saw it as a sign of familiarity. Something this woman didn't have.

"I don't want Max feeling left out today. Will he be involved in the... celebration about to happen?"

Daddy chuckled, knowing what I was doing. "Of course, Kitten. Max is too important to both of us to be left out of anything in our lives."

"Don't worry yourself," Max said. "You and Mr. Blackstone keep me happy and content," Max said, kissing the top of my head affectionately.

With that, the three of us slipped into Daddy's office. Once the door was shut, I burst into giggles.

Daddy sighed, shaking his head as he fought a grin. "Kitten. Are you trying to cause problems?"

"Not at all, Daddy. Just making sure everyone understands Max is ours and not to be messed with." Daddy burst out laughing and opened his arms to me. I jumped into them and he held me close. Max stepped in close behind me and we all three stood there for a long moment. "Kitten's right. You're ours, Max. And not to be messed with."

"No reason to ever think I'd let anyone mess with me," Max said. "I have everything I need right here."

I giggled again, then pulled everyone in for a kiss. Daddy and Max both seemed shocked, but Daddy just chuckled and rolled with it. For long moments it was an erotic tangle of tongues and lips that I was sure had both Max and Daddy remembering the conversation earlier. I know I was, and I fully intended to push that situation in the near future.

When it was over, Daddy sighed. "Everyone will be here in less than thirty minutes. Max, I want you focused on Kitten through the whole thing. If she gets anxious or nervous, it's your job to calm her. But if there's reason for her anxiety, you're to remove her from the situation."

"Do you anticipate a problem?" Max asked.

"Not at all. I just want it clear that you're in charge of Kitten. You do not have to have my permission to pull her out if you feel it's necessary for any reason."

"Understood, Daddy Jacob."

"If either of you need to freshen up, I suggest you do it now. I want both of you out here and ready in fifteen minutes."

Max and I went to the private bathroom in the back. I used the toilet and washed myself once more, making sure I was fresh and comfortable. I was wet with all the anticipation as well as the playing I'd done with Daddy and Max already. Washing would only help for a while, but I was clean and free of sweat. For now, anyway.

I was nervous, but also excited. The second I was out of the bathroom, I ran for Max, jumping into his arms and kissing him thoroughly. Max's arms went tightly around me as he kissed me back.

"You're gonna have a great time, Kitten. This will introduce you to a world of different sensations. It's possible Papa Victor will be here. Daddy Jacob didn't say anything but he's usually in this group. And he's Daddy's right-hand man."

"Will you be OK with it if he is?"

"Certainly, Kitten. Papa Victor did the wrong thing for the right reasons. And his actions allowed me to prove myself to you and Daddy. So, yes. I'm OK if he's one of the men who gets to taste this delectable body." Max grinned at me. "Besides, it'll be me and Daddy Jacob who get to fuck you. Not Papa Victor."

I giggled just as Daddy opened the door to the bathroom. "You two about ready?" He had an impatient look on his face.

"Is something wrong, Daddy?"

"What? No! No, Kitten. Nothing's wrong." He reached for me, pulling me into his arms and finding my mouth with his. "But you're in here with Max. And he's taking up all my time alone with you and it makes me more than a little jealous."

Max clapped Daddy on the shoulder. "What can I say, old man. The girl is partial to young studs." It was the first time Max had dared to tease Daddy and it warmed my heart. It meant that he was truly comfortable here. With Daddy.

I glanced at Daddy. He looked shocked, but then broke out into a grin. "Oh yeah? You might rebound faster than I do, but I have greater staying power. I can fuck her while you recover." He winked at me. Max laughed, kissing my cheek.

"You do that. I'll help you get her to come in case you don't know how to use that stamina."

This time, Daddy laughed. He pulled me closer and hugged me tightly. "I'm the luckiest man in the world to have two such wonderful people in my life."

"I love you, Daddy," I said, kissing him. "Is it time?"

"It is. Everyone will begin arriving in the next few minutes." He gestured back to the main office. "Shall we?"

Max and I went back into the office. Max sat on the couch near the large conference table and Daddy indicated I should sit at his feet. Once I was settled,

Daddy patted his lap.

"Turn to face me, Kitten. I need you." He unzipped his pants and pulled out his cock, offering it to me. I accepted eagerly, taking him deep.

I was just getting into the blow job when I heard the door open. Men entered, talking loudly. Making plans. All of them ready and eager to present Daddy with their progress on the plans he'd set to make them all even more rich and powerful than they already were. I really didn't care about the conversation or the content because Daddy's cock was hard and weeping for me and I wanted nothing more than to swallow him down.

"Ah, Jacob," a masculine voice rumbled deep. "I see you've brought your little Kitten with you today. Victor tells me you're quite happy with her."

"I am. She's everything that I've been missing in my life."

"Not many women I know would tolerate our needs. Even trained pets often balk at some of the things I've asked of them. Yet, you picked yours from the street? Untrained."

"I think I fell in love with her the moment I first saw her. She's willing to give me what I need, no matter what I ask of her. Once she knew she has my heart and I'll always take care of her, she realized everything I do is for our mutual satisfaction and pleasure -- even if I say it's all about me. She knows better. She knows she's mine alone and I'm hers."

"Wait. You gave her your heart? A *pet*?"

"Oh, Stanton. She's much more than a pet. She lets me put her in that role because it's what I need, but she's my woman in every way that's possible. She'll be the mother of my children, and, once this business is concluded, I'll make it more official."

I gasped and looked up at Daddy, but I didn't take his cock from my mouth. I knew Daddy loved me, knew I was his woman. He'd said so on more than one occasion. But *make it more official*... what did that mean? Did he... Was he going to ask me to marry him?

Daddy looked down at me, caressing my face gently. I could see in his eyes that's exactly what he planned. I was sure a tear beaded down my cheek, and it wasn't because of how deeply I was sucking Daddy. I needed the words. Later, though. In private. Now wasn't the time.

"I see. We'll see if she's so willing to be what you need then." The man chuckled, sounding as if there was a huge joke and it was all on Daddy.

I let go of Daddy's cock and looked up at the man. He was handsome, I suppose, looking fit and lean in his dark suit. Not a hair out of place. "I will forever do as Daddy requires. I'm his, and I'll love every second I'm with him. I'll be whatever he needs me to be because I love him."

"You withhold your money from her then?"

"Daddy gives me anything I want," I said, narrowing my eyes at him. "But that doesn't matter. All I want is him. Daddy and Max give me everything I need to be happy. They love me."

Stanton glanced over Daddy's shoulder at Max, who was now standing at the ready instead of seated comfortably. "So you share with your other pet."

"We are a family," I snapped. Then turned to Daddy. "I don't like him, Daddy."

"Easy, my lovely Isabella. If you don't like him, you don't have to be around him." Daddy leveled a look at a man he called brother. One of his inner circle.

The man looked taken aback. "I thought this was an incentive party of sorts. We were told..."

"You were told what I was willing to give you as a reward for your hard work, but you've managed to get on the bad side of the kindest, most gentle woman I've ever had the pleasure of knowing. It's her body. If she's not willing to give it, I'm not letting you take it. And I'm not forcing her to do something she doesn't want to do."

Stanton raised his hands in surrender. "Forgive me, young Isabella. I meant no offense."

"Yes, you did," I said, looking him straight in the eye. "I understand your concern. You don't believe anyone could love Jacob for who he is instead of what he has. But he knows people well enough to tell the difference. Max and I are just happy to have found Jacob. He saved me. Victor saved Max. Victor put Max with me and Jacob and it was the best thing that could have happened to any of us."

"Again, forgive me, Isabella."

Stanton looked appropriately contrite. Perhaps he understood now. Still didn't mean I was letting him off the hook. "I appreciate the apology."

Daddy chuckled. "But she's still not letting you play with her."

With a shrug, I went back to Daddy's cock. I have no idea what happened next, but I knew Daddy had my back with this.

"Everyone!" Daddy called for everyone's attention. "You all have your assigned tasks. Some of you are well on your way to completing them. We're making better progress than I'd anticipated. I want to thank you all." Murmurs all around. "I trust you all remember Isabella. Kitten."

"While I'm sure we all would appreciate your Kitten's willingness to be our reward, I don't want the girl to feel like she had to do anything she doesn't want to." I wasn't sure who said this, but after the confrontation with Stanton earlier, I welcomed the concern.

Enough was enough. "I appreciate you looking out for me," I said, "But I've been anticipating this all morning. And last night. And, in anticipation of everything to come today, I've not been allowed to come. So, suffice it to say, if you refuse to let me come today, this Kitten may have to bare her claws."

That got laughs all around. I looked up at Daddy. He looked as proud of me as I'd ever seen him. He was also wryly amused. "I seem to have created a monster." More laughter. "Up you go, Kitten." Daddy helped me to my feet. "You all know the rules. Max will be here to enforce them. Once everyone had had a taste of my wonderful little Kitten, Max and I will take care of fucking her."

Daddy turned me around and unzipped my skirt to let it pool at my feet. My tail was still firmly in my ass. He helped me off with my sweater, careful of my kitten ears, then urged me up onto the table on my knees.

"Ass in the air, Kitten," he demanded. Daddy rubbed my ass cheeks, massaging them before swiping his tongue through my pussy lips. I gave a sharp cry of surprise when he touched my clit. Though I was turned on beyond belief, his small touch wasn't nearly enough. I canted my hips, trying to get him to do it again, but he just smacked my ass.

"Not again," I groaned, going limp, my ass still up in the air. Several of the men around me chuckled.

"Such a beautiful pet, Jacob. And willing as well."

"She's hot blooded in the extreme," Daddy said. "Keeping her sated and happy is my primary concern in life."

I felt another hand on my ass. This one wasn't Daddy's and I assumed it was the man who'd spoken. He rubbed my upturned cheeks, kneading them over and over. "Never have I seen such an exquisite ass." I felt his breath on my pussy and I whimpered. "Or such a pretty, responsive cunt. Too bad you won't allow us to fuck her, but I will take the taste you offered and be grateful."

He spread my cheeks apart, urging my legs wider. The next thing I knew, the man was beneath me, his shoulders between my legs as he pulled me down onto his face. The second his lips latched onto my pussy, his tongue came in contact with my clit. Two flicks later and I exploded. The orgasms I'd been denied built up tightly inside me, they just seemed to let go all at once. I screamed and screamed, my pussy gushing with my orgasm. I was as wet as I'd ever been and the man between my legs ate me up.

"OK, that's enough. Let me have a taste." The man left me only to be replaced by another. The licking and lashing of my pussy continued and the orgasms seemed to trip over one another. This guy swatted my ass once, but not hard. He squeezed and kneaded my cheeks while his tongue worked magic between my legs.

Another man got on the table, laying down so his cock was right in front of me. I got to my elbows and reached for him, pulling his cock into my mouth to suck. That seemed to break the ice because I was suddenly surrounded by half a dozen men. All of them with their cocks out. Some had taken off their expensive suits, some just had their dicks out of their flies. All of them were looking at me as they stroked their cocks.

The next time I came, I was flipped over to my back. My tail got in the way and I yelped in surprise, shifting my hips upward to accommodate the extra appendage stuck in my ass. I pulled my legs to my chest, spreading them wide while another handsome man buried his face in my pussy.

"She's so Goddamned wet! Look at that juicy pussy!"

"She seems to come every time you touch her clit. Watch this."

The man brushed his finger over my clit and, sure enough, I came in a wet rush, my lower body clenching and spasming with the glorious pleasure flooding through me.

"Fuck me," another guy said. "The girl can suck cock like no one I've ever seen. What the fuck, Jacob? You get this every day?"

"Anytime I want it," Daddy said with a chuckle.

"She's the most passionate woman I've ever been with." Victor came up beside me, locking gazes with me as I sucked on someone's cock. "My beautiful little Kitten," he said as he took his cock out and stroked. "Your Daddy is very generous to share you with us like this."

I wanted to answer, but not only was I sucking a cock, but I was reaching that point where I simply embraced my own pleasure and took what was happening to me in stride. There was nothing but pleasure.

Victor fastened his lips around one of my nipples, pulling strongly. "Good Kitten," he praised before lapping at my tit with the flat of his tongue. "Sweet Kitten."

"Victor," I breathed as the cock in my mouth pulled out and another man moved to take his place.

"You're doing well, Kitten. So beautiful when you come."

"Mmmm…" I sucked the cock offered to me, soaking up Victor's words. I saw Max standing close, watching me for any sign of discomfort. His presence steadied me when I was overwhelmed by the pleasure.

The cock in my mouth pulled out and I gasped. Again I was repositioned, this time with my head hanging over the edge of the table. Again, there was a mouth between my legs, sucking and tonguing my clit with merciless force. My body was soaked in sweat and coated with cum, my mind in chaos. But I was loving every single moment. Daddy had been right. Not letting me come all day yesterday and this morning had been the right call. I was so wound up, so needy, pleasure seemed to ripple constantly through my body.

The reason for positioning my head over the edge of the table soon became apparent. With my neck bent backward, the next cock that was fed to me pushed in deeper than I'd ever thought possible. I gagged slightly and Max reached out to the man, pulling him back. But I wanted this. I grabbed the backs of the man's thighs, pulling him closer. He went slower and more carefully this time and it wasn't long before he was fucking my face with long, slow steady strokes.

"Fuck me," he gasped. "Fuck me!"

I hummed around his dick, urging him on with my nails digging into his thighs. He picked up the pace until I felt him swelling inside me. He was going to come. And I wanted to swallow everything he had to give me.

"Gonna fuckin' come! Goddamn! Goddamn!"

I gripped him tightly, pulling him to me.

Holding him until he exploded cum down my throat with a hoarse shout. "Mother fuck!"

"She's swallowing him down," someone said. "Such a hot little piece."

"I want her mouth," another said. The second the other guy left my mouth, it was replaced by someone else. Meanwhile, someone else got between my legs, pushing them higher.

"I want to remove her tail, Jacob."

"I'll do it." Daddy was there. I recognized his touch. He kissed my clit, flicking it so I came when he gently pulled the plug from my ass. I would have cried out but my mouth and throat were stuffed full of long, thick cock. I managed to squeal when the plug in my ass was replaced by someone's tongue licking all around my opening. The sensation was foreign, though Daddy had briefly explored that area with his tongue once. But this guy…

He licked and sucked the skin around my anus, snarling and growling as he did. Gripping my inner thighs hard, he kept me open when my every instinct was to pull back. To escape his invading lips and tongue. Someone's tongue found my clit at the same time the other guy was reaming my ass and I bucked and thrashed with my orgasm.

The sound I made must have been more vibration than the guy I was sucking off could stand because he came and I swallowed every drop of cum he had to give me. This happened over and over. I lost count and I didn't pay attention to exactly who was with me. Victor was the only man I connected with and he made sure I knew when he had his turn.

"Now, Kitten," he said. He held my head as he leaned down and kissed my lips, heedless of any lingering cum on my face or in my mouth. "I get to give you my cum. Will you swallow me down like the good, greedy Kitten I know you are?"

"Yes, Papa Victor," I answered automatically. I opened my mouth, eager for his cock.

"Here you go, Kitten." Victor fed me his cock, still cradling my head in his hands as he did. It was a long slow glide, his cock sliding in over my tongue like a caress. I groaned, eager for him to take what he wanted. I reached back with my hands and gripped the muscled cheeks of his ass. He was naked and I got to run my hands over his thighs, the thick muscles bunching beneath my palms. Once he had sunk inside my mouth as far as he could go, I started urging him on. Faster and faster.

"Easy, Kitten." His voice sounded strained and his thighs bunched with tension. "I don't want to hurt you."

"Ung…" I grunted around his cock, swallowing when he landed a particularly deep thrust.

"Mother fuck! Goddamn mother fuck!"

"Victor?" That was Daddy. He was so close, I could reach out and touch him." So I did. I found his hip with one hand and clung even as I urged Victor to fuck me with the other.

"She swallowed me. Literally. Her throat… trying to take my cum from me!"

"You ready to give it to her?" Daddy sounded calm while Victor sounded like he was in distress.

"No! I want this to last! It's not often I get a taste of your sweet pet and I want as much time as I can have!"

Daddy chuckled. "Greedy for her, are you?

"Not too proud to admit it, Jacob. I've never met her equal. In anything."

Daddy moved my hand to his cock. I gripped it

tight as he used my hand to masturbate himself. "You know you can come to us anytime you need to, my friend. I owe you much."

"We owe you much, Papa Victor." Max spoke. He was close and I let go of Victor to reach out blindly for him. As always, Max was right where I needed him. He gripped my hand, bringing it to his lips to suck my fingers into his mouth. I couldn't see him, but he must have been squatting down next to the table where I lay on my back with yet another man grunting between my legs as he feasted on my weeping pussy.

The thought of what I looked like, laid out on Daddy's conference table like a pagan offering to some male virility god, set me off again. I screamed around Victor's cock, opening my mouth so he could fuck it at his leisure.

Tears streamed from my eyes. Thick saliva and some cum trickled from my mouth and streaked up my face where I hung upside down. I knew I was a mess, but it didn't seem to matter. My pussy ached to be filled. My orgasms, though hard and nearly debilitating at times, didn't seem to fulfill that aching need inside me. I needed Daddy, and I needed Max.

"I will call on you, Jacob," Victor said. "God help me, I need to take you up on that offer. She's fucking addictive."

Daddy chuckled. "She definitely is. I can't go many hours without my own fix of her."

"I love her," Max said, starkly. "And I love watching her like this. I've never seen such a sensual creature as Kitten."

"Fuck!" Victor bit out the word as he gripped my head tighter and fucked my mouth as roughly as he might my pussy. His heavy sac bounced against my face with every thrust forward. I relaxed my muscles and just took what he needed to give me. "Gonna give you my cum now, Kitten. Drink it all! Swallow every fuckin' drop, Goddamnit! Fuck! Fuck! FUCK!" Victor roared, emptying his balls of thick cum. I swallowed and swallowed, doing my best to take every drop he gave. Daddy moved my hand faster and faster on his cock while Max stood and wrapped my wet fingers around his own dick and masturbated over me.

Finally, Victor's cock twitched only occasionally. I continued to swallow, but started to caress him more than milk him. When he began to soften, I let him slip out of my mouth but moved my head so his dick trailed over my face in wet streaks. With Max and Daddy using my hands, it was the best I could do. I took him deep once more, swallowing around the head as he softened, then released him as he pulled away.

Victor knelt over me, finding my lips and kissing me deeply. I moaned into his mouth, eagerly kissing him back. "You want me to set a date with your Daddy to come over and fuck you, little Kitten?" His whispered question sent shivers of desire coursing through my body.

"Yes, Papa Victor," I answered in a breathy whimper. "If Daddy allows it, I'll accept it eagerly."

"Very well, sweetheart. I'll give you what you want with your Daddy's permission."

"Max, too?" Did I imagine it or did Victor's hands tighten in my hair? When he kissed me again, this time with a more aggressive slant to his lips, I knew I hadn't imagined it.

"Yes," he said huskily. "Max, too." Yeah. Papa Victor needed to fuck Max as much as he wanted to fuck me.

"Jacob, this is the best present you've ever given us." I was brought back to reality when someone spoke to Daddy from between my legs as he finished his own taste of me.

"She's perfect, Jacob. Congratulations." That came from someone else. Hands petted me from different directions, lingering on my breasts and bare mound.

A Force To Be Reckoned With

"I'll do anything you want me to do if you'll just let me fuck her. Please, man. I bet that's the tightest, greediest pussy in the world."

"Pull this deal through, and I'll see what we can arrange. I have no problems sharing her as long as she's willing. But you have to earn my Kitten. She's worth more than just your best effort. She's worth the win." Now, that was a challenge if I ever heard one. Daddy was good at getting what he wanted.

My gaze found Daddy, my eyes locking on to the man who meant so much to me. Next to him, Max. Always close. Always looking out for me.

"Daddy," I whispered, gripping both of them tightly. Max was naked. He let go of my hand to encase his cock in a condom. Daddy was naked, his cock thick and long and gloriously bare. I'd take him deep inside my body and he'd plant his cum there. Just the thought made me have a mini orgasm. My body clenched and my pussy wetted itself in anticipation of receiving him.

"Get under her, Max. You'll take her ass while I fuck her pussy."

Max moved us to the center of the big table, sliding underneath me with ease. Once I lay on top of him, my legs braced on either side of him to help him get me into position, he turned my face up to him for a long, wet, deep kiss. While he kissed me, he pulled my legs high before guiding his cock between my cheeks to my asshole.

I sucked in a breath when the tip slid inside. He paused, continuing to kiss me but letting me get used to his girth. His fingers played with my pussy, stroking my clit and plucking at my lips while he worked his way inside me.

"Fuckin' hot!"

"Look at her taking his big cock."

"You gonna let us fuck her like that, Jacob? Gonna let us take her ass?"

I thought that was the man who'd eaten out my ass like it was his favorite treat.

"You have just a bit more of a fetish with ass than I'd like, Roman, but since your part is the most important, you pull it off, and I'll let you fuck her ass." Daddy sounded amused, but also horny. I had no idea why he loved seeing me being pleasured by other men, but I thought I might be glad of it. He made it a safe experience and always made sure I enjoyed myself. Even if it meant I was denied orgasms *forever* before today's sex fest. It was worth the discomfort to experience this. I'd need to remember to thank him and Max for this. Assuming I didn't pass out first.

Then I felt Daddy's cock at my entrance. The head slipped inside and I gasped. Max continued to kiss me, but allowed me to make the noises they needed to hear so they knew I was accepting what they were doing. It was the first time I'd taken them together. I wanted to savor the moment, but my orgasm was already hovering near. Once I started coming, I knew I wouldn't stop until they both came.

"Fuck," Daddy bit out. "That's a tight fit. You good, Kitten?"

"Yes!" I screamed, to the delight of everyone around. "Fuck me, Daddy, Max!"

Both men did as I demanded. Max surged up inside my ass from his position flat on his back on the table, Daddy as he gripped my thighs, pulling me forward to aid in his pounding my pussy. It was a rough, hard ride, one where I was filled with cock. I was so stuffed I wasn't sure how they fit so easily. Both my pussy and ass burned, but it was just the right amount of pain to muffle the pleasure and allow me to last just that little bit longer.

I lay limply, letting the men take me the way they needed to. I imagined seeing so many of Daddy's friends licking me, forcing me to suck their cocks, then making me come over and over, made Daddy and Max need to stake their claim. Leave their marks. Victor, though he'd just come in my mouth, stood next to us, stroking his rapidly stiffening cock.

"You look so beautiful, Kitten. Your men fucking you hard. Using your body. Look how hard just watching you has already made me." He continued to stroke his long, thick cock, precum already leaking from the tip.

I wanted to answer him, but my mind had blanked, the pleasure and intensity of the situation overwhelming me. All I could do was open my mouth and stick out my tongue in anticipation of Victor's cum.

"Fuck, she's even hotter when she's getting fucked."

"What a beauty."

"Wet dream come true."

"Perfect little body."

Everyone was talking at once. I couldn't keep up, but they all praised me.

"Fuck her, Jacob. Fuck her hard. You coming in her pussy?"

"Absolutely, I'm comin' in her pussy," Daddy bit out. "Puttin' my cum deep. So fuckin' deep!" Daddy shook his head, sweat flying in all directions. He was trying to hold off, I could tell. He wanted this to last just a little longer. Max was grunting with every thrust into my ass, his body, too, was sweating with his effort and the need to come.

"I need Daddy's cum." I whimpered out my demand for Daddy. I wanted this to last, too, but when he came inside my cunt, I knew my orgasm would be positively nuclear. "Need Max to cum in my ass. Need to feel his cock pulsing against the walls inside my body. Want to feel it all, Daddy! Make me come!"

"Ah! Fuck! FUCK!" Daddy pounded inside me now, his cock swelled, stretching me exquisitely. "You ready, Kitten? Ready for my fuckin' cum?"

"Yes, Daddy! Yes! Give me your cum!"

"Max, you ready?"

"I'm comin' Daddy Jacob! Fuckin' comin'!"

Max swelled inside me, then shouted his release. I turned my head to watch his face contort in an almost painful pleasure. The tendons stood out in his neck and his arms tightened around my body as he fucked up into my ass, letting his orgasm overtake him.

Daddy's cum splashed inside me, hot and wet. The second he did, I screamed so loud, I was afraid it would bring security. I couldn't bring myself to care, but still! Never had an orgasm been so hard, fast, or long. It seemed to go on forever, my body clamping around the two cocks inside my body.

The next thing I knew, Victor yelled, his cum erupting from his cock and splashing over my chest and belly. He was followed by several more until I was covered in white, sticky cum. Max didn't get by unscathed either. His arms, where he had them wrapped around me were striped with it.

Daddy sat back on his heels, heaving in breath after breath. Sweat ran down his body in rivulets like he'd just stepped out of a pool. He shook his head, flinging sweat in all directions. "Whoo!" He grinned down at my cum-covered body. "Kitten, I've never seen you look sexier."

"Daddy," I sighed happily.

Daddy looked around the room, his gaze touching on every single man in the room. I noticed Stanton still lingered in one corner. He was fully dressed but had apparently watched the entire scene. Daddy pinned him with a hard gaze.

"I trust everyone is on board?" The question was directed at Stanton, but everyone else, other than Victor, seemed oblivious to the byplay. Victor glanced from Stanton to Daddy and gave Daddy a slight nod. "If not, tell me now. I'll replace whomever I have to for this to work."

"You've got my support," someone volunteered.

"And mine." The sentiment was repeated until every man but Stanton had pledged his support of the deal they were all working toward.

Stanton stepped forward then, looking down at me as he approached. "You truly have a remarkable woman, Jacob. She's special. And a force to be reckoned with." He met Daddy's gaze then. "You have my support. And my sincerest apologies for insulting your woman. I'll complete my task to the best of my ability. I won't let you down." He didn't refer to me as Daddy's pet and I understood the distinction. He also let Daddy know he was still on board, even though I'd cut him out of his incentive. Stanton was acknowledging my place in Daddy's life. Then he looked back at me. "I'm truly sorry, Isabella. I'll never doubt your loyalty to Jacob again. You are worthy of my brother."

"I never doubted you," Daddy said. He gave him a sheepish look. "I'd shake your hand, but I probably have cum on me." Everyone laughed.

Stanton grinned and stuck his hand out anyway.

"Take my hand. What's a little cum among friends." The two men shook hands and grinned broadly.

"Glad to have you on board, Stanton. You are crucial to this working."

"You can count on me." He glanced back at me. "But I'd appreciate it if you'd talk me up to your Kitten. Get her to forgive me so I can partake of her delights at a future date."

"I'll see what I can do," Daddy said.

I wanted to tell Stanton that, if Daddy was good, I was good, but I was just too tired. Max slipped out of my ass and I gave a sharp cry as another orgasm rippled through me. Daddy swore and gave several sharp thrusts into my pussy again before letting his softening cock slip out of me. Again, I came, though nothing like I had earlier. My body was spent, covered in cum. And I was happy. I was sated and happy.

Max lifted me into his arms and took me to the bathroom, and into the shower. I could barely stand up I was so tired. Somehow, Max got me clean and dressed in a long T-shirt. Daddy entered the bathroom soon after and kissed me tenderly before running through the shower himself. Then he and Max both wrapped their arms around me as we sat on a padded bench.

"You good, Kitten?" Daddy murmured against my ear.

"Yes, Daddy. Just… tired…"

"Sleep, baby," Daddy said. "Sleep. Tomorrow, we have things to discuss."

"Me, you, and Max?"

"Yes. And maybe Victor."

I smiled. "OK, Daddy." We could talk about the future later. Right now? All I wanted was sleep. And dream about Daddy. And Max.

Kitten's Christmas
A Razor's Edge Daddy Dom Erotica Short
Wanda Violet O.

It's their first Christmas together, and Daddy has a special Christmas present for his Kitten. Kitten knows what she wants -- her men, together, sharing. What she doesn't know is, she may have a special present for Daddy and Max, as well. But how will their changing relationship effect their growing commitment to one another?

A Hungry Kitten

Only two days till Christmas and I'm all out of sorts. No one should feel discombobulated this close to Christmas. I haven't told Daddy or Max because they'd make a fuss about it and probably make me go to a yucky doctor. Thankfully, I felt better this afternoon. Enough that I made my way to Daddy's office before he was done for the day. He's working from home today because he was worried about me when I asked to sleep in. Yeah. My Daddy loves me.

At the door, I stripped as I was supposed to, leaving Max's T-shirt, the only thing I'd put on this morning after crawling back into bed, folded neatly on the table outside. I didn't wear panties much around the house. Or anywhere else for that matter.

I opened the door to find Daddy on a video conference call. They seemed to all be talking at once while Daddy patiently listened. I didn't think he noticed me. I intended to sit at his feet on my cushion as I usually did, but the second I neared him, Daddy held out one arm for me and pulled me into his lap.

I could see myself in the corner of the screen curled up on Daddy's lap, naked as the day I was born. I tried to shift so they couldn't see my breasts. Daddy didn't seem to mind, even when a couple of the men on the call leaned forward, their eyes wide.

Daddy kissed my temple and murmured, "You know I'm not ashamed to show you affection. Let them gawk, my beautiful, naked Kitten."

Well, when he put it like that…

After the months I'd been with Daddy, I should be used to him showing me off by now. Normally it didn't bother me in the least. Today, I was self conscious. Probably because I'd felt so out of it the last couple of days. I snuggled closer, putting my arms around his neck and my lips on his skin. He grunted his approval and kissed my forehead before opening a side drawer at his desk and pulling out my favorite blanket to cuddle up in, wrapping his arms around me and turned his full attention back to the meeting.

I must have dozed off. I had no idea why because I'd already slept practically the whole day. The next thing I knew, Daddy was carrying me up the stairs. Max met us at the door to the bedroom. "She all right? Do I need to call the doctor?"

"I'm not sure. She seems worn out. Have the two of you been playing today?" It didn't sound like an accusation. Exactly. I could tell Daddy was worried though.

"No. She woke up a little late then went right back to bed. I checked on her several times. As far as I can tell, she didn't get up again except to go to the bathroom or get a drink of water. I tried to coax her to eat some fruit, but she picked at it. She wouldn't even eat her peanut butter and jelly sandwich."

"I'm fine, Daddy. Honest." I looked up at him where he still had me wrapped in the blanket. "I was under the weather this morning, but I'm better this afternoon. I don't feel too bad. Just a little nauseous and drained."

"If you've not eaten, you have to be hungry." Daddy's brows drew together in worry. I hated to cause him that.

"I'm not hungry." I grinned up at him. "At least, not for food."

"There's my Kitten. I don't like it when you feel bad, sweetheart." Daddy brushed a lock of hair off my forehead. I crawled out of his lap, shedding the blanket. He sat on the edge of the bed so I pushed him back so he lay down. Then I unzipped his pants and pulled out his rapidly hardening cock. "Not sure I should let you do this, but I have trouble denying you anything."

"I'm hungry for this, Daddy." Then I engulfed him deep. Normally, I loved sucking Daddy's cock. It was a comfort sometimes as well as my happy place. Daddy knew this. Which was probably why he allowed it now. But it might have been too soon to try after this morning's nausea. I abruptly pulled back when I gagged unexpectedly.

"I don't think you're quite ready for that, Kitten." Daddy said. He stood, removing his clothes. "Why don't we try me going down on you instead of the other way around."

"But what about you, Daddy? I want you to have fun, too." I knew I sounded a little whiny, but I was still out of sorts. I wasn't sick, per se. I didn't feel right. Like myself.

"Oh, I think I'll enjoy myself plenty, sweetheart. You lay back and spread those sweet thighs of yours. Let me take care of you."

I did. I spread my legs and Daddy lowered his face between them. The pleasure was gentle but sublime. Exactly what I need. Daddy had always been adept at knowing what I needed. It was one of many reasons I love him so much.

"How about I take care of Daddy Jacob while you watch and enjoy." Max tossed his shorts and T-shirt on a nearby chair. Giving his cock a lazy pump, he urged Daddy to lay over on his hip. Then, to my utter and complete delight, Max took Daddy's cock between his lips and slowly moved down his length. He took Daddy all the way. Both men growled and my clit pulsed under Daddy's tongue. The sight was the most hottest, most erotic visual I'd ever had the pleasure of witnessing.

I thought back to the conversation we'd had before Daddy had first taken me to his office to be an enticement to his partners. I'd confessed wanting to have Max and Daddy pleasure each other while they were with me. Daddy had said he and Max would discuss it when they weren't in the heat of the moment. I guess they'd done that because Max was definitely all in.

"Fuck…" Daddy gasped before kissing my pussy gently.

I got the feeling he was trying his best to be gentle and not overwhelm me. I appreciated that because, while I wanted this, I also wasn't certain I could take the vigorous pleasure Daddy and Max usually gave me.

"Feels fuckin' good, Max," Daddy said.

"*Mmm…*"

I loved the sound of Max's deep, masculine growl. He made similar sounds when he had his mouth on my cunt, but this was different somehow. Rougher. Not necessarily more intense, but with no hint of tenderness or restraint.

"That's it, Max," I whispered. "Daddy loves what you're doing. I think you love it too."

Both Max and Daddy grunted their confirmation, and I knew they'd both needed this. "Does it feel different when Max sucks you, Daddy? Different from when I suck you?"

"Yeah, Kitten." Daddy's lips brushed my clit as he spoke. He sank two fingers inside me, stroking gently but insistently. "Can definitely tell it's a man sucking my cock."

Daddy lay on one hip as he ate me out. He had

his legs bent and spread wide with Max between them, his mouth working vigorously as the seconds ticked by. Max and Daddy both grew more and more worked up. Daddy broke out in a sweat while Max growled and grunted as he sucked Daddy's thick cock.

Max reached up to pinch Daddy's nipple and Daddy shuddered. He groaned against my clit before flicking out with his tongue. "Mother fuck, Max! What the Goddamned fuck?"

Max didn't stop and Daddy's free hand shot out to bury itself in Max's hair. He pushed Max's head down, forcing Max to swallow more of Daddy's cock. Max didn't seem to mind. In fact, I watched in fascination as Max sucked Daddy all the way down and held himself there. His throat worked as he swallowed several times. I knew from experience that was a hard thing to do. I also knew how much Daddy loved it.

"Oh, wow, Max! That's so fucking hot!" I tunneled my fingers through Daddy's hair. Not to hold him to me, but to grind myself. And him. I could tell he was enjoying himself and made a mental note to thank Max later.

"Fuck! Fuck!" Daddy finally laid his head on my belly. He continued to stroke my pussy, but he gave up trying to eat me out, which was fine with me -- I was enjoying watching the expressions on his face as Max continued to suck his cock and play with his balls. I stroked his hair and brushed his face tenderly as Max became more aggressive, growling every time he took Daddy deep. "What the fuck, Max?" Daddy didn't sound angry. Just so on the verge of losing control he was losing his mind.

Max let Daddy's cock go with a little *pop* of his lips. "Tell me you hate it and I'll stop."

"Don't you fucking dare!" I giggled as Daddy tightened his hold on Max's hair and shoved him back down. Max chuckled as he engulfed Daddy's cock once more.

Daddy used his hold on Max's hair to control the pace. He alternately made Max speed up and slow down, sometimes making Max hold Daddy's cock deep. Whenever he did, Max swallowed several times. Saliva leaked from the corner of Max's mouth, dripping down to cover Daddy's balls.

Normally, I'd be eager to join. Instead, I was glad Daddy's attention was focused on Max and the sensations the other man created. Even though I'd started this, I wasn't sure if I could continue. The nausea that had plagued me all day was coming back with a vengeance.

"Max!" Daddy shuddered as he yelled out. His cock pulsed in Max's mouth. The other man sank all the way down onto Daddy's cock, taking Daddy down his throat to the balls. One trickle of cum leaked from the corner of Max's mouth. "Mother fuck! Fuck! *Fuck*!"

Daddy continued to roar his release. It went on and on, his cock pulsing and throbbing. Max continued to drink the sticky seed. If the look on his face was any indication, Max was supremely satisfied. His own cock was angry looking, the head purple with a pearly drop of precum beading on the tip.

Once Daddy was spent, he let go of Max's hair. I'd bet he was so weak he couldn't hang on any longer. It had been a while since Daddy had come that hard and I was glad it was with Max. It made me smile that the two of them could find this kind of pleasure in each other.

"Get the lube and a condom, Max." Daddy gasped as he spoke, having trouble catching his breath.

"I don't think I can suck you off at the moment, but you can fuck my ass until you come."

"Oh, God." The whispered plea escaped before I could censor it. I wanted to see that more than about anything in the world.

"I think Kitten likes this idea." Daddy grinned at me. Then he moved further up my body so he could wrap his brawny arms around me while he kissed me. I accepted him eagerly, wishing I could participate more but knowing my tummy wasn't ready.

"Next time, Kitten." Daddy always knew me so well. "You know I'd never willingly leave you out of this. Right?"

"I know, Daddy." I felt tears of frustration prick my eyes. "I don't know what's wrong. I don't feel *bad*. I'm a little nauseous."

"It's OK, Isabella. I promise everything will be wonderful. Just relax and know I'll always take care of you." He kissed me again, lingering, but not pushing or deepening the kiss. His touch was comforting and I found myself relaxing. Daddy never called me Isabella unless he needed me to understand he was very serious. If he said he'd take care of me, I knew he would.

I sighed as Daddy broke our kiss only to nibble his way down my chest to latch onto a nipple. I winced and gasped. The nubs were sensitive. Painfully so. Attentive as ever, Daddy stopped immediately and looked up at me. "Tender, Kitten?"

"Yes, Daddy. It's close to time for my period though."

"Sometimes you get tender, don't you."

I nodded, tears wanting to form again. Daddy stroked my cheek and smiled up at me. "Just relax, my beautiful Kitten. I promise I'll take care of everything."

* * *

Max approached the bed again, his cock standing out proud and eager, already encased in a condom. His hand worked his shaft with lubricant, his fingers gleaming as they moved up and down his cock.

"Stretch me first, Max," Daddy commanded. "I've not done this in a while."

He took the bottle of lube and slipped open the cap. "I'm so fuckin' ready for this, I'm afraid I'll go too fast."

"You won't." Daddy sounded supremely confident. Max met my gaze and I smiled at him, nodding my head. Daddy trusted Max as much as I did. "Just take your time. Make it good for me."

If the noises Daddy made and the way his body shuddered were any indication, Max was definitely making it good for Daddy. Every so often, Max would squirt out more lube over Daddy's ass before Max would start fingering and stretching him again.

"Goddamn! Fuck! That's it, Max. Stretch my ass. Get me ready to take your cock."

"I can't wait for this." Max's body gleamed with sweat. Daddy's too.

Daddy still had his arms wrapped around me and he nuzzled my chest between my breasts. He was on his knees with his ass up in the air while Max played with him. Even though he'd come, Daddy was still hard. I could see his cock bobbing below his belly with every move he made, with every thrust of Max's fingers. Daddy's thick cock pulsed angrily, precum leaking from the tip. Daddy had always rebounded fast, but this was a new experience with me and Max. It was easy to see how he enjoyed this. How he wanted everything Max could give him.

I wanted this for Daddy. He was so good to me

and Max. Pleasuring Daddy was the least we could do for him. Max was going to enjoy himself as well, but I knew this was more about Daddy's pleasure than Max's.

"Do it, Max," Daddy hissed. "Put your cock in my ass."

With a grunt, Max pressed himself inside Daddy. I could see the euphoria overcome both of them. Max's eyes closed in bliss while Daddy's lips parted and he breathed out a sigh, like this was the greatest relief he'd ever had. Maybe it was. Both men had fucked me together multiple times, but they'd never taken pleasure from each other. In my opinion, this was way past time this happened.

"You both look so beautiful." My voice was a whisper. I continued to stroke Daddy's hair, to pet him the way he loved to pet me. "Does it feel good, Daddy?"

"It does, my perfect Kitten." His voice sounded strained, but also in awe. "Never felt anything like it, even the few times I've let another man have my ass."

"So fuckin' tight." Max gripped his hips and eased his way in until his abdomen rested against Daddy's upturned buttocks. "Gonna fuck you good, Daddy Jacob. Just like you need."

"Do it, Max," Daddy snapped. He laved my nipple gently, the opposite of his harsh tone. "Fuck me like you mean it."

Max didn't need any further encouragement. He gripped Daddy's hips and pounded him with rapid, hard snaps of his hips. Daddy groaned, tightening his arms around me, continuing to nuzzle my breasts. Even though I wasn't feeling my best, the sight and sounds, and the looks of bliss on both Daddy and Max's faces gave me a kind of euphoric high. My pussy dampened and my clit ached with need until I whimpered and wiggled against Daddy to get friction where I needed it.

"Does my little Kitten like what she sees?" Daddy looked up at me, his beautiful face expressing a plethora of emotions. I saw lust and love and pleasure as well as a desperate need he'd never shown me before. It confused me. My Daddy obviously needed something and I wasn't sure what it was. Or who he needed it from. I wanted with all my being to give him what he needed, but this was something only Max could give him.

"I do. You and Max are so sexy together. I could watch you all day."

"Are we making you wet?"

"You are, Daddy. My pussy aches." The second I said it, I knew I'd expressed the right thing. The look of relief on Daddy's face satisfied me in a way I hadn't realized I'd needed. "Will you fuck me while Max fucks you?"

"Ah fuck!" Max slammed into Daddy's ass hard, holding himself deep. "You sure you're up to it, Kitten?" Max looked equal parts concerned and eager.

"I wasn't until a few moments ago. Now I feel like I'll die if I can't be a part of this." It was true. Lust hit me with such force I cried out, thrashing beneath Daddy. I scooted further beneath him, trying to get to his cock. Needing to feel him inside me.

Daddy didn't resist. He let me scoot further underneath him until my pussy kissed the head of his dick. I looked up into his beautiful face, the face of the man I loved with all my heart. Watching as I urged him deeper, I saw his eyes glaze over and a look of so much pleasure cross his face my heart swelled to bursting.

"Daddy…" I sighed his name like a homecoming. That's what it felt like. I had no idea what was different this time, but I knew it was. This was everything. One of those moments when you knew your life was getting ready to change.

"Sweet Jesus." Daddy lowered his face to mine. He kissed me gently as his cock sank inside me until he could go no deeper. Once he stopped, Max started moving again. First slow and gentle, then harder and with more purpose. Immediately, pleasure engulfed me.

"He's fucking both of us, Daddy." My voice was barely a whisper as Daddy and I locked gazes while Max continued to pound Daddy's ass with his long, sure strokes. I knew exactly what it felt like to have Max fucking me like that. He was into it with his whole heart. Daddy too.

"I know, baby."

"It's blissful…"

Daddy kissed me then, dropping his weight on top of me. Max followed him down so that I was pressed into the mattress by both men. It should have been suffocating, but it was perfect. It was exactly what I needed and I reveled in it.

It wasn't long before we were lost in each other. Daddy. Max. Me. This was my family. My home. I belonged here more than I'd ever belonged anywhere. Daddy had taken me in when I had nothing and made me his world. In the process, he'd become my world, as well. Max balanced us out. I doubted I'd be completely whole without the two of them.

"Fuck… *Fuck*!" Max chanted the word over and over as his movements became faster and faster.

"Daddy!" I screamed as my orgasm crashed into me with all the finesse of a raging bull. It came out of nowhere, catching me by surprise when I normally waited for Daddy to give me permission. Would he punish me for the transgression? I wasn't sure I could take a punishment, though I sometimes welcomed it. Just not today.

"Ungh!" Daddy grunted and his cock throbbed inside me. Two thrusts later, Daddy came inside me in great pulses of his seed. I felt his cum explode deep inside me and I wanted to hold it inside me forever. Daddy's orgasm must have triggered Max's because the next thing I knew, Max threw back his head and bellowed to the rafters. The muscles stood out in his chest and arms as he thrust deep.

When everyone was finally spent, we lay there, the men still on top of me. I wasn't uncomfortable. It was peaceful. Comforting.

"You good, Kitten?" Daddy kissed my cheek as he spoke, caressing me with his face.

"I'm wonderful, Daddy. Thank you." I looked up at Max. "Thank you both." I gave them a watery smile, my emotions suddenly overwhelming me. "I love you both so much!"

Kitten's Visitor

Max moved off Daddy and Daddy pulled me against him as he rolled to his side, taking me with him. The next thing I knew, Max was cleaning between my legs, then between Daddy's cheeks.

Daddy kissed my temple before getting up to dress. "Call Dr. Wilson, Max. Tell him Kitten needs a check-up and maybe something for nausea."

Damn it, I thought I'd distracted Daddy from that thought. I hated doctors! "But I'm all better, Daddy! Please don't call the doctor."

"It'll be all right, Kitten. But we need to do this. I promise I'll stay with you through the whole thing. We might even find a way to make the exam a bit more pleasant." Daddy sat back on the bed and pulled me onto his lap, kissing my temple gently, tightening his arms around me in a brief squeeze.

I wasn't sure I believed it would be all right, but Daddy had never lied to me. If he said he could make it better, then I chose to believe him.

* * *

Fifteen minutes later, a man I recognized from Daddy's inner circle stepped into our bedroom. He was an older man, but very fit, with thick, muscular arms. His hair was a rich salt and pepper with more gray at his temples. Max followed him in, but Daddy waved him off. Max raised an eyebrow but said nothing.

"Give us a few minutes, Max," Daddy said. "This may be a private ordeal for Kitten. I promise to fill you in the moment we're done." Max nodded and shut the door as he left.

I looked up at Daddy. "We don't need to shut

Max out." My voice was barely above a whisper. I had my eyes on Dr. Wilson. It wasn't that I didn't trust him. Daddy had let the man lick my pussy at his office. No, I was nervous about him being here as a doctor. After all, doctors often had needles and other unpleasant things with them.

"I know, baby. But right now, this needs to be about me and you. We'll tell Max everything when we're done. At least, as much as you want him to know."

Well, *that* wasn't cryptic or anything.

"Don't look at me with such fear in your eyes, Kitten." Dr. Wilson sat on the edge of the bed and took my hand. "You know I'd never hurt you or Jacob wouldn't let me near you."

"I don't like needles," I blurted out before I could stop myself.

"Most Kittens don't." Dr Wilson smiled before handing me a cherry sucker. "But I think Kittens like sweet treats. Yes?"

I slowly reached for the sucker, sticking it in my mouth. It was very flavorful and I closed my eyes and moaned in pleasure.

Dr. Wilson chuckled. "I thought you might like that." He shifted his gaze to Daddy. "It has a mild sedative that is safe for her to help her relax. I don't want to cause her distress."

"I appreciate that, Robert. I fear I spoil her, but I don't regret it."

"Nor should you." Dr Wilson winked at me. "Should you decide she's not the right woman for you, Jacob, I could give her a good home."

"She's the *only* woman for me." Daddy squeezed me again, still not letting me go. He sat with his back against the headboard and me firmly against his side.

He smiled down at me as I looked up into his face. "She's my most precious possession."

"Well then. We can't have such a beautiful Kitten as little Isabella here feeling under the weather. Let's see if we can figure out what's wrong and make it all better."

I peeked over Daddy's arm to find Dr. Wilson's gaze. He smiled kindly at me as he put his stethoscope in his ears and warmed the bell between his hands. "May I listen to your heart and lungs, Kitten?" His voice was gentle and he didn't make a move to touch me until I gave my consent. Daddy didn't urge me to comply with the doctor or anything. He left the decision up to me.

I knew Daddy thought having the doctor check me out needed to be done, that it was his wish I let the doctor do his job. That knowledge was the only thing that gave me the courage to nod my head. The second I did, Daddy kissed the top of my head and released me for Dr. Wilson to look me over.

I was still naked. Daddy had said Dr. Wilson would need to examine all of me. Daddy would be with me so there was no reason to dress until the doctor was finished.

The physical exam was pretty straight forward. He put the stethoscope against my chest and listened, moving it around. Then did the same to my back. He examined my breasts in a very clinical manner. "No lumps. You said she's due her period, so there might be some fibroid tissue, but that's nothing too abnormal. Do your breasts become tender when you have your period?"

"Sometimes."

"Not too badly?"

"No." I looked up at Daddy, hesitating.

"Tell him everything, Kitten. He's here to help you."

I took a breath. It wasn't embarrassing. Exactly. But I was afraid there was really something wrong. I'd been feeling that way for several days, trying to ignore my fears. "They've been really tender the last few days."

"I see." He smiled and put away his stethoscope and pulled out a specimen cup from his bag. "Do you think you can give me a urine sample?"

I nodded and took the cup. Daddy helped me off the bed. "Do you want me to go with you, Kitten?"

I wrinkled my nose. "That's gross! I can do it by myself."

Daddy chuckled. "All right then. If you want to put on a T-shirt, there should be one on the vanity. Do not put on panties."

"Yes, Daddy." I glanced at Dr. Wilson who smiled at me. I thought I might like Dr. Wilson. He'd eaten my pussy at the office, but I hadn't really had any meaningful interaction with him before now. I should have known he would be a good person. Daddy didn't have bad people in his inner circle.

I still had the sucker in my mouth, the sweet, cherry flavor tasty and oddly comforting. When I pulled it free with a little *pop*, Dr. Wilson spoke. "The sucker might make you lightheaded. If you get the least bit dizzy, you call out and Jacob will come to you."

"Yes, sir."

My response was automatic, but Dr. Wilson seemed pleased. "Good girl," he praised.

It didn't take me long to collect the sample then finish peeing. I put the lid on the small container and set it on the counter before cleaning myself and washing my hands. By that time, though, the sucker was starting to give me a high. I kind of liked the feeling. I could easily see myself laying back and forgetting everything but Daddy. Maybe he'd let me suck his cock when Dr. Wilson left.

I leaned against the counter, the sucker still in my mouth, remembering what Dr. Wilson had said. "Daddy!" I raised my voice, but tried not to sound like I was in trouble. I didn't want to distress Daddy when I was buzzed. The thought made me giggle for some reason.

The door opened slightly and Daddy stuck his head in. "You good, Kitten?"

"Yes. Just a little dizzy." I giggled again. "I think I'm getting high."

Daddy chuckled. "Robert said you might be." Scooping me up, Daddy kissed my nose. I smiled and wrapped my arms around him. I hadn't put on the T-shirt but didn't care. Daddy would take care of me. If I needed a shirt, he'd get me one.

"I take it the sedative is hitting?"

"I'm buzzing." I grinned at Dr. Wilson, talking around my sucker. "I really like my sucker. Thank you."

"You're quite welcome, Kitten. Now. I'll be right back."

Oddly, Dr. Wilson went to the bathroom and fiddled with the urine sample I'd given. He left the door open as he opened a package and took out a small, white cartridge. Then he took a dropper and placed several drops of my urine onto the cartridge.

"What's that, Daddy?"

"He's testing your urine. Nothing for you to worry about."

"I don't think there's anything wrong with my

pee, Daddy," I whispered loudly, giggling as I did.

Daddy smiled down at me. "I'm sure there's not."

Dr. Wilson washed his hands then walked back into the room. "Now we wait. Less than five minutes."

"Kitten? Dr. Wilson's been very nice to come here with no notice. Just to help you."

"Thank you, Dr. Wilson." I smiled up at him. "Thank you for my sucker, too. I'm high."

He chuckled. "Yes. I think you are." He reached for his bag again.

I couldn't see his movements and Daddy distracted me with a kiss before I could look too closely. I always got lost in Daddy's kisses, but with my head spinning like I'd never experienced before, all I could process was the exquisite feel of his lips and tongue as they slid along mine. The next thing I knew, there was a small pinch at the bend of my elbow. I sucked in a breath, but Daddy kept kissing me and I rolled with it, moaning as he built my lust expertly.

"There now," Dr. Wilson pressed something against the place where the small prick had been. "All done."

Daddy ended the kiss gently, smiling down at me when I looked up at him. "Not so bad, was it?"

"What?"

"Dr. Wilson taking your blood."

I gasped, my eyes going wide. "He did what?" I immediately held out my arm. There was a small bandage with princess crowns on it stuck in the bend.

"Just some routine blood work, Kitten." Dr. Wilson smiled at me. "I'll get this to the lab and we'll have the results later today."

"But I didn't know you were going to stick me." I wasn't really complaining. I was glad it didn't hurt. I felt the need to put up a protest. Might get me another sucker.

"Just so. And I didn't hurt you either, did I?"

"No." I admitted, rolling my eyes. "Don't think I don't see what you're doing. You got me high and Daddy distracted me with his yummy kisses. But I still don't like needles."

"I would never expect you to like them. But I do expect a kiss in payment for me coming all the way out here to take care of you."

"Well, it was nice of you. I suppose it wouldn't hurt." I looked back at Daddy. "If Daddy says it's OK."

"You may give Dr. Wilson a kiss. In fact, he may want more from you. If you feel up to it."

"What else would you want, Dr. Wilson?"

He leaned in and kissed my lips gently. "I'd love to taste your sweet cunt one more time, Kitten. Will you allow it?"

Again, I looked to Daddy for guidance. I would always look to Daddy for approval in anything I wanted. My Daddy would never lead me wrong.

"It's your choice, Kitten. I can pay Dr. Wilson, or you can. From me, he'll accept money. From you, he'll want your body. He knows the boundaries and I'll be with you to stop him before he goes further than I want. But only if you're up to it."

"I'm much better after you and Max…" I trailed off, not meaning to reveal what the three of us had done in front of someone other than Max and Daddy. "That is, my tummy isn't being naughty anymore."

"Did Kitten have a sick tummy?" Dr. Wilson asked with a look of concern on his face.

I nodded. "For a few days. Usually in the mornings, but sometimes it's all day. Especially if I don't have much to eat."

"We can fix that. I brought something with me and can get you a prescription for longer use. But first I'd love to taste your pussy again."

"I'd love that."

Daddy urged me to lay back. "Spread your legs, Kitten." Daddy slid his arm under one leg up and hooked it over his elbow. I pulled my other one up so my legs were spread wide.

"What a beautiful sight." Dr. Wilson petted the inside of my thighs and I shivered beneath his touch. "Just a small taste. Maybe make you come." He kissed my mound before taking a long lick through my folds.

His groan nearly drowned out my whimpers as he licked me over and over again. He licked my clit several times before plunging his tongue into my opening.

God, that felt good! I looked up at Daddy. His eyes were filled with heat and he flashed me a cocky grin. "I love watching you, Kitten. You're the most sensual creature I've ever met." He leaned down and I met his kiss eagerly, whimpering into his mouth.

Daddy cupped one of my breasts, tweaking the nipple gently. It hurt a little, but I didn't mind. It was like there was an invisible string tying my nipples and my clit because each time Daddy tugged one, my clit would throb under Dr. Wilson's tongue.

It wasn't long before I was panting and crying out in pleasure. My body seemed to have a life of its own, thrashing about while the men played with me, making my pussy vibrate with need.

"That's it, Kitten. Can you come for us?"

No sooner had Daddy asked the question than I came with a scream. "Fuck!" Dr. Wilson exclaimed as he continued to cover my pussy opening with his mouth, sucking hard while I came. I was sure I came with a flood. Dr. Wilson kept licking me with that wicked tongue, drawing out my climax each time I thought it was ebbing.

Finally, when I couldn't take anymore, I pushed at his head. "No more," I whimpered weakly. "Please."

Immediately, Dr. Wilson stopped and sat back on the bed. He swiped his mouth with the back of his hand, licking his lips like he'd enjoyed my taste thoroughly. "Sweet as ever."

"That she is," Daddy agreed. He nuzzled my cheek and neck, bringing me down gently.

"I'll check the test."

I was aware of Dr. Wilson moving away from us, but now, I wanted my Daddy. I snuggled closer to him, wishing Max was here with us. I knew I was being clingy, but I couldn't help it. Daddy was right that he'd spoiled me. Was I clinging too hard?

"I don't like that look on your face, Kitten." Daddy frowned at me, gently tracing my brow with a fingertip. "What thought did you have that upset you, baby?"

I bit my lip. I wasn't afraid to express myself to Daddy, but I wasn't sure how I'd take it if he indicated that he'd help me get over my clinginess. I kind of liked being the center of his attention. "I'm sorry if I'm too needy, Daddy," I said, looking away. "I know I need to be more self-sufficient --" Before I could finish, Daddy kissed me again. This time, he dominated me with his kiss. There was no denying him control when he was in this kind of mood. He was making a point.

Daddy thrust his tongue deep, licking the inside of my mouth before nipping my lip only to stroke his tongue against mine again. "You listen to me, Isabella. Really listen well because I don't want to have to repeat myself." I blinked up at him, a little startled but still buzzing and more than a little lust stupid. "I *want* you to cling to me. I never want you to try to be on your own or to avoid me because you think you're taking up too much time or whatever other silly notion you have that I don't want you close. You are the single most important thing in my world. While I love Max, he's not my Kitten. He's not my woman. You are. I need you to cling to me, and to Max. We're a family. Understand, Isabella?"

My sigh of relief nearly brought me to tears. "I'm glad, Jacob. Because I can't imagine my life without you."

He hugged me close. "You'll never have to, honey. You'll never have to."

* * *

Dr. Wilson cleared his throat. He looked pointedly at Daddy, waving the little cartridge in the air. "Positive," he said, then winked at me. "I'm leaving some medicine and some vitamins on the dresser. There are instructions on the bottles as to how you're to take them. Jacob, if you have questions or need anything else, you know how to get hold of me. I'll set her up an appointment in the next couple of days for an ultrasound so we can see exactly what we're dealing with."

"Thanks, Robert. Will you tell Max to wait in the sitting room? I'll call for him when I'm ready."

"I will. Make sure she gets as much rest as she needs for the next couple of weeks. No restrictions unless there's pain or bleeding. Just be mindful of her condition." Then he left.

"My condition?" My eyes got wide and my breath started coming in pants. "Is something wrong with me?"

Daddy chuckled. "No, baby. There's nothing

wrong with you."

"Then what's going on?"

Then, Daddy gave me the most glorious smile in the world. I held my breath. I had the feeling my life was about to change forever. "You're pregnant, Kitten."

For some reason, this didn't compute. I stared at Daddy, not understanding what he was saying. "I'm sorry?"

He chuckled, pulling me to him and rolling so that he lay against my side. "You're going to have a baby, sweetheart. My baby."

"A baby?"

"Yeah."

I had no idea what to say so I looked up at Daddy. He looked so supremely satisfied, I couldn't help but giggle. Then I began to laugh for the sheer joy of it. "A baby!"

"Yeah, Kitten. A baby."

Then a thought occurred to me and some of the joy left me. "But… what about Max?"

"What about him?"

"Is he… I mean, will Max still be part of our family?"

Daddy brushed a lock of hair off my forehead. "I suppose that's up to you and Max. I already told you Max is part of our family as far as I'm concerned, but if you don't want him to be part of this, then he won't. Same goes for him."

"What if he doesn't like that the baby isn't his, too?" I could feel my heart breaking. I wasn't sure I could stand it if Max left us.

"Perhaps we should talk to him before you get too upset. Yes?"

"I suppose."

Kitten's Fantasy

Daddy called for Max, who he immediately opened the door, stepping inside the room. His gaze locked on mine, then went to Daddy. "Is Kitten all right, Daddy Jacob?"

"She is. Come, Max." Daddy held out a hand and motioned to the other side of the bed. "We all need to have a talk."

"This sounds serious." Max sat cross legged on the bed next to me. "What's going on?"

Daddy smiled. "Kitten is pregnant."

Max's lips parted in a grin. "Well, that explains a lot."

"It does. She's worried you might have concerns."

"Concerns?" Max's brows drew together in confusion and he met my gaze. "What concerns, Kitten?"

"Well, the baby. Only Daddy is allowed to cum in me. I will only ever carry his child."

Max's frown deepened. "So?"

"I mean… That is…" I wasn't sure how to word it. I didn't want to offend Max. Or, worse, hurt his feelings. If he hadn't realized that he'd never be the biological father of my child, I didn't want to be the one to tell him.

"Are you going to be all right with any children Kitten has being mine? You won't be expected to have a part in their lives, but I can't imagine Kitten not wanting you to."

Max scowled then, but his anger was directed at Daddy, not me. "How can you possibly ask me that?"

My heart sank. Max deserved to have children of his own. Not to watch as Daddy gave me babies while not allowing Max the same pleasure. Would he leave us now? Tears pricked my eyes at the thought.

"Any child Kitten has is mine, too. How could you even think I'd not love that child as my own? Of course I want to be part of her life! I'm Kitten's protector. I'll be her daughter's protector too."

"Daughter, huh?" Daddy smiled. "So sure, are you?"

"I'm positive." Max leaned down and pressed a soft kiss to my belly above my mound. "She's having a girl and her name will be Andromeda."

Daddy laughed. "Fine, Max. If she has a girl we'll name her Andromeda."

"She's having a girl," Max insisted.

I let out a breath I hadn't realized I'd been holding. "Oh, Max!" I pulled him to me so his big body rested on the other side of mine. I clung to both him and Daddy, needing the connection to both of them. "I love you both so much!"

"I love you too, Kitten," Max murmured before kissing me tenderly. "I'll always love you."

"You're my beautiful, brave Kitten," Daddy said, kissing my hand and rubbing his face against it. "I love you with all my heart."

"I need you, Kitten." Max's husky voice tugged at my heart. "Can I have you? Are you up to it?"

"Yes, Max. I need both you and Daddy now." I looked over at Daddy, pleading for him to allow me this. "Please, Daddy?"

"I can't say no to you." Daddy smiled at me. "Max, take her sweet pussy. I want her ass."

My heart sang and my pussy throbbed. Daddy always seemed to know what I needed -- sometimes even before I did.

Max rolled to the nightstand and pulled out a

condom, rolling it on.

"Get on top of me, Kitten," Daddy ordered. "Lay on your back. Max, get the lube while you're over there."

"With pleasure." Max winked at me and my insides fluttered.

I was having a baby -- with the full blessing of both Daddy and Max. I was so happy the flood of emotion nearly overwhelmed me. Tears prick at my eyes.

Daddy kissed my cheek. "What's the matter, sweetheart? Are you sure you're up for this?"

"I am! I'm so happy."

He cupped my face and kissed me gently. That was when I felt Max probing my ass. He'd slickened his finger with the cool lubricant and it slid inside me with ease. I sucked in a breath at the burn, but there was no pain. He quickly added a second finger and stretched me gently.

"Listen to our little Kitten purr." Max smiled at me as he continued to work my ass. "I love the sounds you make. Love watching you lose your mind with us."

"Feels so good…"

"She's a miracle." Daddy cupped my breasts gently, ever mindful that I'd confessed to them being tender. "Our own Christmas miracle." He turned my head to him for a kiss as Max prepared my ass for Daddy's cock.

I opened for Daddy eagerly, lapping at his tongue when he swept inside my mouth.

"Mmm…" Daddy groaned as he continued kissing me. "So fucking sweet."

I whimpered, letting my men do whatever they wanted to me. "Put me inside her, Max. Guide my cock inside her ass."

Max did. There was a small resistance until the flared head of Daddy's cock popped inside the tight ring of muscle. I sighed, sliding down on Daddy's cock, working my hips to feel the exquisite burn and gain friction. "Oh, God! That feels so fucking fantastic!"

Daddy grunted, moving his hips in time with mine, fucking me several times before his fingers bit into my hips to hold me still. "Let Max inside you. We want to fuck you together."

"Please, Max! Please!"

Without a word, Max slid his cock inside me, his big body shuddering above us. Once he was in to the balls, both Daddy and Max started moving inside me, each at his own pace. Max moved leisurely while Daddy seemed desperate for me, pounding his cock inside me with hard, fast thrusts.

"Fuck... Fuck..." Daddy chanted the word like a prayer. "Never needed you so fucking badly!"

"I'm yours, Daddy. Take me however you need."

"Fuck!" Daddy pulled out of my ass with a snarl. "Put a fucking condom on me Max." Daddy was in full Dom mode. Max responded, pulling out of me to reach for a condom. Daddy gripped my neck, turning me to kiss him while Max gloved him up. "Now. Me and Max are both going to fuck your pussy, Kitten. We're going to take you carefully, but we're both going in. You tell me if we're too much."

I shuddered, my body breaking out in a sweat. This was going to be perfect. And I'd dreamed of this for months!

"Holy shit! Her pussy got fucking wet! Like *really* wet!" Max swiped his fingers through my cunt, raising his gleaming fingers so Daddy could see. I reached out and snagged Max's hand, pulling his fingers to my mouth to lick them clean.

Daddy immediately turned my head and thrust his tongue between my lips. "Mmm..." He growled into my mouth, his tongue tangling with mine. "So fucking sweet!"

The next thing I felt was someone probing my pussy with a condom covered dick. Judging by the way Daddy stiffened, it was him. Once he was inside me, he pounded me several times, shuddering beneath me. His body dampened with sweat and slid against me in an erotic glide. "Fuck!" he bit out. "Get inside her, Max. I'm not going to last long. Be careful!"

Max barked out a laugh. "*Be careful*, he says. You do realize we're putting both our dicks in her tight little pussy. Right?"

"Fuck!" Daddy's fingers wrapped around my shoulders, his grip like iron, his muscular arms nearly covering my back as he held me for Max. "Just... fuck!"

Max drizzled lubricant over my pussy and his cock as he found room beside Daddy and slid home. I was stretched to bursting. "This is the most incredible feeling in the world!" I assured them, rocking my hips, trying to get them to move.

Max swatted my inner thigh. "Be still, Kitten." I whimpered but did as he commanded.

It wasn't long before they both moved inside me, slowly at first. Daddy picked up the pace first and Max groaned and picked up his rhythm, coming along for the ride.

My legs were spread wide, an open invitation for both of them. I lay there in Daddy's arms and let them have me. I trusted them to see to my pleasure, and, God! What pleasure! I loved the burn. Loved the friction.

Max used his thumb to rub my clit and I tripped into my first orgasm. Screaming at the top of my lungs, I came, squeezing them both with almost painful intensity. I could feel their heartbeats through their cocks inside my body. When the first spasm hit, Max cried out, stopping his movement. "Not gonna fuckin' come yet! Not gonna do it!"

Daddy growled, moving one hand to my throat and holding my head to his shoulder as he continued to fuck me. He fucked me hard and fast, his heels digging into the mattress for leverage.

"Don't you fuckin' stop, Max! Don't you fuckin' dare!"

With a defeated groan, Max started his own hard, driving rhythm, fucking me with nearly vicious strokes. Another orgasm made my body spasm. This time when I clamped down on them, both men bellowed to the rafters. I could feel the pulsing of their cocks as they came. My only regret was the condoms. I'd have loved to have both men bathing my cunt with their soothing cum.

Max collapsed on top of me, his breathing hard and deep. He found my lips, sweeping his tongue inside my mouth to stroke mine. When he finished, Daddy fisted Max's hair and pulled him down for his own kiss. Theirs was rougher than either man would kiss me, and I thought they might be developing their own wants and desires with each other. It made me giddy with happiness.

"What a wonderful Christmas present." Max beamed down at me, then Daddy.

"It is." Daddy slid one arm from around me and put it around Max. "She is. The best Christmas present ever."

"Merry Christmas." I looked from one of them to

the other, hoping they could see my love shining brightly in my eyes. "Merry Christmas."

Kitten's Vacation
A Razor's Edge Daddy Dom Erotica Short
Wanda Violet O.

Warning: This is a Razor's Edge Daddy Dom BDSM Erotica short story. Expect limited plot and character development, and lots of heat. If you're looking for a lengthy plot driven erotic romance, this is not it!

Being a mother is absolutely one of the best things to ever happen to me. I never thought I could love anyone so completely as I love our daughter. The other best things ever to happen to me? Daddy and Max. Daddy is my rock. The one person in my life who grounds me. Max and Daddy together make me feel safe, wanted, and loved.

But something's just a little bit off... Daddy hasn't taken me and Max to the office since I'd found out I was pregnant, and Max always finds a reason to keep me upstairs in our rooms whenever Daddy has his inner circle in our home.

I still love Daddy with all my heart, but I'm beginning to worry. Has he replaced me?

Daddy's Breakfast

"Kitten, honey. Everything all right?"

Daddy leaned against the door frame, his satisfied gaze landing on me where I sat feeding Andi. The child was happily sucking away at my breast even as her eyelids drooped.

"Yes, Daddy." I smiled at him and I hoped he could see how much I loved him. "Everything's wonderful."

"You seem a little restless."

I shrugged. "Just anxious, I guess."

He frowned. "What about? Is there something wrong?"

"Oh, no! Nothing's wrong. I was just concerned… I mean… I haven't gone with you. You know. To the office? I know you've had meetings here and you've never called for me."

"I thought you could use a break. Even with my and Max's help, you sometimes seem overtired. You and little Andromeda are my most important priorities. I can't help you breastfeed so I'm doing my best to make sure you have time to rest during the day." He frowned. "Do you want to accompany me?"

That was a question I wasn't expecting and had no idea how to answer. "I-I… Yes, Daddy. If you need me to help you, I'll always be…" A thought occurred to me and I felt the blood drain from my face. "Has my body changed too much?"

"What?" Daddy straightened, his expression growing dark. "Explain what you mean."

"Well, my belly hasn't bounced back. Probably would help if I'd work out with Max more often. And my hips got wide. My boobs are big, but also messy." When he scowled at me angrily, I held his gaze with my wide-eyed one. "Did I do something wrong?" My voice was barely a whisper. If I'd made Daddy mad, would he kick me out? Replace me? But that was absurd! Daddy loved me! He'd promised he'd always love me. Right?

With a sigh, he came to me, kneeling in front of me. He smiled at Andi and lightly ran his fingertips over her downy hair. When he met my gaze there was tenderness there. Love. "No, Kitten. You've done nothing wrong. Yes, you've had changes in your body, but you're still my perfect, beautiful Kitten. Your body tells the world you bore my child. How could you think I wouldn't love your body even more now than I did before?"

I shrugged, suddenly shy. "I'm sorry."

"You've got nothing to be sorry for, Isabella. Now. Tell me. Is being a gift to my inner circle something you need? You're the most sensual creature I've ever met. Do you need me to share you? I'll always give you what you need."

I tilted my head to the side, not understanding what he was getting at. "I want what *you* need, Daddy. You said you needed me to be a reward to your men for all their hard work. I'm still able to fulfill that. I mean, if you think they'd still desire me." It felt weird to talk about how his men might see me now when we never had before. Maybe because now that we had a baby, our relationship had changed? Me and Daddy were still very close. If anything, I thought we were a better couple for having Andi in our lives. Max was every bit a part of that life and he doted on Andi. There was no denying the child had two fathers. And I felt like I had two partners. But had this changed our sexual situation?

He sighed. "Maybe I've made... other

arrangements."

At first, I wasn't sure I understood what he was saying. When it hit me that there was another woman taking care of Daddy's needs, I felt like I couldn't breathe.

"What?"

"Honey, you need to focus on taking care of Andi and yourself. The last thing you need is a bunch of horny men salivating over you. I know you're exhausted."

"So you replaced me." It wasn't a question. I felt lightheaded and sat back abruptly on the couch where I still had Andi at my breast. The child grunted in protest at being jostled but didn't stir. Just continued to suck contentedly.

We were in the sitting room outside our bedroom in our suite. It was just me, Daddy, and Andi, though I'd intended to put my sweet child down for a nap after her lunch. She had a crib in her own room in our suite. That would leave me and Daddy to talk this out, but I wasn't sure I really wanted to.

I knew my voice sounded thready and weak, but I couldn't help it. Though Daddy shared me with his closest friends and had given me Max as a guardian and lover, I'd never thought of sharing Daddy. I'd accepted that someday Max might need someone other than me, but I didn't want to share Daddy. Not at all. The thought made me want to throw up.

"Honey, only for my men. They don't get you anymore. At least not for a while."

"But you picked out a woman for them." I tried to hide my hurt. To hold it inside. "She had to have been someone you approved of."

He moved to kneel in front of me. "Baby -- Isabella. There hasn't been a woman for me since the day you moved in with me. I let Victor take care of my associates and I've never been at the office when it's happening. They don't do it here either. I don't even know what the women look like."

I had no idea what to say. I was relieved yet at the same time terrified I'd somehow disappointed him.

"Talk to me, Isabella. What questions do you have?" Him calling me by my name meant he was serious. This was outside of the play that had become our reality. If you could even call it play anymore. I was Kitten more than I was Isabella, and I wanted it that way. This was the way we lived. Daddy and Kitten.

"I've disappointed --" Before I could finish my sentence, Daddy wrapped his hand behind my neck and kissed me. Deeply. Roughly. It was delicious. He hadn't kissed me like this since before I'd given birth. I'd missed this rougher side of Daddy.

"Don't even think it, Isabella," he snapped. He pressed his forehead to mine and I could actually feel his pain. "You are the most important thing in my life, baby. You and Andromeda and Max. There is no other woman I'll ever want. And I could never imagine bringing another man into my life." He barked out a laugh. "Never imagined I could bring a man into my life at all. Not like we did Max."

"But... you like showing me off. Letting other men play with me."

"I did." Daddy kissed me again. This time with love and tenderness. "I *do*. It's something I've always enjoyed. I'm not saying that I'll never enjoy it again, though I'm pretty sure having you with Max will fulfill that need inside me. There's nothing I love more than watching the two of you together. Except when you include me. But ever since we found out you were pregnant I've been absurdly possessive of you. I've had times where it's even hard to let Max have you." He shook his head, frowning. "No, it's more than that. Max is a huge part of our lives, but sometimes, I..." It was uncharacteristic of Daddy to be hesitant about anything. Or indecisive. "Sometimes I need you all to myself. No Max or Andi -- even though I love the two of them beyond reason. I love you *all*. I'd kill for any one of you."

"I know you would, Jacob." I smiled up at him, taking a deep breath, needing to have everything spelled out. Despite how much I knew Daddy loved me, I suppose I was still insecure. "My body's really changed. You once said I was perfect, but now... I look different, and I'm afraid I'll never look like I did before. Are you ashamed of me now?"

"Isabella..." Daddy's voice was a low warning. "You're still perfect. *My* perfect. Do you think the signs of your body cocooning my baby, nurturing and loving her, would be less than perfect to me?"

"I have stretch marks. My hips are bigger, to say nothing of my tits. They have stretch marks too. And when they're empty of milk they sag."

Daddy reached over to cup my free breast in his big palm, feathering his thumb over the nipple through my maternity bra. I couldn't help but arch into his touch.

"And I love every single one of your new curves. You're more beautiful now than the day I first brought you into my home." With a smile, Daddy took Andi from my arms and took her to her crib. When he came back, his gaze was firmly fixed on mine. Intense. So very intense...

Thinking about what Daddy had said made me feel better, but my tummy was still messed up. "I couldn't bear it if you replaced me, Daddy." My throat was tight. I felt tears well in my eyes and tried to hold them back. I'd never been able to keep my true feelings from Daddy. I think it was like a Pavlov reaction at this point. Daddy had demanded everything from me. My thoughts and feelings, most importantly. Holding back from him wasn't something I was capable of.

"Never, baby. There isn't anyone who could ever replace you. You're my woman. My friend. My lover. And my Kitten. The mother of my child. My everything."

I threw myself into his arms, savoring being wrapped in his strength. I'd never felt as secure anywhere or with anyone else as I did with Daddy. I loved Max just as much as I did Daddy, but he was different. I still needed him, though he served a different purpose in my life than Daddy did. "I love you so much, Jacob!"

"I love you too, baby. I love you too." He kissed me again, this time, he didn't stop. Lifting me into his arms, he took us to the bedroom. Andi's crib was in the room next to ours with a camera monitor where we could watch her and hear if she cried.

"Daddy?"

"I need you, Kitten. Can I have you?"

"You know you can. You don't have to ask."

"Isabella…" He hesitated, like he needed to tell me something but wanted to be careful about how he worded it. "I've tried to treat you with respect and let you know you always have a choice, but I fear we've taken the Daddy and Kitten personas further than the superficial. We live that life now and so does Max. I never want you to forget you have choices, though. If you don't want me touching you, you don't have to let me. It's not my right to take what I want from you."

"And you never would, Jacob. I trust you with everything I am. I know I have choices and I'd exercise that right if you treated me badly."

"Then tell me. Do you really believe I'd replace you because your body changed from having my child?"

I sighed. "No. I'd only just now realized you hadn't been taking me to the downtown office and that Max had been keeping me in our rooms when you had meetings in your office here and in the conference rooms. I guess I panicked. A man like you can have any woman he wants. I know some men want young, perfect wives. I didn't think you were shallow in your feelings for me, but…"

"It's human nature to worry."

"Yes. I suppose it is."

Daddy lowered me to the bed and covered my body with his. We were both still dressed, but I was pretty sure that would change very soon. Sure enough, he stripped off my shirt and shorts. I still had on my maternity bra with the pads in place to catch leaking milk, but my nipples were ultra-sensitive to his touch.

Daddy nuzzled the curve of my breast just above the edge of my bra. I moaned, arching into his touch. I loved everything he did to me. Always. But this seemed somehow much more intimate. Maybe it was because it was just me and Daddy. It happened sometimes. One of my men would take me when the other wasn't with us, but rarely. That's just the way we were. So, yeah. It had been a long while since I'd made love with Daddy alone.

"I can't wait to get my mouth on those heavy, full breasts." Daddy's growl made my insides flutter with pleasure and anticipation.

"They leak. You may get more than you

bargained for." I was sure he knew what he was doing, but better to warn a guy. Right?

"Oh, baby. I'm counting on it." He gave me a decidedly wicked smile as he slid his arms behind me to unfasten my bra. I was still apprehensive, but if he was willing to try it, who was I to deny him anything?

Once my bra was off, he squeezed my breasts gently. Milk dribbled from my nipples, especially the one Andi hadn't nursed, and I gasped. "We're going to make a mess," I muttered.

"Probably." Daddy chuckled as he closed his mouth over one nipple and sucked gently.

"Oh, God!" I arched my back, but couldn't tear my gaze away from the sight of Daddy sucking me. His eyes were closed and he groaned. I watched his throat work as he swallowed the milk he'd sucked from my breast.

"Abso-fucking-lutely delicious."

He switched to the other breast, giving it the same treatment. I'd just fed Andi from that breast so there couldn't have been much left, but Daddy devoured me, moaning with every swallow.

"Daddy…" I sobbed, need hitting me hard and mean. "I need you!"

"What do you need, my beautiful little kitten?"

"I need you to fuck me. Fuck me till I come!"

Without another word, Daddy stripped and crawled up my body, laying fully on top of me, his naked muscled body between my thighs, his cock poking at my pussy lips. "What my Kitten wants, my Kitten gets." He slid deep, working his hips in a slow, steady rhythm, his gaze focused on mine. My lips parted on a gasp and a moan. I wrapped my arms around Daddy's neck, but he quickly snagged my wrists and pinned them in one of his big hands above my head.

"Daddy?"

"Hush, Kitten. Let me play."

With a cheeky grin, I repeated his words. "What Daddy wants, Daddy gets."

He chuckled. "Damned straight."

As he fucked, me, Daddy shifted so he could take one breast in his mouth. He fed from my breast as he fucked me and there was something so insanely erotic and intimate about the action that I came in a rush. Pleasure swamped me. My breast tingled where Daddy gripped and milked it. I loved watching Daddy's throat working to swallow the milk from my tit. "That's so hot, Daddy..." My voice was barely a whisper, my words difficult to form as Daddy increased the force he fucked me with. He rode me hard, shifting to the side so I had to hook my leg over his thigh while he gripped the tit he sucked.

"Fuck," Daddy gasped out. "Holy shit!"

His cock swelled inside me and he never stopped drinking. A euphoric feeling draped over me like a warm, fuzzy blanket. Daddy let go of my hands, but I kept them over my head, unable to do much more than breathe, whimper, and simply let Daddy take what he wanted from me.

"Gonna get my breakfast every day after Andi finishes hers." His voice was harsh. Sweat slickened his skin where he rubbed against me. In all the time I'd been with Daddy, this was the most intimate situation we'd ever been in. Daddy drank from me. Drank down the life-giving milk I gave to our daughter. With each strong pull at my breast, my pussy spasmed in a mini orgasm. It was continual and rhythmic, and oh so delicious!

"Daddy!" I gasped as my breathing became more

and more erratic. "Daddy! I'm gonna come!"

"Then come, Kitten. Let me have your pleasure."

As if his words flipped a switch inside me, my whole body tensed before a powerful orgasm pushed its way through me. I screamed, throwing my head back and letting the sensations take me over like Daddy demanded of me. Then his cock swelled inside me and with a strong pull of his mouth on my nipple, Daddy came deep inside my pussy while nursing at my breast. It was heady. It was erotic. Maybe even a little bit kinky and taboo, but I loved every blistering second of it.

When he'd emptied himself of his seed, Daddy leaned in to kiss me. I tasted my breast milk on his tongue and shivered again. This new experience was like nothing I'd ever even dreamt of. Nursing Andi sometimes gave me a euphoric feeling. Nothing sexual, but like I was drifting on a calm sea. Nursing Daddy took that euphoric feeling three levels past anything gentle or soothing. I wanted this experience with Daddy again.

"Daddy…" I sighed his name, finally moving my hands from above my head to hold him close to me.

"How was that, Kitten?" He murmured his words as he gently kissed my lips, my jaw, my neck.

"Wonderful."

Again, he latched on to my breast while he cupped and squeezed the fleshy mound above my nipple. He sucked strongly again, swallowing every drop he took from my tit.

"Love your taste." His voice was gruff. Husky. I glanced down and saw that, though his cock was covered in both our cum, it hadn't gone down. Daddy was still hard and ready to fuck me again.

"I've never felt anything like that." I was drowsy.

Sated yet... not. I wanted more but wasn't sure I could manage.

"Me neither, baby." He continued to gently suck my breasts, back and forth while he milked them with his hands. "But I plan on repeating the experience. Often."

Flight Attendance

With a happy sigh, I stretched, offering my breasts to him as I arched my back. "Take what you want, Daddy. I loved every single second of it."

"Good. Because I think it's time for you and me to spend some quality time together."

I stilled. "What?"

Daddy smiled down at me. "How would you feel about getting away from everything and everyone for a couple of days?"

God, I wanted to, but… "I don't think I could leave Andi." I glanced at the monitor to see my child sleeping peacefully in her nursery.

"Max and the nanny that you never use will be here to look after her. Besides, I'm not talking about a week. Just a couple of days. You've got plenty of milk stored for Andi so they won't need to use formula, and I know for a fact Max knows how to take care of her. He does just as good a job as you do. We'll take my private jet so we can leave whenever we want. We can also add on an extra day or two if you're comfortable enough. I promise we won't go far."

I bit my lip, thinking about it for a long time. Then, I grinned up at Daddy. "I think I'd like that."

He gave me the most beautiful smile. Daddy didn't smile nearly enough, though he'd been doing it more and more. Especially when he looked at me and Andi when we played or cuddled. He looked at me and Max like that occasionally, but usually he was just giving us hungry looks before we all ended up fucking like mad. Which I loved.

"Good. Pack a bag with a couple days' clothing. Though, if I have my way, you won't be using any of it." The smile he gave me this time was more like I was used to seeing. Positively wicked.

* * *

It was hard to leave my little Andromeda. Max had named her before we even knew if she was a boy or a girl. Max had been determined she'd be a girl and he got his wish. And Max was a wonderful father to Andi. Between him and Daddy, I was certain the child would want for nothing. Especially affection. She would most certainly know she was loved by all of us. Max promised to never leave her side while we were gone, even though the nanny Daddy had hired would be there. I suppose it was good to know Max had backup, though he'd insisted he could look after one little girl himself. I was kind of looking forward to seeing how that worked out for him.

I'd kissed Max, then Andi. Mine and Daddy's things had been loaded into the limo and we'd sped off toward the airport. Now we were in Daddy's private jet waiting to take off. I still wasn't sure where we were going, but I decided it didn't really matter. Daddy would take care of everything. I was here to relax and enjoy myself. Though, I'll admit, I already missed my sweet baby. And Max.

"Don't worry, Kitten. Max and Andi will be fine. Max won't hesitate to get help if he needs it and we'll only be a short distance away. We can be home in a couple of hours if we have to."

"I know." I smiled up at Daddy. He'd fastened me securely into my seat for takeoff but held my hand firmly in his. "I miss them, but I trust you to make sure they have what they need while we're gone."

"That's my very good Kitten." Daddy leaned down and kissed me softly, which made me squirm because I wanted more. I also knew there would be more the second Daddy could manage it.

"Would you like some champagne while you wait, Mr. Blackstone?" The woman who spoke was dressed in a flight attendant's dark, conservative skirt that hit her below the knees. She wore a white blouse with a vest the same color as the skirt. She had a welcoming smile on her face but it seemed to be only for my Daddy. I frowned but kept my mouth shut. If I didn't, I was sure I'd say something that would get me into trouble.

"What do you think, my lovely Isabella? Would you like something to celebrate our first mini vacation together since Andromeda's birth?"

"I…" I was unsure what to do. I knew I shouldn't feel like I was inferior to this woman, but it was hard. She was slender and beautifully made up while I felt exactly the opposite. I didn't welcome my new curves, even though Daddy had worshiped them just a few hours earlier.

Though I'd been with Daddy for a well over a year now, I'd yet to be on his private jet. There had never been a need. As such, this wasn't a woman I'd ever met. Considering the way she was looking at my Daddy and ignoring me, she obviously didn't see me as someone who'd be around for any length of time. Which was stupid of me to think because I'd been with Daddy almost constantly since he'd claimed me for his own.

Daddy didn't rush me, though I saw a flash of irritation on the attendant's face. "No, thank you Jacob." Since he'd used my first name, I used his. I wasn't at all comfortable with this woman being around me or my Daddy.

"No?" Daddy looked surprised, then he glanced up at the woman and his expression darkened. "Ah. I see." He sounded very much like he *did* see. "Thank you, Jacinda. That will be all."

"I've personally prepared your private room, Mr. Blackstone. If there's anything else I can help you with, don't hesitate to call me." She gave my Daddy a brilliant smile and I wanted to claw her eyes out. It took a considerable amount of discipline for me not to hiss at her.

Except I might have. Just a little one.

"I'm so sorry to bother you, Mr. Blackstone." One of the male flight attendants stepped just inside the private cabin, his gaze appropriately demure as he addressed me. "I'm Adam. I'm terribly sorry about the mix up. Jacinda wasn't supposed to be on this flight." The man, who appeared to be close to the same age as Max, gave the woman a disapproving look.

"Barbara was sick," Jacinda said hastily. I could tell by the look on her face, the way her eyes widened fractionally, she knew she was in trouble.

"I said, that will be all, Jacinda." This time, Daddy's features hardened and he gave Jacinda a look that would have had me running away. She sucked in a breath and took a step back, but she didn't seem to get the hint. Not really.

"Very well, Mr. Blackstone." She turned and left, having never acknowledged me. "I'll be near if you need me, sir." Jacinda looked subservient, but when she slid me a narrow gaze, I knew she was only putting on a front for my Daddy.

"She won't bother you or Miss Isabella, Mr. Blackstone. I'll see to it personally." Adam nodded politely to me, acknowledging my presence like Jacinda hadn't. Almost as if I were an equal to Daddy.

Daddy sighed. "I knew I needed to clean house." He brought my hand to his mouth and kissed my fingers. "Thank you, Adam. I appreciate your help."

Wanda Violet O. Daddy's Kitten

Adam gave Daddy a slight bow, then left. Once we were alone again, Daddy kissed me gently. "I haven't been on the jet in over a year, Kitten. Since before I brought you home to me. I forgot about Jacinda. Should have explained things to her and made sure she knew you were mistress here. That's on me."

"It's OK." I smiled up at him, but I felt like I was big as a house, especially compared to the tall, willowy flight attendant -- who knew how Daddy liked his private room kept.

Before I realized I was even going to say anything, I blurted out the one question I didn't want to acknowledge I needed the answer to. "Have you fucked her, Daddy?" I couldn't help it. It was there in the forefront of my mind and I knew it would only fester if I didn't have the answer. Even if I wasn't a hundred percent sure I wanted to know the answer.

"What?" Daddy's surprised gaze snapped to mine. "No, princess. I've never fucked her nor have I wanted to. She wanted me though. Made no secret of it. She didn't make a nuisance of herself so I didn't do anything about it before I met you. This is my fault. I simply... *forgot* about her." He unfastened my seat belt and pulled me onto his lap. Once his strong arms were around me, I curled up and snuggled into Daddy's chest, breathing him in to soothe my mind and heart.

"I'm sorry, Daddy." I sniffed, the tears close even though I didn't have a reason to cry.'

"No, baby. If this is anyone's fault it's mine. I've sheltered you away from everyone, even before Andi's birth." He curled a finger under my chin and tilted my head up so I had to meet his gaze. "I wanted to hide you from everyone because I was possessive. I didn't want everyone to see how beautiful you were with my child in your belly. Then I wanted you to myself after

Andi was born. You, Kitten… You. Are. *Everything* to me. I should have made sure everyone was clear on your place in my life."

To my complete and utter horror, I burst into tears. I wrapped my arms tightly around Daddy's neck and sobbed. Maybe it was the hormones that still caught me by surprise sometimes. Maybe I hadn't realized how much I'd been afraid Daddy was tiring of me. All I knew was, the breakdown I was currently having freed something inside me. Tension I hadn't realized had built up was released like water from a floodgate.

Daddy rubbed my back and murmured soothingly to me as he kissed my forehead and temple. "I've got you, princess. I'll always have you. My perfect, beautiful Kitten."

"I love you, Daddy." My voice wasn't very strong, but I got my point across. "So very much."

Daddy hugged me even tighter. "I love you too, Isabella. Now. This is supposed to be a fun and relaxing adventure. I'm sorry we got started on the wrong foot. From here on out, though, I promise everything will be better."

"Mr. Blackstone." Adam appeared from the doorway again. "I'll be taking care of you and Miss Isabella on this flight. Again, I apologize for the problem earlier."

I nodded my head even as I snuggled deeper against Daddy. Had he done this or had the woman decided not to come back on her own?

"Thank you for taking the task on yourself. I know you hadn't planned on being on this flight."

"Not at all, sir. I'm happy to help." Adam gave us both a warm smile. "Now. What would Miss Isabella like to refresh her?"

"How about that champagne, Kitten?" Daddy smiled down at me. Lord, he was beautiful! I could stare at my Daddy all day and never get tired of looking at him.

"Thank you, Daddy." My response was whispered and I wasn't thanking him for the champagne. Of course, Daddy knew what I meant.

"Of course, Kitten. I only want you to be comfortable."

"Then yes, please. Thank you, Adam." I gave the new attendant a tentative smile.

"My pleasure, Miss. Sir? Champagne for you as well?"

"Scotch for me. Once the plane is in the air, I'd appreciate it if you'd replace everything in my suite with fresh linens and pillows. I want anything already in there removed."

"Absolutely, sir. In fact, it's already being attended to. Will there be anything else before we take off?"

"Make sure Jacinda is transferred. I don't want her anywhere near me or Isabella again."

"Mr. Jackson has already been made aware. He will find a suitable place for her."

Daddy gave Adam a slight grin. "Thank you, Adam. I appreciate you anticipating our needs."

"Again, my pleasure, sir. Ma'am." He acknowledged both of us, his smile genuine.

"I'm too emotionally sensitive since having Andromeda," I whispered. "I'm so sorry, Daddy. I'm sure it will get better. You didn't have to send that woman away." Though I was glad of it. I tried to chuckle a little, to lighten the mood even if the very last thing I felt like was laughing. "I'll be back to being your naughty kitten in no time."

"I won't hear another word about it, Isabella." His tone was gentle and he smiled down at me. "This is your vacation. If you're not comfortable with someone or something, you're to tell me immediately. Hell, everything I own is yours, too, so you definitely have the right to change anything you don't like. I thought you knew this, but I can see I need to be more exact in expressing those kinds of things. I don't care why you're uncomfortable, only that you are. I'll fix it. You never have to explain to me, though I'd appreciate it if you did so I can keep it from happening again. I want you happy, Kitten. *Always*, above anything else, I want you to be happy and healthy."

"Thank you, Daddy." I snuggled against him even harder, clinging to him like a baby monkey. Daddy knew I needed him when I felt insecure. As bad as it made me feel when I had to take up Daddy's time for him to soothe my injured feelings, he never seemed to mind. He was never impatient with me or indicated in any way I was a bother. Or more trouble than I was worth. In fact, Daddy seemed to thrive on my need for him. I thought that maybe he needed me to need him every bit as much as I did. Taking care of me fulfilled something deep inside him he kept back from the rest of the world. I was glad. Because I needed him to take care of me.

I looked up at Daddy, hoping he could see how much I loved him. When he smiled down at me and pulled me to him for a long, deep kiss, I knew he did.

Surrendering to Daddy was never hard. The second his lips touched mine, I opened and let him have what he wanted. As always, his kisses were drugging. Soon, I was lightheaded and panting with need. My whimpers filled the cabin but I didn't care. If Daddy didn't want me to make noise, he'd tell me so.

"You are so beautiful, Kitten." He murmured against my lips, barely breaking contact when he spoke to me. "So Goddamned sensual, you drive me crazy. I'm a lucky man to have you in my life."

"I love you, Daddy."

"I love you too, Isabella."

Daddy unfastened his seat belt and urged me to straddle him. I rarely wore panties for this reason. Daddy liked to have access to me whenever he wanted. I trusted Daddy to make sure I was covered or not in a position to show more than what he desired me to show. Otherwise, I didn't worry about it.

Daddy cupped my mound before thrusting two fingers deep inside my pussy. I let my head fall back even as my hands gripped his shoulders. I held on and let Daddy do as he pleased. He fingered me for a long while before moving his fingers to my back hole. I'd learned to love this act almost more than Daddy or Max fucking my pussy. I loved having my ass played with and it seemed to delight Daddy to no end.

"My sexy little Kitten. Are you horny, my love? Do you need my dick fucking you until you scream?" His words were decidedly wicked, his tone sexy as hell.

"Yes, Daddy." I whimpered my answer, meaning it. "I need you to fuck me. Hard and fast. Then I need you to put your cum deep inside me."

"Where do you want it, Kitten? Where do you want me to fuck you."

There was only one way to answer that. "My ass, Daddy. Will you please fuck my little asshole? I need you to stretch it." I kissed him between my words. "Fuck it. Put your cum in it." I knew Daddy loved the dirty talk as much -- or more -- than I did. He loved knowing what I wanted and what I was feeling. What he was doing that I especially liked or my fantasies. He had a penchant for turning the last into reality at the earliest possible convenience.

"Fuck!" Daddy gripped my bare ass before delving his fingers between my cheeks. He wet his finger with my dripping pussy before circling the hole with the wet digit.

"Yes, Daddy," I whimpered as I pressed myself against his finger. I was so horny for him and he knew it.

"You want my cum in your sweet ass?" he asked breathlessly as he continued to assert pressure on my back hole.

"Yes, Daddy. Please."

"I think we need to get you ready first. Don't you?"

"Are you going to stretch my ass? Did you bring a plug?"

Daddy chuckled. "My naughty little Kitten. I have something better than a plug."

I shivered in anticipation. Whatever Daddy had in mind would ultimately bring me pleasure. When I first came to be with Daddy, when he'd first started fucking me, he'd told me it was about his pleasure. Not mine. While he might say that now, I knew better. Daddy never did anything that didn't bring me pleasure. Eventually. He'd never let me down and I trusted him with my life and my heart.

"Tuck your knees beside my hips, Kitten. Rest your head on my shoulder so your lips are at my neck." When I wiggled into position, Daddy wrapped his arms around me, pulling my skirt up over my bottom. God, I loved this feeling! It was almost like a high. A sex high. Whatever was about to happen, Daddy would be with me and he'd enjoy it. He'd also make sure I enjoyed it.

"Reach back and spread your cheeks, Kitten. Show off that little asshole for me."

"Daddy!" I gasped out his name as I reached back to do as he instructed.

"Are you ready Kitten?"

"I -- Ready?"

"Oh yes, Kitten. I find I still have a need to share you, even if I'm not ready to take you back to my colleagues. I won't do it much while we're gone, but I will fuck you at the resort. Wherever I feel like it. No matter who's there."

"Oh, God!" My clit throbbed. I wasn't touching it, couldn't touch it, but I knew if I could move to where the little nub scraped over the material of his suit, just once, I'd explode like a bottle rocket.

"Do you like the thought of that, Kitten? Do you want everyone at this resort to know and witness who you belong to?"

"Yes, Daddy. I want you to show them that you own me."

"Sweet God, Kitten! You drive me fucking *mad* with lust!" Daddy sounded almost angry now. Not in a scary way. Like he had reached the limit of his control and was about to snap. My favorite way for Daddy to fuck me. "Spread those cheeks wide. Pull them apart as far as you can and hold them."

I did, feeling deliciously exposed. I wondered if Adam or Jacinda where close enough to see me? While the thought of the first only made me hotter, I didn't want the woman to see me. Unless she was being made to watch as punishment for making eyes at my Daddy.

"Adam is going to help me, Kitten. Unless you object?"

I shivered. Adam? The flight attendant? Daddy

had only shared me with his friends. His close inner circle. Though he'd fucked me in front of men he had no intention of sharing me with, this was the first time he'd ever suggested something like this. Not that it mattered. If Daddy wanted, I was more than willing to give him everything.

Kitten's Trust

"No Daddy. I don't object. I trust you." I nibbled on the skin of his neck below his jaw line. Daddy tilted his head to give me better access. I wanted to latch on to him like he had my breasts. I could mark him so Jacinda and anyone else who wanted my Daddy could see he was mine.

Daddy chuckled. "I can practically hear you thinking, Kitten." He tilted his head further. "Go on then. Mark me. I'll wear your mark like a badge of pride."

With a happy "Mmm" of delight, I sucked the spot just below Daddy's ear. He shuddered around me, his big body as helpless as he made mine.

The next thing I knew, another hand was stroking my wet pussy then dragging the wet digit to my ass. I jumped and squealed but Daddy calmed me.

"It's all right, Kitten. Adam is just going to help stretch you. Do you mind if he plays with your beautiful ass?"

"No Daddy! Please let him!"

"My sexy, sexy kitten. I know I said I wanted this trip to be just me and you, but I find watching other men play with you gives me great satisfaction. They want what I have. I give them a taste so they know how lucky I am to wake up to you each morning. To go to sleep with you each night. And to fuck you senseless in between."

"And knowing how much satisfaction it gives you thrills me, Jacob." I smiled up at him, then met his mouth with my own, kissing me with as much passion and lust as I felt. "I hope you're always glad you claimed me."

"Do it, Adam," Daddy growled. "Play with her

ass. You may dredge your fingers through her pussy lips, or eat it if you want. You may not penetrate her pussy in any way."

"Understood, sir. And may I say, with all sincerity, thank you for trusting me to help you pleasure your woman, Mr. Blackstone."

Immediately, Adam gripped my cheeks gently, pulling them apart so I could move my hands. Then he swiped his tongue through my cunt all the way up to my ass. I squealed in delight and arched my back to give him better access. The other man gave a grunt, then settled his tongue over and around my puckered hole, which made me supremely gratified I'd kept up the Brazilian wax routine.

Daddy kept kissing my mouth while Adam worked on the other end. It was bliss. Daddy might need to see me with other men, but I was beginning to think I needed it too. Not because Daddy wasn't enough for me, but because Daddy seemed to thrive on it. The more he liked it, the more I liked it. He growled and grunted into my mouth as he kissed me. I shivered, clinging to him even as Adam was licking and sucking my ass like mad and making his own sounds of appreciation.

"Sweet, isn't she, Adam?" Daddy chuckled when Adam made a noise like he was just fucking defeated.

"She's addictive, sir." Adam spoke between licks and slurps. "Never tasted anything like her. Never saw another woman respond with as much abandon as she does."

"You're deserving of a reward for understanding that my Kitten was uncomfortable. Thank you for taking action so quickly."

"Everyone working for you knows how important Miss. Isabella is to you, Mr. Blackstone."

Adam spoke against my ass, his voice strained. "Jacinda knew it too. She chose to ignore that. Which meant she needed to go."

Daddy grunted but was otherwise silent as he returned to kissing me. I was so close to my orgasm I was panting and whimpering constantly. Daddy threaded his fingers through my hair and pulled so I had to meet his gaze when he pulled back.

"Adam." Daddy might have spoken to the man so fervently eating out my ass, but he looked directly at me. "How would you like to fuck my Kitten's sweet ass?"

The other man groaned and sucked even harder at my ass. "Please, sir. Don't tease me. Not like that."

"Not teasing. You deserve a reward. Kitten loves being fucked. I love watching her when she's getting fucked. Win all around."

"You'd really let me fuck her ass?"

"Kitten?" Daddy raised an eyebrow at me even as one corner of his lips lifted in a grin.

"Yes, please, Daddy. And may I suck your cock while he fucks me?"

"Sweet God," Adam groaned. "Is she always like this?"

Daddy chuckled. "Yep. She's a sensual little thing. More so than anyone I've ever come across. She loves sex and all the pleasures of the flesh. And she loves sucking my cum straight from my cock, don't you, Kitten?"

"I do, Daddy." I licked at Daddy's lips, demanding he give me his tongue. Daddy met my kisses and licks head on, taking what I offered and giving me so much more.

"Get Enzo. He'll have lube and condoms."

"My bodyguard, Daddy?" This was the first time

Daddy had let his employees engage in sex with me. I'd have to ask him about this later, but I wanted to be fucked too badly to question it much.

"Yes, Kitten. At this point I don't trust anything left in my suite. Enzo knows to always be prepared in case I want someone to fuck you."

"Do you want him to come to this section of the plane, Mr. Blackstone?" Adam spoke between licks and kisses. "If not, I'll go to him."

"Yes. Have him come here, Adam." When Adam stopped what he was doing to call for Enzo, Daddy smiled at me. "You may leave on your top if you're not comfortable, Kitten, but I want the skirt off." His voice was soft and compelling. "Then I want you to bend at the waist and suck my cock with your ass in the air. Adam will prepare you. Then he'll fuck you. If you're a good Kitten and hold off coming until I give you permission, I may consider letting Enzo fuck you as well."

My eyes widened. Enzo was… huge. Taller and more heavily muscled than Max or Daddy, his dark, golden skin stood out against the white shirt he wore. Tattoos crept up the side of his neck almost to his shaved head. He was more than a little scary, but that was mostly because I'd never actually spoken to him. Enzo was always in the background, standing between me and everyone other than Daddy and Max. "Enzo?"

"Unless you're opposed."

"No! I'm not opposed. I just… never thought…"

"About fucking Enzo?" Daddy looked amused, but like he understood all too well, even if I hadn't said anything. "You know he'd never hurt you. Right? He's big and scary looking, but he'd never hurt you, Kitten."

I grinned at Daddy, feeling more like myself than

I had since I'd found out I was pregnant nearly two Christmases ago. "Yes, Daddy. I know. And yes, I'd like him to fuck me." I scrambled from Daddy's lap to do as he asked. I started to take off my shirt and bra, then remembered I would be leaking a lot. I hadn't pumped in a while and it had been a few hours since Daddy had sucked me before.

Daddy must have seen my indecision because he smiled gently at me. "It's your call, sweetheart, but I promise you, everything about you is sexy as hell. Besides, sex is much more fun when it's messy."

I bit my lip, not sure what to do. "Maybe I'll just save that for you?"

"As you wish, my beautiful Kitten.

"Seems silly with both men about to fuck me." I tried for a giggle but it just sounded nervous and insecure. "Adam's already had his tongue in my ass, for crying out loud!"

"Nothing about you is silly, princess. And I'm honored to keep that for us alone. Thank you for giving it to me."

God, I loved it when he looked at me like this. When he did, I felt like I was his entire focus. Like nothing else in the whole world mattered so much as me. I let out a breath I hadn't realized I was holding, then stepped out of my skirt and did as Daddy ordered. Bending at the waist with my ass in the air, I took out Daddy's cock and engulfed it eagerly.

As always, the salty, slick fluid of Daddy's precum hit my tongue like a shot of adrenaline. I braced my hands on his thighs and sucked him down.

I absolutely *loved* sucking Daddy's cock! He was thick and long and I struggled to take him all, but I always did. I forced his cock down my throat until I was taking every single inch of him. Daddy gripped my head and forced me up and down but never making it so much I couldn't handle it. I was so lost in enjoying myself that I forgot about Adam and what he was about to do.

The next thing I knew, warm liquid trickled between my cheeks. I squealed around Daddy's cock even as I wiggled my ass, an invitation for anyone behind me to fuck me. A big, rough palm rubbed over one cheek before squeezing gently.

"You have a beautiful woman, Mr. Blackstone." Was that Enzo? Did it matter? I trusted Daddy. If there was a man touching me while I was sucking Daddy's cock down, that it was all right. I canted my hips, wanting more of that deliciously rough touch.

"I certainly do, Enzo. You have condoms, yes?"

"Oh, absolutely. No one gets in the way of your sweet Kitten when she needs to be fucked. I've made it my personal mission to make sure there are always lube and condoms." The man sounded amused but I couldn't be bothered. Not when Daddy's cock was hard and leaking cum.

"Give one to Adam. He earned this reward for anticipating Kitten's comfort when she didn't like Jacinda. He was kind, courteous, and respectful of the most important woman in my life."

"As he should be. Your Kitten is a special woman."

"Kitten? Do you think you'd be up to letting Enzo have you once Adam is finished?"

"Mmmm..." I hummed out, never taking Daddy's cock from my mouth. I'd do whatever Daddy wanted. And, honestly, I enjoyed it when he shared me. Probably only because he seemed to enjoy it so much, but it was always great fun. And Daddy hadn't shared me in a very long time. At least, not anyone other than Max. Until this very moment, I hadn't realized I'd even wanted it.

"I need words, my beautiful Kitten."

Reluctantly -- and only because Daddy pulled me up by my hair -- I released his cock. "Yes, Daddy. Oh yes. Absolutely." I grinned before looking Daddy straight in the eyes as I lowered my mouth back over his thick, hard cock.

"Christ," Daddy bit out, his hand firmly back in my hair. "What you do to me, woman!"

"I can see that one's a handful." Enzo chuckled. "Not what I'd call overly aggressive, but she knows how to get what she wants."

"And she knows I'll deny her nothing."

"If you're offering her ass for my enjoyment, I'll not say no, boss. I'd never covet your woman, but I'll take what you'll give me end enjoy every fuckin' second of it." I wasn't sure I'd ever heard Enzo say so much. At least not where I could hear. He wasn't as refined as Daddy or Max, but his rough words were a turn on.

"Then once Adam finishes, you may have her ass as well."

"You're very generous, boss." Enzo's voice was a dark, compelling seduction. "Not sure I deserve this honor, but I ain't refusin'."

"You're Kitten's protector. You've watched me letting other men fuck her. While you're as vigilant with her safety as Max is with her wellbeing, you've never let your gaze linger on her for long. Only to gauge her comfort in case I or Max were too engaged with our own pleasure to miss it if she's uncomfortable. I know because I pay attention to the dangerous men in the room. You're always in the top two."

"As if you and Max wouldn't be completely in tune with her." Enzo's rough hand stroked down my spine from my neck to my ass again. God, I loved it when he petted me! "I noticed her. But I also know she's too good to fuck a roughneck like me, Boss. Ain't too proud to admit it either. That one's special."

"Believe me, I know." Daddy petted my hair while I continued to suck his cock. "Now, Adam. Do what you want. You may penetrate her ass, but not her pussy. And only with a condom."

Adam wasn't in any hurry. He licked, slurped, and sucked my pussy and ass. He followed Daddy's directions to the letter. Several times, he swiped his fingers through my pussy, but only to brush my clit or to wet his fingers, even though Enzo dribbled a generous amount of lube over my back hole. He didn't even get close to disobeying Daddy, though. Just seemed to love touching and tasting me if the sounds he was making were any indication.

"Christ!" Enzo's voice was even more husky than before. He sounded as turned on as I was. Daddy, too. Both men groaned as Adam continued to eat me out. Adam sounded like he was a starving man given a banquet. And the man was very talented with his mouth. He reminded me of one of Daddy's friends at his office. That man liked eating my ass too. Adam did it like his very life depended on him getting his next taste of me. "She loves that!"

Daddy chuckled but it sounded strained. "They both do."

Enzo just grunted. He'd moved up beside me and Daddy so that, when he undid his pants and slid them down his thick thighs, his cock bobbed right in front of my face. All I had to do was turn my head and he could feed me his dick.

"Do it, Kitten." Daddy hissed in my ear. He gripped my hair, holding me to him while his hips thrust upward, ruthlessly fucking my mouth. "Suck him!"

Daddy yanked me off him, turning my head toward Enzo. I took the big bodyguard deep before swallowing, letting the back of my throat massage the head of his cock. Enzo groaned. His hands were in fists at his sides, the veins roping up his arms standing out in stark relief as his muscles tensed.

"God, she feels good." Enzo growled, his words harsh and guttural. He thrust his hips at me gently, but there was no doubt he was in control.

"It only gets better." Daddy tugged me back to his cock and I eagerly took him deep. Then I felt fingers prodding my ass. Two slipped inside me and I arched my back. Daddy held me tightly to him when I might have let his dick go to scream my pleasure. I still squealed around him. Then Daddy shot his cum down my throat, his cock pulsing over and over and I swallowed every single drop.

"Fuck!" Daddy shouted, his hands tightening in my hair until he pulled my scalp. The sharp pain was its own stimulant. Lust shot through me in a mean punch. I wanted -- needed -- to come. I felt like something was alive inside me, crawling through my blood, trying to drive me mad. "Do it, Adam. Fuck her ass. Now."

"Yes, sir." Adam sounded less refined than he had when he'd first presented himself to us. He was more… primal. Adam stripped in quick, snappish movements before rolling on a condom and coating his cock liberally with lubricant.

Adam gripped my hip with one hand while he guided his cock to the entrance of my ass. The flared head of his dick pressed against me insistently until it popped just inside the ring of muscle. At once the way his cock stretched my ass burned painfully and hit me with a punch of lust. The sensation was overwhelming. I'd had sex countless times in countless different ways, but this seemed to hit me harder than usual. All I could do was scream.

Adam surged forward, gripping my ass as he pushed until I felt his abdomen resting against the globes of my ass. He pushed harder and faster with each stroke. Sweat dripped onto my back. It wasn't long before Adam was pounding into me in hard, sharp snaps of his hips.

"Fuck... fuck... fuck!" With a harsh cry, Adam buried himself as deep as he could, his cock pulsing out his cum into the condom. I was so fucking close I could taste my own orgasm! I wanted to come with a fierce abandon. I was wild inside, insatiable. Maybe it was because this was the first time I'd had Daddy share me since we found out I was pregnant. Maybe I'd needed this more than I thought. I was pretty sure Daddy did. He hadn't been this fierce in fucking me in a long time.

I'd braced myself with my hands on Daddy's thighs. I looked up at him now. Adam busily fucked my ass into oblivion and I looked up to meet Daddy's gaze, trying to let him know how much I needed this and how much I knew he needed it, too. Daddy's eyes were dark with ferocity, letting me know he understood.

Gradually, Adam's movements slowed, his orgasm finally waning. He slipped out of my ass before I heard him lean heavily against the bulkhead separating the two sections of the plane. "Fuck..." he groaned. I heard him toss something into the waste can. Probably the condom. "Thank you, Mr. Blackstone. That was the best experience of my life so far."

"You're welcome, Adam. I'm sure I don't have to tell you that you may only touch Isabella at my discretion. And I'll only allow it when I feel you've earned it."

Adam gave Daddy a slight bow as he collected his clothing. "I'd never expect liberties with your woman, Mr. Blackstone. I'll just look forward to earning the privilege again."

With a nod at Daddy and another, longer one to me, Adam left our area of the plane. I only hoped he stopped in the small attendants' section between the front and the back to dress because he hadn't taken time to before leaving us with Enzo.

"Your turn, Enzo," Daddy instructed. "Give her what she needs. Make her come so hard she screams."

Enzo grunted. I felt him push against my back entrance. His cock was larger. Maybe not quite as long as Adam's, but wider. Thicker. He pumped in shallow thrusts a couple of times before pulling me upright with my arms behind my back. He hooked his own arms through mine and held on tightly before beginning a hard, punishing rhythm.

I stood with Enzo at my back while he fucked me. He was taller than me and each time he surged up into my ass, I rose up on my toes. I gasped out every time his body slammed into mine, little whimpers escaping.

"Fuck, yeah, little Kitten." Enzo's voice was gruff in my ear. "You feel so fuckin' good around my cock. That's it. Squeeze me with that tight little ass."

I was helpless to do anything but obey him. Enzo could be hard when it came to safety, but this was a side I'd never seen from him. He wasn't as commanding as Daddy could be, but he was even more immovable. More... domineering. I recognized then that Enzo wasn't as indulgent as Daddy. This was a man who'd take complete control. He was more like Daddy had been the first time. When I'd pushed him into pulling me completely into his life. His world of sensual pleasures and dominance and submission. Enzo was like that. I figured it was why Daddy had put him with me in the first place. If I ever was in danger, Enzo wasn't a man who'd give me any choices. He'd take charge, do what he thought was best for me, and never apologize for it, no matter the outcome. I'd known this before but hadn't realized it until he had his dick up my ass. Why now? No fucking clue. I only knew that something had happened for Daddy to suddenly introduce Enzo into our play. And Adam.

Then I couldn't think about it anymore. Enzo erupted inside me with a brutal roar. My ears actually hurt though I had very little time to process much before I tripped over the edge into my own orgasm.

I was up on my toes, Enzo firmly, deeply in my ass. One of his arms let me go only to circle my body and pin me even harder against him. He bit down on my shoulder, an Alpha animal holding his partner steady beneath him. Daddy was in front of me, his mouth fastening on my clit and flicking it with his tongue while Enzo continued to grunt aggressively, riding out his own pleasure.

I came twice more before Daddy stood, hooking one of my knees around his hip before shoving his way inside my pussy. Enzo slid out of my ass but stayed at my back, his hands firmly on my hips while Daddy fucked me where I stood.

"My fucking little sexy Kitten," he rasped. "So

Goddamned fucking sexy!"

"Daddy!" I gasped out his name, clinging to him while he drove in and out of my pussy. "Daddy, please may I come?" My question was desperate. I didn't always ask, but it felt important after the way Enzo had taken me. That had been nothing short of a claim. It had been exhilarating, but also disconcerting. If Enzo truly was like Daddy, he'd take what he wanted. By asking Daddy, I'd let Enzo know that Daddy held the ultimate key to my pleasure. Even if it had been Enzo who'd fucked me, my loyalty would always be to my Daddy.

"Yes, Kitten," Daddy bit out. "Come around my cock! Fucking take me with you!"

I did. Daddy shouted, the muscles and tendons standing out in his neck and shoulders. I screamed, my head falling back against Enzo's chest. Enzo latched on to the side of my neck, kissing and licking at the tender skin there. Daddy's hot cum dripped down my leg when he pulled out of me. I groaned at the sensation.

"Keep her there while I get a towel, Enzo."

I stiffened. "Daddy?"

"Hush, Kitten." Daddy cupped my chin, leaning in to kiss me softly. "I know what you're thinking but I swear this is for your safety. We'll keep Enzo close. Maybe introduce him to Max. Since Enzo doesn't need to guard you at the house, they've never met. Would you be good with that?"

I glanced back at Enzo who stood motionless and silent, his warm, chocolate gaze hot enough to burn me if I stared at him too long. When I looked back at Daddy, I was sure he saw my concern. His features went soft and he smiled at me.

"Enzo is a trusted friend. Very few people know, but we grew up together. Enzo will be protective and possessive of you, but he will protect you like no other. Max is your last line of defense, but Enzo is the first, with me in the middle."

"I don't understand." I trembled as Enzo held me securely in his arms.

"Let me clean you up and I'll explain."

When I nodded, Daddy got a warm, damp cloth and cleansed me gently. When he was done, he joined me and Enzo on the spacious and plush couch along the side of the cabin.

"I'm bringing Enzo into our lives, Kitten. Now that we have Andromeda to look after, I want to make sure you're both protected. It will take Enzo a while to feel comfortable in our home with you and Max, but I have no doubt the two of you can make him feel welcome."

I glanced up at Enzo once more before taking a breath and voicing my fears. "Daddy, Enzo is a lot like you. But he's... more."

"That he is, Kitten. Are you worried he'll take you from me?"

I gasped. I shouldn't have been at all surprised Daddy knew what I was thinking. Daddy knew me better than anyone except Max. "Yes, Daddy." I couldn't help the guilty look up at Enzo. "Sorry," I whispered.

Enzo just chuckled. "Little Isabella, I've been watching you from a distance since you came to be with Mr. Blackstone. Yes, I won't deny I've always thought you beautiful, and maybe I've been a little jealous of Mr. Blackstone's colleagues when they've been allowed to fuck you. But you're Mr. Blackstone's woman. No matter how much I enjoyed fuckin' your ass, you're not mine. I'll take what Mr. Blackstone gives me, but that's as far as it goes. Jacob is too happy for me to take that away from him."

Daddy scowled. "So sure you'd succeed if you tried?"

"Oh, absolutely, Jacob. It's only out of respect for you I didn't run off with her the first night she came to live with you." Enzo's lips twitched as he fought to hide a smile.

"You said you'd never covet my woman." Daddy's scowl was fierce. Except he chose that moment to wink at me.

"And I wouldn't. Unless you gave me reason to. Like not makin' her happy, or not lockin' her down once and for all." Just like that all traces of humor were gone from Enzo. I stilled, not wanting to add to the tension.

"Are you calling me out, Enzo?"

"I am, sir. That girl deserves your name."

"She deserves more than that. Never worry. I'm about to take care of that the second we land."

"What?" Did he mean what I thought he meant?

Then, with both of us naked, Daddy got down on one knee and held out a small box. He opened the lid and the most beautiful ring I'd ever seen rested on velvet. I gasped out my surprise, tears springing to my eyes.

"My beautiful, sweet, Isabella. Will you be my wife? I promise to always love and cherish you. I'll always see to your wellbeing and pleasure. You will be my queen, my beautiful princess. I'll give you more babies and surround you with all the love I have in my heart. Will you marry me, Kitten?"

I was so shocked all I could do was burst into tears. Then I threw myself at Daddy. He caught me without us both bowling over. A warm chuckle from Enzo reminded me we weren't alone. But I didn't care.

"I love you, Isabella. I always will."

"I love you too, Daddy. Thank you so much for everything you've given me. Thank you for asking me to be your wife."

"Well?" When I looked at him quizzically, he chuckled warmly. "Will you marry me, Isabella?"

"Oh! Oh, yes! Yes, Daddy! Absolutely I will! Yes! Yes! Yes!" I rained kisses over his face while he laughed and held me tightly.

"Hold out your hand, princess." When I did, Daddy took the ring from the box and slid it onto my finger. "Never thought I'd have to ask a woman to marry me twice. I guess I should be thankful you didn't reject me outright in exchange for Enzo over there."

"No, Daddy." I grinned and laughed in pure delight. "I like Enzo and I think he could come to mean as much to me as Max does, but only *you* are my Daddy."

"As it should be." Enzo pushed away from the wall, still naked. "Now, why don't the two of you get some rest. You don't want to be worn out when we get there." He glanced at his watch. "It's only a couple more hours. I'll wake you when we land."

"Thank you, Enzo." Daddy scooped me up. "That sounds just about perfect."

Daddy hurried with me in his arms back to his private suite. He lay me gently on the plush bed and crawled in behind me. Before I could say anything else, Daddy tucked the head of his cock against the entrance to my ass and pushed inside me slowly.

"I'm not going to be the only one who's not had this ass tonight."

"Feels so good." I groaned, draping my knee over his thigh, opening myself up to him.

"That's it, my beautiful Isabella. Let me have you."

"I'm yours, Jacob," I whimpered. "All of me, all that I am, is yours."

"God, I love you!" His voice was fierce, his movements becoming harder and harder. "Love every fucking thing about you!"

"I love you too, Jacob! I love you too!"

He reached around to stroke my clit while he came deep inside me. I was helpless to do anything but follow him into that lovely, lovely madness.

When it was over, he held me close, his cock still firmly embedded in my ass. He brought my hand to his mouth and kissed the skin of my finger directly in front of his ring.

"I have the ceremony all set up. We'll be married the second we land."

"What about Max?"

"This was a surprise for you, honey. Max knew. We'll have a public ceremony later, but this is for us. Max volunteered to stay with Andromeda to ease your mind over leaving her for the first time. He's completely happy with this. And with the possibility of bringing Enzo into our little family."

"You really expect Enzo to be part of this with us? I doubt he'd be as accepting as Max."

"You underestimate him. Enzo is loyal to me. He always has been. He's as close to me as Victor. Closer, even, because we've known each other all our lives. He's my eyes and ears. My bodyguard, but more. This is a good thing, I swear to you."

I smiled up at him, because Daddy -- Jacob -- was everything to me. If this is what he wanted, I'd be more than happy to give it to him. "I know. I trust you."

"Good. Now, rest. You've earned a nice long

nap."

"Will you wake me up fucking me?"

Daddy chuckled. "Oh yeah, Kitten. I think I can manage that."

With one last sigh, I closed my eyes and slept. Daddy was right. I had needed a vacation. And what an adventure...

I love my life!

Kitten's New Collar
A Razor's Edge Daddy Dom Erotica Short
Wanda Violet O.

After an exhausting, but fun, flight to paradise, Kitten is looking forward to spending quality time with Daddy. Feeling completely free for the first time since giving birth to their daughter Andi, Kitten enjoys every decadence Daddy can provide -- and he can provide quite a few. Not to mention fabulous sex. But things are about to change for Kitten. And a wedding isn't always about rings and flowers. Kitten wants a new collar.

Slippery Nipple

I had no idea where we were when we landed, but the flight was only about three hours long. Not that I noticed. Daddy kept me busy the entire flight. After he let our flight attendant, Adam, and my bodyguard, Enzo, fuck me, I was exhausted. Daddy had taken me to his private master bedroom at the back end of the cabin and I had dozed occasionally. Between rounds of vigorous sex, that is.

Now that we'd landed, the weather was sunny and warm. A cool breeze ruffled my hair and I turned my face into the sun, closing my eyes and basking in the warmth.

"Feel good, Kitten?" Daddy smiled down at me with so much love and affection my heart swelled.

"It does, Daddy. I love feeling the sun on my skin. It's like a warm hug."

He chuckled. "That it is, Kitten. There will be plenty of that over the next couple of days. Did you check in with Max?"

"Yes, just before we landed. He says he and Andi are getting along fine."

"Good. Let's get upstairs to the room. You can shower if you like, then we'll begin our adventure."

With a glad cry I threw myself into Daddy's arms. He chuckled and hugged me back, squeezing me tight. He set me down and let me walk beside him hand in hand through the hotel lobby up to the room. I was hardly able to contain my excitement. Once inside our suite, I didn't even stop to take in what I was certain was magnificent decor. Instead, I threw myself at him again, this time peppering kisses all over his face before wiggling free and shedding my clothing as I hurried to the bathroom. Daddy's laughter followed me as I scampered to the shower.

As I'd hoped, it wasn't long before Daddy joined me. Snagging the shower gel, he eyed my hungrily. "We're going have so much fun, Kitten."

I smiled as I wrapped my arms around his neck, stretching up on my tiptoes even as I pulled him down for a hot, wet kiss. Water sluiced over us as Daddy's soapy hands slid easily up and down my back, then to my ass as he squeezed and kneaded. "I think my little Kitten needed this time away."

"Maybe. I love being home with our little family, but I feel like I've been let out of a very big, very gilded cage." I grinned up at him, knowing he'd understand what I meant.

As I expected, Daddy chuckled, leaning down to kiss me again, his hands never stopping their soothing stroking. "I understand completely. Before we continue, though, I need to explain my thoughts with regard to you."

I cocked my head, a thread of worry slinking through me. I knew I was still insecure with Daddy. As long as he'd been in my life, I'd have thought I could feel comfortable. He'd even asked me to marry him! But there was still that last little bit of doubt that told me I wasn't good enough.

Daddy had picked me up from a very low time in my life, a woman with no one and nothing, and brought me into his world as his pet. A treasured pet, but a pet nonetheless. He'd assured me time after time that I was so much more, that I was his woman and I would always be with him, that I was his and he was mine. Sometimes, though, I remembered that Daddy was not only good looking but exceedingly, *obscenely* wealthy and could have any woman he wanted. Most men I'd known would have, given the opportunity. I didn't believe Daddy was like that. Not at all. I just needed reassurance sometimes. This was one of those times.

"I brought Enzo into our circle. I let one of my valued, trusted employees partake of your sweet body. That's not always going to happen. I allowed Adam to fuck you because he'd pleased me, but mostly because I knew you needed it. I think you need me to share you as much as I need to share you. I chose Adam because he was available and had taken care of both of us, anticipating both our needs. I chose Enzo for a very different reason, though."

"Because he guards me. You wanted to reward him."

"Partly, yes."

"Partly?"

He bent down to take one of my nipples between his lips and sucked. I knew he was drinking my milk. I hoped that was how he planned on me emptying my breasts the next couple of days. The sensation was... indescribable. So different than having my daughter nursing even though it was the same act. A euphoric feeling washed over me, almost like a drug. My legs buckled and Daddy's wrapped his strong arms tighter around me as he continued to pull from my nipple.

"Mmm..." He groaned, his eyes fluttering closed. I wrapped my arms around his head, holding him to me with what little strength I had. "Delicious."

"Daddy..." I gasped out his name, losing myself in the moment.

With a little *pop*, Daddy released my nipple, swiping his tongue over the stiff peak several times. Then he moved to the other breast. By the time he finished, I was so relaxed I was literally like a sleepy kitten he had to peel off his chest. Hormones. Gotta love 'em.

Daddy smiled down at me. My eyes were so heavy I could barely open them to look up at him. "Feel better, Kitten?"

"What was that? Did you drug me?" I knew I had a goofy grin on my face. "I feel like I've had the most fantastic sex and am basking in the afterglow."

That got a louder laugh from him. "Good, my sweet Kitten. That's what I want. I want you so relaxed and content you don't want to move. Just let me take care of everything."

I stretched, realizing I was in Daddy's lap on a wide ledge along the back of the big shower. No idea when he'd sat us down or moved us there, but I curled up in his lap and sighed happily. "Mission accomplished, Daddy."

"Good," Daddy replied, his voice a soft rumble. His lips found mine in a slow, gentle kiss. There was a slightly sweet taste when he swept his tongue into my mouth. I'd tasted my own milk before out of curiosity, but this was something completely different. I could get addicted to the taste coming from him.

He smoothed my wet hair off my face as he smiled down at me. There was no doubt about the love in his expression. As always, Daddy proved any insecurities I had were unwarranted. In this case, I knew whatever Daddy had planned with Enzo would be to our mutual benefit. Knowing Daddy, it would be more for me than him, but I indulged him. Because he always indulged me. "Now. Enzo."

"You said you were rewarding him for guarding me."

He kissed the end of my nose. "I said partly. Something happened a while back. Something you had no knowledge of, and that is the way I wanted it."

My brow furrowed in confusion. "I don't understand."

"I pay my security people an obscene amount of money to protect all of us. If they do their job right, if there is ever a threat, the only person who knows is me. They tell me the moment a threat is detected and take action to make sure it's extinguished well before it ever gets close to any of us."

My heart pounded. "What are you saying, Daddy?"

He sighed. "There was an incident. Rivals of mine decided they'd make a play for you and little Andi to reach me. Do you remember Ronald? From when you first decided you were ready to embrace our new relationship?"

I frowned. "He was mean. And you made him leave. I remember Papa Victor said he would give you trouble."

There was a pause as something passed over Daddy's face. Pain? Betrayal?

"Victor's your best friend. Right?" Something didn't feel right.

Daddy smiled. "He was. The only person, other than you and Max, I was closer to than Victor is Enzo. He's had my back my entire life. So when Enzo got an inkling something was up, he took care of it. In the process, he was hurt."

I gasped. "He was gone for over a month! You just said he was due a vacation."

"He was. But I didn't want you to worry about him. Enzo was fine. He just needed some recovery time."

"He got hurt keeping me and Andi safe." Tears sprang to my eyes. "But he's fine now? You promise?"

"Yes, Kitten. You saw him with your own eyes.

Did he look like he had any lasting effects from his injury?" Daddy smiled at me gently, stroking my cheek with the pad of his thumb, a soothing gesture.

I thought about the plane ride on the way here. Yeah. Enzo was definitely in top physical condition. And, as a character on a popular science fiction television show would say, he was most certainly *fully functional.* "No, Daddy."

"He could have avoided injury, but it would have meant the threat got closer to you and Andi, and Enzo wasn't willing to let that happen. So he took care of the threat. Even though it cost him. I trust him as much or more than any other person outside our family, and he proved his loyalty yet again. He's always been like a brother to me."

"Wait." I tried to think, needing to put this all together. "You're talking like Papa Victor isn't your friend anymore."

"That's not for you to worry about. All you need to know is that Enzo will be around much more now."

"So Enzo won't be in the background any longer?"

"When we're out, you won't see him. But he and his crew will always be watching over all of us."

"But when we're home? Or in a place he feels is safe?"

Daddy grinned down at me. "I like the way you phrased that, Kitten. You understand. If Enzo doesn't believe it's safe, you'll never see him. He'll always be in charge of our security. Now, he will have the rest and peace he needs when we're all safe."

"Me."

"Yes. I'm taking you away from my men. You have a need to be… used. I have a need to watch and participate. More, I have a need to control the situation."

"Haven't you always had control?"

A shadow came over Daddy's face before he shuttered it. "I thought I did."

I frowned. "Something happened, didn't it?"

"Nothing you need to worry about, Kitten. All is taken care of." He bent to kiss my lips. I had questions. I wanted to know what had happened. What *would* happen. But when Daddy kissed me, I forgot everything around me and surrendered completely. I was his. Heart, body, and mind. When he wanted me, I was his.

He took his time, kissing me until my toes curled and I was once again on the edge of sanity. My little cries and whimpers echoed in the shower. In Daddy's strong grip, I swayed and moaned, consumed by an exhilarating blend of lust and surrender. His tongue, deft and insistent, explored the depths of my mouth, igniting a fire within me that burned brighter with each touch, each caress.

Our bodies melded, lost in a kaleidoscope of sensations that defied reason. I knew Daddy owned me, but I don't think I had ever appreciated it as acutely as I did now. There were things I wanted to know. Important things. Because I was pretty sure someone Daddy trusted had betrayed him in some way. I could almost feel his pain. It was something I'd have to explore later. Perhaps Max could help me. Just now, though, it didn't matter.

Daddy's expert hands worked down my body, caressing me in just the right way. He knew exactly what I wanted, what I needed. His breath became ragged, and I knew he was getting close to losing himself, much as I was. Soon, we'd both be deep in the passion we shared and the world around us would cease to matter. I clung to him, my nails digging into his back as he filled me with his kisses. Then he reached between my legs and thrust two fingers inside me, his thumb brushing my clit. I cried out, my head falling back.

Daddy moved me to straddle him and I grasped his cock. His jaw clenched as the head kissed my entrance once before I sank down on his hard, throbbing cock. "My God, Kitten! What you fucking do to me!" His voice was harsh.

With every thrust, my lust surged. I wanted to touch him, to taste him, to let him know how much he meant to me. I reached down, my fingers sliding over his chest, his nipples hardening beneath my touch. He growled, his hips moving faster, pounding up into me with surprising intensity.

Since he'd found out I was pregnant, we'd had a few rounds of rough sex, but not nearly as many as before. After the birth of our child, he had been careful, afraid I was still sore. Now, though… this was amazing!

I moved in sync with him as I absorbed his power. My thighs burned, but I kept going, determined to satisfy both of us. With each thrust, I felt a surge of pleasure that radiated through my lower body where we joined. Thrusting my breasts out, I offered them to him and he wrapped one arm around my back and pulled me to his mouth.

I rode him like a demon, moving up and down on his stiff cock, feeling the blood pulsing in my veins as I throbbed with ecstasy. Daddy held my hips, guiding my movements, ensuring that I felt every inch of his dick. With each thrust, he groaned around my nipple, the sound making me even hotter, the slight vibration pulsing through the stiff peak as he sucked harder, urging me faster, harder.

With every movement, our passion surged, my body convulsing around him as small orgasms swept through me, hinting at the pleasure to come. I wanted to touch him, to taste him, to let him know how much he meant to me. I let my fingers slide over his chest and his nipples hardening beneath my touch. He growled, his hips moving faster, pounding up into me with an ever-increasing force that sent shocks and thrills coursing through me.

My mind swirled with dizzying pleasure as I continued to ride him, the warmth of his arms and the water in the shower surrounding me and making me feel safe. *Wanted.* I loved the way he owned me, the way he made me feel so protected and cherished. His words echoed in my head, his praise a sweet melody to my ears. I was his, he was mine, and that was all I ever needed.

I bit my lip, pulling myself away from his mouth as I felt the first tremors of an intense orgasm surge through me. "Daddy, I'm going to come," I whispered, my voice trembling.

His eyes were intense with heat. "I know, baby girl. I can feel it too."

Daddy moved to lay me on the bench, our bodies never separating. He placed a hard kiss on my mouth before pushing up, pulling one of my legs over his shoulder. Using that leg as leverage, Daddy pounded into me, a hard, driving rhythm that jarred my entire body with every thrust.

I gripped my breasts, curling my fingers into my skin to keep them from jiggling too much. They were much bigger than before I got pregnant and, now that Daddy had drained most of my milk, not nearly as firm.

"Stop," he snarled at me, nipping my calf hard enough to make me yelp. "Do not cover your breasts unless you're playing with them, Kitten."

"But --"

"No buts! You're trying to hide them and I won't fucking have it."

"They… move." I didn't want to let go. I wanted Daddy to see me as perfect. Like I used to be. I know he'd told me on the plane that he loved my new body, but I was still self-conscious. Especially about my boobs.

"I know. I love watching your tits jiggle when I fuck you." He continued to drive into me, his muscled abdomen rippling with each movement. "When I'm done with you here, before we make our way to the beach, I'm going to fuck you from behind at the vanity. Gonna watch those perfect tits move every time I slam my cock into you. And you're going to let me."

"Daddy!" I screamed as my orgasm crested, pushing me into bliss.

Daddy held himself deep, growling as my pussy squeezed around his cock but he didn't come. "That's it, Kitten. That's it." He leaned forward and I gasped, my back arching as his lips clamped down around my upturned nipple. The sensation as I was still coming was electric, sending more zings of pleasure through me. Daddy sucked and licked, his tongue swirling around my aching nipple. I moaned, trembling with pleasure.

"Goddamn, Isabella! You're so fucking hot!" His animalistic growl sent a vibration through my breast that triggered another orgasm from me. That sexy, rough voice of his was like another hand he used expertly to pet me to a fevered pitch.

When his mouth left my nipple, I sucked in a

ragged breath, still shaking. Daddy straightened and gave me a blinding smile. "Good girl. Now, let's get to that vanity." He reached for my hand, pulling me up from the bench. I stumbled, my legs weak from the intense pleasure he'd so expertly built.

Daddy wrapped an arm around my waist to steady me, nipping my neck as he did. I cried out, the slight and sudden sting startling me, but awakening something inside me that had been sleeping since before the birth of our child.

"Daddy!" I screamed as he took us out of the shower. He lifted me and walked the few steps to the vanity.

When he set me on my feet, he shoved my back so that I sprawled over the cool, smooth marble surface. I tried to push up but Daddy moved his hand to my head and held me. "Stay down," he growled. "You move when I say."

This was a side of Daddy I hadn't seen in a very long time. Max was usually the more aggressive male while Daddy was content to watch. When it was the two of us alone, he was intense, but gentle. This was a side of him I reveled in.

In a swift, rough move that took my breath, Daddy entered me hard and deep. He waited only long enough to set his feet and get a good grip in my hip before he started pounding me. He fisted my hair in the other hand, pulling me up slightly so I had to look at both of us in the mirror. My tits bounced with each brutal thrust. Daddy bared his teeth at me as we both watched ourselves. I gasped, loving the erotic image we made.

"Watch yourself, Isabella." He spoke directly at my ear. "Watch yourself as I fuck the shit out of you." He jerked my head to the side so I caught our reflection in the full-length mirror on the door. Daddy plowed me from behind. My tits swayed and jerked with every thrust.

Finally he let go of my hair and wrapped both arms around me so tight I could barely breathe. His hips jerked as he fucked me. His breathing was as ragged as mine. Little cries slipped from my throat, punctuated by the slap of flesh on flesh as Daddy continued to fuck me.

Finally, Daddy threw back his head and bellowed to the ceiling. Both his arms were still tight around me as he spilled his seed inside me, his dick not leaving my pussy for several minutes as he held me upright. I had no idea how he managed not to collapse in a heap on the floor, but Daddy stood there holding my weight as we both caught our breath.

"Daddy…"

He kissed my temple before sliding free of my pussy. Scooping me up in his arms, he carried us back inside the shower and cleaned his cum from my thighs and cunt. When he'd finished, he kissed me gently. Like I was used to. "Was I too rough with you, Isabella?" His voice was tender, if rough from his recent shouts.

"You know you weren't, Jacob." Daddy had started trying to pull us out of Daddy and Kitten from time to time. I knew he worried I wasn't his equal and he was right. No matter how much he reassured me, I always felt I could be replaced. Wasn't that what wealthy men did? Replace their women when they got tired of them?

Daddy had tried his best to make me understand, but I was nothing when he found me. It was hard to fully accept he was mine just as much as I was his, and I knew it frustrated him sometimes.

"I want to give you everything you need, baby. I think you've missed the rough sex."

I smiled even as my eyelids drooped. "I did. I love everything we do together, but sometimes I need you to completely dominate me."

"I promise I'll do my best to see you get that as often as you want it. I'm sorry I neglected that side of our relationship, but I wanted to make sure you'd healed enough physically. I never want you to hurt, Isabella. Mentally or physically."

I turned in his arms, wrapping mine around his neck. "You always take care of me, Daddy."

"I'll always take care of my Kitten. But I want Isabella to be taken care of too."

This was just one of many, many reasons I loved my Daddy.

Daddy dried us and carried me back to the bedroom. The suite Daddy had gotten us was enormous. There were two bedrooms, a sitting room, a full kitchen and bar, as well as an enormous hot tub on the balcony. Daddy had only the best, but I was still in awe of the place.

"My sweet Kitten." He laid me gently on the bed and pulled me against him when he climbed in after me. "You are so very special. I've never met your equal. You complete me like I never thought possible."

"I love you, Jacob," I whispered as I drifted off to sleep.

Blowjob

I woke with Daddy on top of me, fucking me slowly as he coaxed me awake with nips and kisses to my jaw and chin. The second my gaze focused on his and I smiled up at him, his movements sped up until he was surging into me with reckless abandon.

He pushed himself off me slightly. I gripped his shoulders tightly, trying to pull him back on top of me but he only straightened his arms further, pulling away from me.

"Daddy?"

"Come for me, Kitten. I like watching your tits bouncing when I fuck you." I glanced down at my chest. A few drops of milk escaped but not the mess I'd have if I'd done more than take a quick nap. "No, Kitten. Look at me." His voice had gone from silky and seductive to hard and commanding in the space of a breath.

"I --"

"Look. At. Me." He never broke his rhythm, surging in and out of me with ever increasing force. "You are beautiful, no matter the changes in your body, Isabella. There is nothing about you I would change. Not even to go back to the very young and innocent woman I first brought into my home. Into my care. That woman led me to the love of my life. Gave me a beautiful daughter to love and cherish and protect." Then his face turned harder and fiercer than I'd ever seen. "So help me fuckin' God, I will make you see you like I do."

"Jacob!" I screamed as I came around him. Daddy didn't stop fucking me. Instead, he pushed up, wrapping his arms around my legs, using them as leverage as he fucked me ever harder. As far gone in pleasure as I was, it didn't escape my notice how my breasts moved with each hard jolt to my body.

I stared into Jacob's eyes. As sweat streamed down his face and landed on my chest, I could see the fierce need and lust shining in his gaze as it focused squarely on my chest. He actually licked his lips as one pearly drop of milk was flung from my nipple to my chin. Instead of whiping it off, he shifted his weight to one hand and scooped the drop up with a finger and brought it to his lips. His expression changed from a harsh demand to one suspiciously close to ecstasy. He closed his eyes and the masculine groan was nearly a growl. The sound sent shivers through me and I just… surrendered.

The second I did, Daddy noticed. He grunted his approval, then blanketed me with his larger frame, pressing me into the mattress. His hoarse groan punctuated the splash of hot cum erupting inside me. My own orgasm gripped me so hard I seized and all I could do was gasp and ride it out.

When the last of my tremors subsided, Daddy kissed me, lapping at the sweat coating the skin of my neck, his breathing ragged. I caressed his back, running my fingers over his damp skin. "I love you, Kitten," he whispered in my ear, his voice shaky. "I always will."

"I love you too, Daddy. Always."

"Good." He shifted to look down at me, stroking my hair gently as he continued to thrust softly inside me. "How do you feel?"

I couldn't help the goofy smile that split my face. "Amazing!"

Daddy's chuckle warmed my insides. "Not too sore? I wasn't too rough with you?"

"No. You were perfect. The sex today was exactly what I needed."

"You're an amazing woman, Isabella. I've never made a better decision in my life than I did when I picked you for my woman." He kissed me again before moving to help me out of bed and taking me to the bathroom to clean up.

"We've still got the better part of the afternoon, baby. What do you say to some time on the beach? Hmm?"

"The beach? Yes! Let's do that, Daddy!" I gave him a quick kiss while he chuckled at me. Then I scampered off the counter where he'd set me to clean me up and went in search of my bathing suit.

My clothes had all been put away by Daddy's staff before we got there. I hadn't gone looking for anything yet but I'd never had problems before. Now, I couldn't find a swimsuit of any kind. There were a few dresses of differing styles and a myriad of accessories - - Daddy's staff always made sure we had anything we could ever need, even if we were only going for an overnight stay -- but no swimsuit. The disappointment rolling over me was enough to nearly bring me to tears. I really wanted an afternoon under the hot sun. I was pleasantly sore but the soothing heat would have felt so wonderful.

"What's wrong, baby?" Daddy came behind me and kissed my bare shoulder.

"I don't have a swimsuit."

"So?"

"So," I huffed, turning around in his arms, unable to control the pout forming on my lips. "I really wanted to lay in the sun."

"Who said you couldn't?" He raised an imperious eyebrow at me as if to challenge me in some way.

"Well, I suppose I could always wear one of

these sundresses, but it's not the same."

"Who said you had to wear anything at all, Kitten?"

I paused, letting the impact of his suggestion sink in. "You mean, go naked?"

He shrugged. "It's a private beach. The only people allowed to be there are guests of this resort. And this place is adults only." He gave me a cocky grin. "And I own the resort."

I felt a thrill of excitement course through me. The idea of being naked in front of Daddy, in full view of the ocean, was both terrifying and exhilarating. Though I'd been naked around his inner circle, being out in the open was a whole other ball of wax, so to speak.

But... damn. Just the thought was a turn on. Would he... would he fuck me on the beach? "Okay!" I grinned. "I'll do it."

"That's my girl." Daddy gave me a heated kiss that had me wanting to climb his body and have my wicked way with him, but he set me firmly away before turning me around and swatting my ass. "Go get your leash, Kitten. You're mine forever and I have the need to show you off."

I remember the first time Daddy leashed me and led me through the lobby of his offices. I'd been nervous but had soon learned the power of submitting to Daddy. He hadn't done it often, but I'd learned to love it. It sometimes garnered unwanted attention, but Daddy always took care of me. *And* anyone who was stupid enough to try to belittle me.

Now, I bounded through the massive bedroom suite to the dresser where my diamond studded leash glittered in the sunlight. I always wore the blue metal collar laced with blue diamonds at my throat. I was allowed to take it off when we were in our home, but I never did. To me, it was more precious than even the beautiful engagement ring Daddy had presented to me. It represented Daddy's ownership of me. His first hard claim on me. I picked up the leash and carried it to Daddy, handing it to him with an excited bounce in my step.

"My, my. Someone is excited to show off her delicious curves."

"Nope! Not at all, Daddy. I'm excited to have *you* show off my curves."

He chuckled and it heated my insides once again. I reached between my legs to find my pussy already weeping even though he'd used me vigorously only a little while before. Holding his gaze, I brought my fingers to my mouth and sucked them clean.

"Mmmm…" I gave Daddy a cheeky grin. "Delicious."

Daddy's nostrils flared. "I'll show you delicious, Kitten." He grabbed my hair and tugged me to him for a rough kiss before shoving me to my knees. "Suck." The word was a menacing growl as he forced his cock deep into my mouth. I gagged slightly but welcomed the demand.

I loved that Daddy finally felt like he could take what he needed. I knew how sexually aggressive he could be at times. I was pretty sure he used Max in order to restrain himself. By letting Max take charge and be the aggressor, Daddy could watch from a distance without unleashing his full dominance. I had the feeling that was about to change. And I couldn't be happier.

"Suck me, Kitten." I loved the rough gravel to his voice. Loved looking up at him as he fucked my mouth. "That's it," he growled. "Such a good little

Kitten. Taking my cock deep." He punctuated his words by thrusting his cock as deep as he could. He couldn't get it all the way in, but I opened and let him do what he could.

I moaned as streams of saliva began to dribble down my chin to my chest. I knew I was a mess. I also knew my Daddy loved the way I looked when I'd been sucking cock.

"Wow."

I started at the sound of Enzo's voice from the doorway, but Daddy held me in place, not letting me turn to face him.

The man could move like a ghost. Or maybe I'd been too busy with Daddy's cock to pay attention. Enzo had fucked me on the plane, but I'd barely seen him since then, and not at all after we landed.

"Now, that's a beautiful sight, Jacob." Enzo's voice was husky and deep. It vibrated inside me in the most delicious way, sending my clit into overdrive.

"Isn't it just." Daddy's grip on my hair tightened and I groaned. I loved it when he took control like this! It was raw and primal, the decadent pleasure with the bite of pain.

"Look at me, Kitten," Enzo ordered, his voice hard, commanding, as he moved to stand next to Daddy. It was impossible not to obey him. "You like getting your face fucked, don't you." He knelt beside me, his hand at the back of my neck while Daddy retained his grip on my hair.

I blinked up at him, unable to speak because of the vigorous fucking Daddy was giving my mouth. When my gaze flickered back to Daddy, Enzo gripped my jaw hard. It didn't hurt but startled me so my attention went back to Enzo.

"That's right. You focus on me. When Jacob is

using you like this, your eyes are on me unless I tell you otherwise."

I didn't understand, but I couldn't say anything because Daddy's movements quickened, punishing my throat as he neared his orgasm. As I continued to stare up into Enzo's face, Daddy grunted, then groaned, and finally, threw back his head and bellowed his release. Jets of cum slid down my throat. I missed some, not able to swallow with his cock so far down my throat, and cum dribbled from the corners of my mouth to land on my chest before he pulled out of my mouth and shook a few more drops from the tip of his dick onto my upturned tits.

"What a naughty Kitten," Enzo tisked, clicking his tongue. "You missed some of your Daddy's cum." He scooped a glob from one side of my mouth and fed it back to me. Then he did the same with the other side. "If this wasn't your first time out, I'd jerk off on your tits and make you wear our cum to the beach and show everyone what happens when a naughty Kitten doesn't swallow all she should. But I'll let you off that hook." He grinned. "This time."

Daddy still had a look of bliss on his face and was stroking his cock. "That'd be so fucking hot."

Daddy seemed to have devolved from the refined presence he normally presented -- even to Max -- into some kind of primal beast. He even looked different. It gave me a moment of pause. My discomfort must have shown on my face because Daddy's demeanor immediately changed and he knelt in front of me.

"Whoa, Kitten. Easy." He stroked hair out of my face and snagged a towel that had landed on the floor earlier. "Get me a washcloth, Enzo." Just like that, Daddy was back in charge. Enzo nodded once before heading to the bathroom without protest. "You OK, Kitten?"

I thought about it. "Yes. It was all so hot for a while. I loved everything. I love knowing I'm going out on my leash with you in a bit. I even loved the thought of what Enzo said." I glanced toward the bathroom, not sure what I wanted to say. I didn't want to hurt his feelings or for him to think I was going behind his back to Daddy. Which was a ridiculous thought because Daddy would never ever make me do something I wasn't on board with. He might have told me once everything I did was for his pleasure, but he never failed to make sure I enjoyed myself. Not once. So if I really couldn't do something, all I needed to do was say so.

"But you didn't like everything."

I ducked my head, feeling like a failure. "I'm not sure I could go that far." My voice was small and timid. "I don't want Enzo to think I'm balking the first time he suggests something."

"Isabella, honey. No one is going to humiliate you. Not for any reason. Ever."

"Absolutely not." Enzo approached and I gasped. I had been looking for him, but I'd focused so completely on Daddy that he still managed to startle me. He knelt beside Daddy, handing him the damp cloth. "I'm sorry I scared you, Miss Isabella," Enzo said. His face was blank and he didn't flinch back, even when Daddy shot him an angry look. Strangely, Daddy didn't actually say anything as he cleaned me.

I nodded. "OK." The whole mood was intense -- as intense as the sex had been. But I honestly wasn't as confident in Enzo as I was Daddy. And it felt like Daddy wasn't the one in control. I wasn't sure how that sat with me.

"It's not OK," Daddy muttered. "You're a bastard, Enzo."

The other man just shrugged. "Never claimed I wasn't."

"You scare her like that again" -- Daddy tossed the cloth in the general direction of the bathroom and pulled me into his arm but looking at me instead of Enzo --"I'll fucking kill you."

"I truly meant no disrespect, Miss Isabella. And I'd never push you to do something you didn't want to do, or weren't ready for."

Daddy turned me so I straddled his lap. His cock pressed against my pussy, parting my lips with its length, but he made no move to enter me. Instead, he framed my face with his hands, looking straight into my eyes. "I should have prepared you more for Enzo, Kitten. When the three of us are alone, Enzo likes to be in charge. He has a need for total control and his desires run dark. That being said, I trust him to never put you in a situation you don't want to be in."

"I said what I did, planted the fantasy in your head, to see how you'd react. Though I've studied you, I don't know you as well as Jacob or Max. I intend to know you better than either of them."

"Daddy?" I looked up at Jacob, not sure what was happening.

Daddy sighed, shaking his head slightly before pulling me close to wrap his arms tightly around me. "Things have changed, Kitten. It's all corporate greed. My inner circle turned on me. I destroyed them. That's how things happened that caused Enzo to be hurt. I was at the top of the proverbial food chain before, but now I'm alone."

I sucked in a breath. "Papa Victor…"

Daddy winced, like I'd actually physically

wounded him.

"Don't ever call Victor *Papa* again," Enzo snarled. "Fucking scum doesn't deserve the title."

"It's all right, Kitten. Enzo and I took care of everything. It's all over. There's a vacuum left where the traitors were deposed, but I'm shoring up things so I have control of everything."

"Were..." I swallowed, terrified to ask my next question. "Were you in danger, Daddy?"

"It's over, Kitten. There's nothing for you to worry about. I swear it."

"But... Daddy!" I threw my arms around his neck and sobbed uncontrollably. The thought of something happening to Jacob was enough to throw me into a panic.

"I swear by God and the Virgin Mary, Enzo, I should kill you where you stand." I'd never heard Daddy so furious. Not even the time Victor had deliberately frightened me to get a reaction out of Max.

"She needs to know it all, Jacob. You know it as well as I do. She's stronger than you think, but not when you keep so many things from her she's blindsided. Victor was a snake. He wanted her for himself and he was willing to kill you to get to her. What do you think would have happened then? While I have no doubt Victor would have treasured your Kitten, she would have lived the rest of her life never knowing what the man was capable of."

"Like she knows what I'm capable of?" The two men stared at each other for long, long moments, neither backing down. Daddy sounded furious. And resigned. No one ever argued with Daddy. The fact that Enzo did, told me more than I wanted to know. Daddy wasn't the only one in charge anymore.

The argument... wasn't something I was used to.

Daddy never raised his voice in front of me, never allowed his men to raise their voices when I was around. From the beginning Daddy and Max had sheltered me from everything, and now with Andromeda, I was certain the two of them would only tighten their safety net around us.

Enzo raised an eyebrow at Daddy before turning to me, a determined look on his face. "You love Jacob. I know you do. I can tell it in every line of your body. The way you look at him and surrender to everything he asks of you. You've never questioned him or balked. You simply trust him to take care of you in all ways."

"Yes," I said, without hesitation. "I love Daddy with all my heart."

"That man loves you just as much, girl." Enzo dropped all pretense at deference, talking bluntly. "There's nothing -- and I mean nothing -- he wouldn't do to keep you and your daughter safe. Not even Max commands his love the way you do."

"I --" I swallowed. "I know he loves me."

"Good. You need to know he's eliminated every threat to you. Every single threat."

"For now," Daddy muttered. "There's always someone waiting to nip at our heels."

"Which is where I come in." Enzo stood, crossing his arms over his massive chest. "I've been your bodyguard, but now I'm closer. I'm head of Jacob's security. I'm also now on all of you full time. Max has someone with him. Andromeda has her own security person."

"The nanny?" I cocked my head, trying to understand even though I could see Daddy wasn't liking this at all.

"Yes. There's also a third in case someone goes after Andromeda and her guard has to run with her.

I've covered everything. If all goes well, you'll never see anyone but the nanny. If Max doesn't need or want her help with your daughter, she'll be in the background. Watching. Waiting. But all of you -- Jacob included -- have eyes on you at all times. Nonintrusive, but always on guard."

"I told you Enzo would be part of our lives now, Kitten," Daddy said softly at my ear. "He's the only one I trust completely. We grew up together. He's had my back as long as I can remember and we've been through many scrapes. But, like I said, his needs run dark. He will be your and Max's caregiver in the event something happens to me."

"But... Victor..."

"Is gone, Kitten. I know you liked him, but I misjudged him."

Enzo snorted. "The only thing you misjudged was Kitten's appeal. When you stopped bringing her to the office, when you stopped sharing her with everyone, that's when Victor lost his Goddamn mind. Hell, if I didn't love you like a brother, I'd try to take her away from you myself."

Daddy bared his teeth at Enzo, his arms tightening around me. "I'd kill you, too."

Enzo raised his hands. "Fully aware. But before her, there was just you and me. I'm a lot of things, Jacob. Most of them not good. But you have my loyalty above everyone else. You know you do."

With a sigh, Daddy relaxed his hold. "I know. But Victor's betrayal is still fucking raw."

"I know." Enzo squeezed Daddy's shoulder before moving to the dresser. "Now, let's take your Kitten outside. She loves the sun. She should have all the sun we can give her while we're here."

Screaming Orgasm

Enzo snagged a large beach bag and tossed sunscreen, a loose cover up, and a wide-brimmed hat inside. "The resort has towels ready at our cabana. I've made sure drinks are delivered."

"But…" I looked from one of them to the other. "Is it, you know, safe? I can stay inside if it's not. I don't mind."

"You'd be locked away in our home if it wasn't safe, Isabella." Daddy stroked my cheek as he smiled at me. Then he leaned in to kiss me gently. "Thank you, Kitten."

I looked up at him in confusion. "For what?"

"For letting me take care of you. You've never once questioned me. The only time you said anything was when you were afraid I was pulling away from you. Which was the whole reason for this trip. I need you to know how much you mean to me and I fully intend to marry you while we're here."

"I love you, Jacob. So much!"

"I love you too, baby. Now." He gave me a smile. "Time to go. You ready?"

I looked down at my naked form sitting on Daddy's lap and laughed. "There's not much to get ready, Daddy." I brushed a finger over my collar. "I'm pretty sure this is all I've got."

The smile Daddy gave me was one of pure satisfaction. The heavy conversation fluttered away, thank God. It was good to see Jacob back in the moment and anticipating the time to come. "It's all you need, Kitten."

"Good." Enzo picked up the diamond chain and handed it back to Daddy. "Let's show off your beautiful pet, Jacob."

Daddy fastened the leash to my collar. As he led me outside through the patio balcony and down the steps to the beach below, I glanced back. Enzo was nowhere to be seen.

"Don't worry, Kitten. He's got our backs."

"But I thought it was safe here!"

"It is. But any time we're out, there's always the potential for danger. It's part of my life I'd hoped would never touch you, but I realize now that was wishful thinking." Daddy glanced back at me. "I won't make the same mistake twice." Then he smiled faintly. "No more talk of this. We're meant to be having a good time. Together."

It would be hard to put aside all Daddy and Enzo had told me, but I'd try. For Daddy. I wanted him to enjoy our vacation as much as I was.

Once we reached the beach, Daddy took me to a secluded cabana. There were others scattered along the beach, but ours was nestled among a copse of palm trees by itself. Of the few people I did see, Daddy was the only one dressed. "You see, Kitten? No one cares if you're nude."

I grinned. "Was all this… foreplay?"

Daddy laughed and I fell in love all over again. Whatever had happened, however Jacob had been betrayed, he needed to be Daddy. And I needed to be his Kitten.

"I suppose it was, Kitten. Though, I'm sure there will be people who see us." He shrugged. "You're mine. I have measures in place to keep anyone away who I don't want to be here."

"And Enzo leads them?"

"Yes."

"And you trust him. As much as you trusted Victor?" I hated asking the question, but I had to. Not for me. For Daddy.

As I'd hoped, Jacob didn't answer me right away. Instead, he contemplated the question. I could practically see him thinking about his answer. When he spoke, it wasn't what I was expecting.

"No." He shook his head slightly before smiling to himself, like he just now realized what he was saying. "I never trusted Victor like I trust Enzo."

"Why?"

"Because Victor never spent time in the hell Enzo and I did. We broke out together. Enzo was always in the background. His choice. Me at the fore. It's how we've always worked. Now, we're going to be closer. Like we were when we were younger. We'll have each other's backs."

"Is it different than with you and Victor?"

Daddy smiled down at me. "Yes. Victor was loyal, but I always knew that, even though we'd been close since I first started my business ventures, as long as I was making us both money, Victor was my staunchest ally. I thought we'd grown close, but Victor was always out for Victor. And he wanted you from the first time he saw you. Looking back, I think he pulled that stunt with Max with the intent of somehow getting Max to steal you away from me. Then he'd bring you both back home or something." He shrugged, shaking his head. The look on his face was one of resigned pain. This betrayal from Victor had hurt Daddy more than he wanted to admit. "I don't think he was thinking clearly when it came to you. He simply wanted you."

"Why did he wait so long to…"

"To come after me?" I nodded and Daddy continued. "I'm not sure. Looking back, I'm surprised he didn't try something as soon as I made him your protector on the event of my death."

"But Enzo won't do that. Right?" Before Daddy could answer I plowed on. "Because he seems like a man who simply takes what he wants."

"You wouldn't be wrong there, Kitten. Enzo is a straight up killer when I need him to be, but he is solidly behind me. He stays in the shadows because that's how he can best protect me. He also prefers it that way. He's never been a man who likes the spotlight. He may want you, but he wants me just as much."

"So, you and Enzo are lovers too?" The thought of Daddy and Enzo, two over the top Alpha types, fucking each other sent a shot of lust through me so hard I gasped.

The smug smile on Daddy's face told me he'd dropped that little tidbit on purpose, just to see my reaction. "We have been in the past. I suspect we will be again. I'm also sure Enzo and Max will get along quite nicely."

I groaned. Yeah. "That would be hot as fuck." Then I frowned up at him. "You're distracting me."

"Not denying that, Kitten. This is meant to be a fun trip. Not turn into something you stress over."

"But you promise Enzo is solid. He's not going to…" My voice tried to catch and I had to clear my throat. "Not going to try to separate us." I couldn't say it any other way. Couldn't think about someone taking me away from Daddy. Or about someone trying to hurt Daddy. I just couldn't.

"I promise. Enzo is the man I should have given you to, but he hadn't expressed interest. Looking back, he was probably handling things behind the scenes and didn't want to be distracted. Because I see the way he looks at you. He's as possessive as I am. But he's also that possessive of me. We've always been together. Just… in a different way. Now, though, we both know it's time for things to change."

"You'll both be stronger together?"

"Yes, Kitten. We will." Daddy took me in his arms once more for a gentle hug. His hands roamed my back, his fingers skimming along my skin and making me shiver. Then he brought his mouth down to mine, kissing me with love and hunger.

When he pulled back, he stroked my chin with his thumb, his gaze roaming my face. Then he smiled. "Now. Let's get you in the sun."

Once we were settled, Daddy undid my leash, wrapping it around my waist so that it hung loosely above my hips like a glittering adornment. He dug through the beach bag for sunscreen. I reached for it, but I should have known better. He merely raised an eyebrow at me and I dropped my hand with a giggle. While I was nude, Daddy was dressed in loose khaki trousers and a white shirt with the sleeves rolled up to just below his elbows. "I should spank you for that, Kitten."

"What? I was just going to put on sunscreen."

"For denying me the pleasure of touching your body. Not happening, Kitten. Which means, I'll get the pleasure of seeing your pink ass after I spank it."

I shivered, but not in fear. Yeah. I liked the sound of that. A lot.

As Daddy rubbed in sunscreen over every inch of me, I noticed he'd tossed two bottles on the couch in the cabana.

"Is that a bottle of lube?"

"Yep. Enzo is nothing if not thorough. He knows I'll be fucking you out here."

"I think I'd like that."

"Good. Now. Come closer and let me make sure I got enough sunscreen on your mound." The wicked gleam in his eyes told me he'd be inspecting me very closely.

I obeyed and Daddy sat on the couch, spreading his knees so I stepped between them. He leaned forward, gripping my hip in one hand while brushing the thumb over my mound. "Why Kitten, I do believe you're wet."

"I am, Daddy."

"What made you wet? The thought of me fucking you? Or spanking you?"

"Both, Daddy."

"Good." His voice was a satisfied purr. Instead of letting me go, he leaned in and swiped his tongue through my folds, sucking gently at my clit before he pulled back.

"Daddy!" I cried out, letting my head fall back. My knees nearly gave out, but Daddy's strong hands gripped my hips to keep me steady.

"Such a sweet little Kitten." Another swipe. "Delicious. Intoxicating." Another swipe. "And all mine." He latched on to my clit, sucking and flicking it with his tongue, making a powerful wave of pleasure build and build until he let go of my hip and smacked my ass. Hard.

The bite of pain pushed me over the edge and, with a ragged cry, I came in a blistering explosion. I think I screamed out Daddy's name, but I'm not really sure. The world seemed to crash around me. The next thing I knew, Daddy was holding me in his lap, kissing my forehead and stroking my hair softly. "That's my good, sweet, little Kitten. Such a beautiful, beautiful Kitten."

"Daddy…" I sighed as I turned my face into his

touch. He leaned down and caught my lips with his. I groaned when I tasted myself on his lips. I always loved it when he kissed me after eating me out. Daddy knew it, too.

"My sweet, sweet Kitten. So very sensual."

I knew my smile was dreamy but I couldn't help it. I loved every single thing Daddy did to me. He never let me down. Never left me wanting unless there was a reason -- usually to prolong my pleasure as long as possible so the resulting orgasm was over the top.

Reaching up, I stroked Daddy's face. He was so handsome. So perfect. "I know there are women all over who want you, Jacob." My voice was barely above a whisper. "Yet you chose me?"

"I did. You're my choice. You always were. From the moment I first saw you."

"When was that?"

He smiled down at me. "When you were just fifteen. It wasn't a sexual thing. Not back then. You… intrigued me. You were this little pixie. Tiny and so very fragile looking." He shook his head slightly as if trying to stave off a memory that threatened to overwhelm him. "Then you tried to help a little girl."

I gasped, jerking upright. "You… saw…"

"I did, Kitten. I saw the girl's father drag her off the playground by her hair. I saw the moment you saw it happen. You ran after them, yelling at him to stop hurting the child. He didn't and you kicked him behind the knee." The memory was painful and I shook my head, not wanting him to continue but he did anyway. "He let the girl go, but turned on you." A muscle ticked at the corner of his eye. "Hit you. He thought no one saw, but my men did. And, yes, it was Enzo who brought you to my attention. The reason he brought me to that park on that particular day was because he knew you'd be there. He knew you were the one for me. That wasn't the first time you'd tried to protect that same girl. It just happened to be the first time no one else was watching. Or so the bastard thought."

"Her name is Tina. I never saw her dad after that and Tina said he'd gone. She didn't know where but she said her mother was glad. Tina was glad too because he hit her a lot."

"He did."

I swallowed, needing to hear the answer to my next question even as I dreaded knowing. "Did... did you..."

"Yes, Kitten. And because he put his hands on you, he died extra hard."

"You... did that. For... me?"

"It's always been you, Kitten. Everything. The only thing I had no hand in was the death of your parents. I had an arrangement with them. One that placed you in my care when you graduated college. I knew your father before he met your mother and he knew I'd take care of you. Understand me, Isabella. I never intended to take you away from everything you knew. I intended on wooing you. Making you want to come into my world on your own. I wanted you to come to me of your own free will, but when they died... When you no longer had anyone close looking out for you, I couldn't leave you alone. I had to keep you close. Especially since you weren't doing well on your own."

Tears threatened and I knew I wasn't going to be able to hold them back. Not with Jacob. Daddy. I couldn't hold anything back from him. "You took care of me. You spoiled me and coddled me. I did come to you of my own free will. It was my decision." I sniffled, swiping at my eyes when two tears overflowed. "All of it, Daddy. You led me in the direction you wanted me to go, but it was always my decision."

"You know that, had you not wanted to be my pet, I'd still have made you my woman. Right?"

He looked so hesitant, almost like he was afraid he'd hurt me when nothing could be further from the truth. I smiled up at him, brushing my thumb across his lip as I stared into his eyes.

"I've enjoyed everything you've shared with me, Jacob. It's been a grand adventure. One I hope never stops. Thank you for taking care of me even when I didn't know you were there. Thank you for giving me Andromeda. Thank you for giving me Max. But most of all, thank you for being my Daddy."

Daddy pulled me close, burying his nose in my hair. His arms tightened around my naked body and I knew I was home. This man was my home.

We held each other like that for a long time. I knew there was a lot of emotion inside him. I could feel it in the set of his body. The way he clung to me told me he was as off balance as I was. This wasn't a conversation he likely ever expected to have. "It's OK, Jacob," I whispered. "I love you. I'll always love you."

"I love you too, Isabella. So fucking much…"

With one last, hard squeeze, he released me. Smiling up at me he settled his hands at my waist. "This is supposed to be a celebration, Kitten. Why are we talking so seriously?"

"Because this was something you needed to tell me and something I needed to hear. I'm glad you told me."

He cocked his head to the side. "Aren't you going to ask if there is anything else I need to tell you?

Any other secrets I'm keeping?"

I shrugged. "If there are, I'm sure you have a good reason. You'll tell me when or if I need to know. That's all that matters."

"I don't deserve you. But I'm selfish enough to keep you."

"Now that you've gotten things settled, how about we do what you came here for, Jacob." Enzo entered the cabana dressed similarly to Daddy. He gave Daddy a half grin. "You should have done this a long time ago. I told you that girl was the one for you."

"You did, Enzo. But she wasn't ready. Now she is."

"Oh, she was ready. You were afraid of scaring her off."

"Not too proud to admit that, either." Daddy grinned before leaning in to kiss me. "How about it, Kitten. You ready to marry me?"

I gasped, looking down at my bare body. All I wore was the collar at my throat and the diamond leash wrapped around my waist. "I can't get married like this!"

"Why not? I told you this is a private beach. You saw for yourself on your way here." Daddy smiled at me, my frustration obviously amusing to him.

I rolled my eyes. "It's just not done."

"Honey, I'm one of the richest men in the world. I can do anything I want. Besides, this isn't a traditional wedding ceremony. You can have one of those later if you want."

"It's not?"

"No, baby. This will be a collaring ceremony. The paperwork is legal, so we'll be officially married. Only the ceremony will be different."

I sucked in a breath, a smile forming before I was

even aware I was going to smile. "Oh, Jacob!" I threw myself back into his arms. I was sure I was getting sunscreen all over his clothes but I didn't care. "I love that idea!"

"That's my good Kitten." He reached up and unhooked my collar. "I have a new one for you. This one you won't take off unless I give you permission."

"I never take this one off."

He smiled. "I know. It pleases me more than you could ever know."

As he took off my old collar, another man approached us. "Mr. Blackstone?" He acknowledged all three of us, and didn't blink at my lack of clothing.

"Yes. Jacob Blackstone, and this is my Isabella. My best man here is Enzo Capella. He'll be our witness."

"So wonderful to meet you all." He smiled at all of us in turn. The man had a slight accent I couldn't place. "Do you need more time to prepare or are we ready to begin?"

Daddy looked at me with such love and tenderness it made my heart melt. "I think we're ready."

"Yes," I said a little breathlessly. "I think we are."

There were nice words said and a blessing to start our union right. All I was concerned with was the way Daddy looked at me. Like I was everything important to him. Like no one else existed for him. It was then I realized that it was the way he always looked at me.

"You have a collar for the young lady?"

"I most certainly do." Daddy reached out a hand to Enzo who handed Daddy a flat, square box. Daddy opened the box and pulled out a choker of sparkling gems. As he held it out for me to see, he raised an eyebrow. Was he looking for my approval?

"It's so beautiful," I breathed. There was a single strand of diamonds and colored gems completing the circle. In the center was a larger green stone that would sit in the hollow of my throat.

"Not nearly as beautiful as you, Isabella. Kitten." He turned me away from him to fasten the collar around my neck. Sure enough, the green gem that was the centerpiece of my collar sat in the niche just below my throat. "The stones in this collar are diamonds, Kitten. Every stone is a diamond. As much as this collar cost, it's not worth nearly as much as you are. You are my most precious possession. I will always protect and love you, for the rest of my days. I will protect you and our daughter with a ruthlessness that will make even the stoutest heart quake. Nothing bad will ever happen to you."

"Jacob..." I whispered his name as he turned me to face him again.

"I love you, Isabella. My wife."

Sex on the Beach

I didn't know what to say so I just looked up at him with as much love as was in my heart. "I love you so much." Tears spilled down my cheeks and Daddy reached out to swipe them with the pad of his thumb.

"May I kiss my bride?" His voice deep and resonant.

"Please," I whispered. He might not have been talking to me, but I wanted his kiss too much not to answer.

He leaned down and kissed me softly, lingering for a few heartbeats before pulling back to look into my eyes. "Mine." The rough possessiveness was so at odds with what I'd experienced with him before. He loved sharing me. I loved it too. But, more than anything, I simply loved Daddy. I loved Jacob. They were one, yet different. Jacob was the strict, dominant Alpha in charge of his entire world and all the people in it. Daddy was the more indulgent man who catered to my every whim. I was definitely about to experience Jacob on my wedding day.

When he kissed me again, this time he did so with more passion and need. Hunger. His tongue explored my mouth, his hands sliding down my body in a possessive caress. I moaned softly in response, melting into him.

A throat cleared and Daddy actually groaned. He ended the kiss, pressing his forehead to mine for brief moments, his breathing ragged. I could feel his cock pressing against me, pulsing with need. "Who do I have to kill in order to be able to fuck my bride?"

Enzo actually burst out laughing before clapping Daddy on the shoulder. "Easy, man. Just need your signature on the marriage license so the Padre can file it with the court."

"Don't I have people for that? I want to claim my bride." Daddy looked and sounded disgruntled, as if any time he had to spend not inside my body was too much. I loved that possessive hunger in his gaze. It thrilled me more than I could describe.

"You do. But since there was no pre-nup in place, your lawyers refused to take any part. There's been a whole fucking floor of lawyers blowing up my phone since I gave them the heads up. I have three versions of one if you change your mind before the paperwork is filed, but I basically told them to fuck off."

"Good," Daddy grunted. No. This wasn't Daddy. It was Jacob. "Fire them all. If I'd wanted a pre-nup, I'd have given instructions for one."

Enzo rolled his eyes. "How about you just threaten to fire them. You have the best legal team in the world. Do you really want to have to start over?"

"Fire someone. Threaten the others into submission."

"Sorry, Jacob. Not my department. Only reason I'm fielding these calls is for your Kitten. She deserves the day with her Daddy without a bunch of busybody legal assholes actually being legal assholes."

"I'll sign a pre-nup," I blurted out. "I don't want your money, Jacob. It was never about the money. I just want…" I sniffed past the hitch in my throat. "I just want you."

"Kitten, honey." Jacob immediately turned into Daddy, picking me up and holding me close to him. His arms were tight, soothing bands around me. I wrapped my legs around his waist and my arms around his neck. "I know that. But it doesn't matter anyway. You're mine and I'm yours. Remember?"

"I don't want to cause you problems with

anyone."

"You're not." Enzo spoke before Daddy had the chance. "They are causing me problems, but not Jacob."

"Kitten, no one causes me problems. I don't want to do something, I don't do it. Sure, they can be vocal about their opinions, but I make the final decision. They don't like it, they can fuck off."

"Does she even know who you are, Jacob?"

I looked from one man to the other. There was tension, but not like there would have been in the office if one of his inner circle had questioned him. It was more like family holding each other accountable.

"Enzo looks cross, Daddy. I hope his face doesn't freeze that way."

Without so much as a glance my way, Enzo quipped, "Can't. Too warm here for my face to freeze."

Daddy barked out a laugh and I grinned, laying my head on his shoulder. I loved it when he laughed.

"That," Enzo said, pointing a finger at Daddy. "That right there is why she's the one for you. She embraces your kinks, but more importantly, she makes you laugh." He patted my shoulder gently. "Maria says little Andi is doing well. Max is having a ball with the child and needs very little help from her." He shrugged. "At least, not in that capacity."

I stiffened. "Is Max all right?"

"Oh, yeah. He's fine. Got a good case of blue balls, but he's fine."

"Tell Maria to help him any way he needs, if they're both agreeable," Daddy said. "What do you say, Kitten? I'd planned on us leaving tomorrow, but do you think you'd be comfortable staying a few days longer?"

I grinned up at Daddy. "Yes. If Max promises to

call us if he gets too overwhelmed."

"Don't you worry about Max." Enzo grinned. He held up his phone to show us a picture. Max and Andi both had on KISS shirts and paint on their faces. Andi was grinning and drooling everywhere while Max had his tongue stuck out like Gene Simmons. "He's enjoying his time with little Andi."

"Sweet Jesus." Daddy chuckled. "All kidding aside, if that makeup hurts her face, I'll have to kill Max."

"Daddy!"

"Well?"

"Maria anticipated that would be your reaction and assured me the face paint is made specifically for babies. Also, it came off directly after the picture." He fiddled with his phone again before turning it around and showing us.

"Fine. I guess Max gets to live." Daddy said it deadpan, but there was a twitch to his lips. "Doesn't mean I won't spank him when I get home."

"Enough of this. Go fuck your woman, Jacob. Knock her up again. Whatever. But don't think about anything else for the rest of the day."

"Pretty sure I'm the one in charge, Enzo. Not you."

Enzo snorted. "Not today. You're off the clock." He took a folded piece of paper from the Padre and spread it out on the coffee table in the tent, then slapped a pen on top of it. "Sign, you two. I'll take care of everything else." Once everyone had signed the marriage license and the Padre had left, Enzo grinned and shook Daddy's hand. "Enjoy your woman, Jacob. You deserve her."

"You've been my Kitten for so long, I sometimes forget Isabella may have needs, too. Are you good with the way our relationship is? Do you need more control over your life? It would be hard for me, I'll admit. But for you, I'll try."

"No, Daddy." I buried my face in his neck and licked the salty sweat beading on his skin. "I like our relationship exactly the way it is."

"If that ever changes, you talk to me. Understand? I don't want to push you away with my bossiness."

"You won't. I like that you're in control. I needed it when you first brought me home. Now, I crave it. I like not having to make hard decisions, but mostly, I like knowing that it makes you happy being in complete control."

"My, God, you're perfect." Then he kissed me. This time, I knew by the way he took me up higher and higher with just his kiss, he meant to fuck me. Here. On the beach. In the cabana where anyone could happen by.

Only, that's not what he did.

Daddy lifted me, urging my legs back around his waist, and walked outside the tent to a nearby palm tree. An air mattress had been arranged on a rug in the sand. A fluffy white comforter was spread over the white sheets on the mattress. There was an assortment of lube and condoms on a silver tray beside the bed for ease of use.

"Now, my beautiful wife. Let's seal this deal."

Laying me down gently, he ran his hand from my throat where my new collar rested to my waist where the diamond leash was wound around my middle. Sunlight filtered through the leaves of the palms, glittering off the diamond leash. I could only imagine what my collar looked like.

"So beautiful," he murmured, leaning down to

kiss my belly, delving his tongue into my navel. I squealed and he chuckled, continuing his way down to my mound. "Need another taste."

He swiped his tongue between my pussy lips before groaning and delving deeper. Daddy lay on his belly, his head between my legs, and shoved his shoulders between them. He shoved my thighs up, giving him unimpeded access. The second he did, Daddy covered my pussy with his mouth and sucked.

I didn't even try to stifle my screams of pleasure. Somehow, the fact we were out in the open didn't bother me anymore. Daddy said it was OK so it had to be OK. If that meant someone saw it, they were either meant to or it just didn't matter.

"So fucking good." Daddy's words were muffled by my pussy and I felt the vibrations through my clit up to my belly. My hands were over my head, thrusting my breasts upward when I arched my back.

"That's it, Kitten. Sing for me." Then he went to work. He tongue-lashed my clit and opening like he was possessed. I was on fire, ignited by the lust and a brutal intensity. Somewhere in the background a hard, driving grunge band played, echoing through the warm air. It served as a soundtrack for what promised to be an explosive round of hard and dirty sex.

"Christ, what you do to me, Kitten!" Daddy pulled himself away from my cunt to shove his pants from his hips then crawled up my body. His shirt remained, but I soon made short work of the soft material. I jerked and the buttons scattered, letting me shove the fabric from his broad shoulders. There was a predatory, maniacal gleam in his eyes as he covered my small body with his bigger one. "Need to fuck you! Right" -- he reached between us --"fucking" -- the head of his cock pressed against the entrance to my pussy --

"*Now!*"

With a brutal shout, Daddy filled me. My own cries accompanied his as another orgasm surprised me by crashing over me like an ocean wave. My muscles seized and I milked his cock as, without further preamble, he fucked me hard and fast.

Jacob's arms slid around me easily with the sweat and sunscreen coating my skin. He pistoned furiously against me, driving his cock harder and harder with every thrust. My hair fanned out around me, sticking to my sweaty skin as our bodies clashed together with each forceful stroke. The scent of salt and sweat filled the air, mingling with the smoky undertones of the grunge music. The sound of the waves crashing against the shore was the perfect cadence to accompany his claim.

The sun was setting, casting a warm glow over us, as our bare skin slapped together in a rhythmic dance. Our cries echoed around the beach, punctuating the music in the distance with the raw, untamed passion that coursed through our veins. His grunts were loud in my ear as was the sharp staccato of flesh against flesh.

With a particularly vicious thrust, Daddy held himself deep for several seconds before pushing himself up to flip me over onto my belly.

"Gonna fuck this ass, Kitten. Gonna fill it full of my cum and you're gonna let me."

"Yes, Daddy," I cried. Vaguely, I knew a few people had started to walk our way, but if Daddy wasn't concerned, I wouldn't be either. It was all in Daddy's hands. I trusted him with everything. Heart, body, and soul.

There was a cool splash of lubricant between my cheeks, followed by the thrust of Daddy's fingers into my ass as he stretched and prepared me to take him. I wiggled my hips, trying to get him deeper. "More!" My cry was a needy demand.

Instead of complying, Daddy smacked my ass. Hard. "Be still," he hissed. "You'll get what I give you and nothing more."

"Daddy!" My pleas grew louder and louder. I didn't care who heard or saw me. If Daddy wanted me quiet, he'd tell me. Or gag me.

"Such a tight, fucking asshole," he bit out. He gripped one of my cheeks with his free hand hard enough I thought it might bruise. The pain felt good and I longed for him to smack my ass again. I looked back over my shoulder, needing to see what he was doing. Not because I was afraid. Because I needed to see what we looked like together like this. His fingers between my cheeks.

Daddy met my gaze and bared his teeth. I did the same, tilting my hips to take his fingers even deeper. Heat flashed in his eyes and he brought his hand down on my ass again. I hissed in pain, but the warmth in my belly only intensified. So I did it again.

"I said hold still!"

"Fuck me!" I demanded. "Fuck my tight little asshole, Jacob. Fuck me hard and fast."

Surprise flitted over his face, followed by a look so intense it was nearly terrifying. Lord knew if he'd leveled that look on me when we'd first met, I'd have run away screaming. Now, I embraced it. I wanted him to use me the way he needed. I thought I needed it as much as he did in that moment.

"Fucking little bitch. Eager for my cock, are you?"

"Always, Jacob. I'll always be eager for it. For you."

He added a third finger. Then a fourth. The burn was intense, bordering on true pain. I gave a sharp cry but still I pushed back against him, needing him deeper.

"God damn it, Bell! God fucking damn it!"

I expected him to replace his fingers with his cock, but instead, he let go of my ass and guided his cock inside my pussy.

I'd been stuffed like this before with him and Max, but somehow, knowing there was an audience of strangers, knowing Daddy was riding the edge of his control -- I could see it in the way the muscles in his jaw flexed and relaxed -- made the sensations so much more intense.

He only thrust a couple of times before he pulled out with a vicious shout, removing his fingers from my ass, too. I screamed, hating the loss. It made me feel empty. Like I'd been cheated somehow. I knew I'd never be satisfied until he came deep in my ass. Maybe not even then.

Daddy backed away from me, still breathing hard, his eyes blazing with a mix of lust and anger. I knew he was trying to calm down. It was his own desire, the need to dominate, that was bubbling over and making him rougher than he would normally be with me. It had been the same before. But this is what I wanted. What I thought I'd die without.

"Please, Daddy. Please," I begged, feeling the loss of his fingers inside me. "Fuck my ass. Hard. *Now*." Because my demand came out as more of a sob, it sounded more like I was begging. Which, honestly, I was.

Daddy stared at me for a moment, his eyes burning with a mixture of desire and frustration. His breathing was ragged, and I could see the struggle playing out inside him. I also saw the exact moment he decided to trust I knew what I needed and gave himself a mental "fuck it" and decided to give me what I asked for.

He picked up the bottle of lube again, and poured it over his dick and my ass. The slick fluid dribbled between my cheeks and into the stretched ring of muscle that had to be gaping open.

"Such a fucking good little slut. Spread your cheeks. Hold them open for me."

I reached back and did as he instructed, readying my ass for him to aim and thrust home.

Jacob didn't waste any time. He gripped my hips and shoved himself deep. The second he was filling inside me, I let go of my cheeks as he pounded into me. His hand cracked over my ass cheek again. I yelped and jerked, the sudden pain startling me but feeding the pleasure building inside me.

"Don't let go of those cheeks, Kitten. You keep offering that ass to me while I fuck it."

I did as he said. My breasts were mashed against the mattress, my ass up to receive the man at my back. My gaze locked on that of a man standing a way down the beach. I wasn't sure what kept people away, but I knew without a doubt more than one of the people currently staring at us wanted a closer look.

Another hard smack to my ass made me yelp. "Attention on me, Kitten. Don't concern yourself with anyone else."

"He's stroking himself. Watching us." I whispered my observation.

"I know. Coveting this ass I'm fucking. Wanting what's mine." The control Jacob normally held tightly in check was slipping. A sliver of trepidation followed almost immediately by anticipation tore through me like the cut of a very sharp knife.

"Show them," I whispered, not sure why I'd spoken but needing to push him just that little bit. Some sick, twisted thing inside me wanted to see what happened when he lost his grip on sanity. Like he always seemed to push me past. "Show them why this ass is all yours."

"Fuck!" That seemed to be all he could take. Jacob shoved my hands away, gripped my hips, and fucked me like a demon.

He slammed into me harder, faster, his pace savage, making me cry out with each thrust. A growing crowd now stopped to watch from a distance, transfixed by the scene unfolding on the beach. I felt like I was on fire, achingly stretched and eager for more.

"Take it, Kitten," Jacob growled at me. "Take my cock and milk my cum."

He didn't just pound into my ass, he ruthlessly plowed it. The swift, hard thrusts echoed in the evening, the contrast between this barbaric claiming and the beauty of the reddening sky sharp. His grunts mingled with my moans. I felt every inch of his cock as he savagely buried himself within me, owning me.

The roughness of the sex only heightened my arousal, the feeling of his body invading mine becoming more and more intense. I screamed louder, arching my back in time with our frantic fucking.

Jacob's powerful thrusts hit a new level of intensity, pushing me higher and higher until I came with a fierce scream as frenzied as the orgasm tearing through me.

Never had I felt so desired, so completely owned. I writhed at the sweet, debasing torment Jacob was inflicting on me. We were no longer in a public place.

We were lost in our own primal passion, our bodies forming an erotic tableau for all to witness.

Jacob's primal shout soon followed me and I felt his cum splashing inside my ass, coating my walls and marking me as his once again. He collapsed on top of me, his body sweating, his lungs heaving, his cock still buried deep in my ass.

I'm not really sure what happened after that. I must have passed out. The next thing I knew, I was being carried. I looked up to find Daddy's smug, satisfied face looking off into the distance. "Daddy?"

His gaze snapped to mine and his grin widened. "How does my little Kitten feel?"

I sighed happily, snuggling against his chest as he carried us inside our resort suite. "Wonderful. And well and truly fucked."

Daddy chuckled. The cool breeze from the air conditioning was chilly and I shivered. Daddy tightened his grip on me, kissing the top of my head. "The shower is waiting, Kitten. I'll get you warm and clean, then we can rest."

He did as he said, cleaning me carefully and kissing every inch of me before placing a gentle kiss over my pussy and my ass. It was like he was praising me for accepting him so freely and willingly.

"You're my perfect, perfect Kitten," he murmured as he stood and turned off the water.

He dried me then himself before carrying me to the bed. Once we were both settled, he took my left hand. He removed the engagement ring he'd given me and slid a diamond band on my finger before replacing the engagement ring. They merged perfectly, forming their own collar for my finger.

"It's official, Kitten. You're my wife, as well as my Kitten."

"Thank you, Daddy." I hoped he could see my love for him shining in my eyes. Because there was no one in this world other than our daughter I loved so much. Not even Max.

One tear spilled down my cheek and Daddy leaned in to capture it with his lips. "I hope those are happy tears."

"They are."

"Then I'm the one who should be thanking you. For giving me a daughter as beautiful as her mother. For being my wife. For being my Kitten."

"Thank you for all those things too, but most of all for being my Daddy."

"You're welcome, Kitten."

"You're welcome, too, Daddy. I love you."

Wanda Violet O.

Welcome to Wanda Violet O.'s world of bedtime fantasy, where you'll find a variety of sexy creatures ready to drink their fill. Wanda specializes in extreme kink. Monsters, BDSM, Role Play… she's got it all. Come take a look for yourself!

Wanda at Changeling: changelingpress.com/ wanda-violet-o-a-226

Changeling Press E-Books

More Sci-Fi, Fantasy, Paranormal, and BDSM adventures available in e-book format for immediate download at ChangelingPress.com -- Werewolves, Vampires, Dragons, Shapeshifters and more -- Erotic Tales from the edge of your imagination.

What are E-Books?

E-books, or electronic books, are books designed to be read in digital format -- on your desktop or laptop computer, notebook, tablet, Smart Phone, or any electronic e-book reader.

Where can I get Changeling Press E-Books?

Changeling Press e-books are available at ChangelingPress.com, Amazon, Apple Books, Barnes & Noble, and Kobo/Walmart.

Changeling Press, LLC

ChangelingPress.com